# The Final Link

## The Gateway Saga Book 1

### By Erin Thornton

This book is dedicated to Influenza A and Influenza B, without which I would have released on time and not had to push back release date a full month. I hope you're happy!

# Prologue

Another day, another customer. Aggie grabbed the plate and carried it out to deliver. "Here's your order. Is there anything else I can get for you?"

"Does this look cooked to you?" Her older customer poked at his chicken but didn't cut into it. She hated it when people actually answered that question. Why couldn't they just nod and go with it, regardless of whether they were happy or not.

"I'm sorry, sir, but I'm not sure. I can't tell from the outside; I'm not the cook. I assume they checked the internal temperature or something before sending it out with me." She knew her tone sounded short, but were they expecting her to look through it with her x-ray eyes?

"I want to speak with your manager. You're obviously too rude to do your job properly." With an eyeroll Aggie didn't even respond. Walking away, she flagged down the manager and pointed at table nine. It was the third table that day and the eighth one that week; that wasn't bad, except it was only Tuesday.

Checking on her last table who already had their food, it was a couple guys closer to her age and had been sure of themselves all night. Aggie was so over the losers who came in and hit on waitresses. It was her biggest pet peeve. "How are you guys doing? Are you ready for your check?" She was supposed to offer dessert but she rarely did because she just wanted the tables to leave so another could sit down. The lingering tables always made her shift feel like it was longer than it really was, and families were the worst.

"Only if that check is going to include your number. If not, then I think we'll need to stick around until we persuade you." The first guy was the leader of the two, which was obvious because the other one just sat and laughed encouragingly at everything the first one said.

"Oh, my number? Of course, because I work here because I can't do better than guys who tip poorly and hope to get laid by a stupid waitress who happens to give them her number. I have nothing better to do tonight but sit by the phone and hope that you call because you need a late-night blow job? I'm sorry, I think I have a better offer from table nine." Aggie gestured toward the old man who'd insulted her. Walking away without another word or a second glance, Aggie went to go print their check. Unfortunately, she hadn't lowered her voice and everyone in the restaurant was staring at her now. She would have cringed if she'd actually cared. It wasn't like this was her dream job. She might not know what she wanted to do, but peopling was really not her thing.

As she approached the kiosk to print the ticket for the pigheaded guys who thought they were God's gift to women, Aggie was quickly cornered by the manager on duty. "Hey there, Aggie, I just finished talking to table nine and after the display you just put on out there for everyone, I think this is just going to be easier if we part ways. I feel like this isn't your best fit. I'm sorry, but they'll have your last check at the end of the week and you can turn in your uniforms then." The manager was a weaselly-looking guy that Aggie thought was more creep than manager. Honestly, it was probably for the best. He was always checking her out when he didn't think she was looking.

This place was really a step down, and she didn't even make that much in tips. Although, that could have been partly her fault.

Regardless, it wasn't going to make her lose any sleep that night. Even if this was her fourth job in as many weeks, she knew she would settle into something soon and then she could move out of her Gran's house. She never had to pay for anything while she was living there, but she wanted her freedom and something to call her own. When that day presented itself, she knew it would be the right time.

# Chapter 1

ggie flopped down on her bed, causing the pile of dresses to jump and a few to scatter to the floor. She had laid them out for the funeral today but couldn't bring herself to put any of them on. She lay there in only her black lace bra and matching panties. Rolling over, she saw the photo of her mother holding her not long after she was born. "Mom, why did you have to go so soon? Now I have to do this on my own." Her Gran had taken on the challenge of raising Aggie when her mother died, while Aggie was still in diapers. Her father wasn't ever in the picture. When she asked her Gran about him growing up, she was shut down with, "Never mind that man; he couldn't be bothered to stick around after your mother found out she was pregnant and then became sick." She had only brought him up a few times in her youth, and was met with the same short and angry answer. Now, Aggie was left to plan and attend her grandmother's funeral.

Glancing from the picture, Aggie began fidgeting with the loose pieces of jewelry on her nightstand. She loved to have at least a pair of earrings or a necklace to complete her everyday look. Unfortunately, she also had a bad habit of leaving them on when she crawled into bed. Instead of crawling out of bed again—Aggie was much too lazy for that—she would just set them on the bedside table. Keeping up with her personality, they tended to stay there until she wanted to wear them again and never made their way back to the bathroom.

Grabbing her cup of water that was always beside her bed, Aggie made her way to the kitchen to refill it. Walking out of her room, she didn't feel the need to put on clothes because there was no one but her in the house. Their house was in the middle of nowhere, at least twenty miles to their closest neighbor. Walking past her Gran's room, Aggie found herself slowing and turning in. She couldn't get past the doorway, but the room still felt like her grandmother was there. Her perfume was still lingering in the air. Aggie didn't know the name of it, but it was a floral scent that always made her nose curl, ever to be associated with Blythe Wasley. With one last look, Aggie turned to make her way downstairs.

Walking down the hallway towards the kitchen, Aggie heard something that stopped her dead in her tracks—the click of the latch on a door that had never been opened the entire time she had lived in that house, which meant her whole life. Turning slowly, she saw that the mysterious door that her Gran would never speak of was cracked open. With a puzzled expression, Aggie walked towards the room. Pressing open the door, she walked inside slowly. What she saw was simply strange.

On every wall, every inch, was a doorknob. There were dull ones, drab ones, rusty ones, all the way to brilliant, shiny, and delicate ones. "What kind of collection is this? Gran, you were always odd but I think this takes the cake." Aggie took a few more minutes to survey the space that had been hidden her entire life, then quickly shut the door.

Time was getting away from her and she had to finish getting ready. Aggie was thankful there wasn't going to be an official wake, given the fact that there was no other family left alive and all the friends were distant. She wasn't even sure how many people would show up for the funeral, let alone a wake if one were held. Even though no one would be coming over to the house it was still shut up tight, as though the house was also in mourning. The curtains were closed, casting dark shadows all over the house. If this had been her first time in the house, it would be a bit spooky.

Making her way back to her childhood room, Aggie felt safe. This room had always been her sanctuary and today it was a refuge. The rest of the house served to remind her of her grandmother. The double bed was her mother's and always made her feel safe and protected, as though her mother was still there somehow. Walking over to her dresser, she pulled out a pair of black hose. Her Gran would have insisted she wore them, because that was proper. Aggie hated them, especially in the heat of summer. This was one time she would wear them without complaint.

She pressed the escaping clothes back into the drawer. Her dresser was getting too small, as it was the same one she had as a young child. As her clothes got larger, space became limited. Aggie never wanted to trouble her grandmother with something so small. She had already taken on a child and Aggie didn't want to be a bigger burden.

Blindly grabbing a dress out of the mess on the bed, Aggie threw it on in a hurry. All of them were black and the best of the best in her closet. Not that she had a lot of dresses, but this was a special occasion; she had to sort out the best from the worst. Glancing at herself in the mirror, she smoothed out the wrinkles from lack of use.

Aggie was a curvy girl, with a flattering shape. She wasn't one for working out, but she loved her snack foods. It was her vice in times of stress, happiness or, in this case, grief. Okay, really, she ate snack foods under any circumstances.

Her chocolate-colored hair was brushed out straight, lying over her shoulders and halfway down her back. She never wore much makeup and this day was no exception.

*****

The wind had picked up overnight and was thrashing Aggie's hair around wildly. *Why are funerals always stormy or severe weather? It's like nature knows someone has died and it's keeping the mood set right,* Aggie thought to herself while sitting graveside. After speaking with the planners at the funeral home, they had opted to do everything in one place given the fact that chances were no one would show besides herself. The funeral home had everything set up and, since that this was an old church graveyard, it was easier to plan the service. The preacher was handling the ceremony and they were waiting until right on the hour to start, giving anyone else a chance to show up.

Aggie closed her eyes so she wouldn't have to just stare at the casket while she waited. Inhaling slowly, she smelled the newly turned earth, making it all the more real that her Gran would soon be living in the ground. Not down the hall from her, harping about what a mess her room was and if she was going to do the dishes after dinner.

A scuffle caught her attention; she noticed a few people making their way through the scattered headstones toward her. She didn't recognize them. Aggie sat up a little straighter as they approached her. The first was a woman who walked straight up to the closed casket, placing her hand on the top, her head bowed in silent vigil. When she moved again, her eyes met Aggie's. They were an odd shade of blue, almost violet. *This weather must be messing with my vision, or she has some elaborate contacts.* The woman was willowy and beautiful. She didn't say a word to Aggie, just took up residence behind her, out of sight. Aggie turned to look to be sure the woman hadn't left.

A few more people approached and they all, like the violet-eyed woman, paid their respects to her grandmother and silently made their way to the space behind her. By the time the preacher took his place at the front of the service, the area behind Aggie was full of people. There were no murmurs amongst them at all. No one took a seat, they just stood reverently, waiting for the service to start.

The preacher broke the silence. "We meet here today to honor the life of Blythe Wasley. We give thanks for her life and ask God to bless her now that her time in this world has come to an end." His words were a prayer to begin the service. "For Blythe Wasley, the journey is now beginning. But for us there is loss, grief, and pain. Every one of us here has been affected—perhaps in small ways, or perhaps in transformative ones—by Blythe Wasley. Her life mattered to us all. It is important for us to collectively acknowledge and accept that the world has fundamentally changed with her passing. We are all grieving. Life will not be the same, nor should it be. Together, let us open our hearts and commemorate the impact Blythe Wasley had on us."

*****

Tossing and turning in her bed, Aggie had difficulty sleeping that night. It wasn't the first time she had been alone in the old farmhouse, but it was the first time she had been alone knowing no one would be with her again. Tears stained her face. She had held it together at the funeral. It helped that others had shown up to show that her Gran's life was equally as important to others. Not that any of those guests had spoken a word to Aggie; she still didn't know who any of them were. They were all different. In addition to the lady with the almost-violet eyes, there was a man who stood enormous in the crowd. He had to be seven feet tall easily. Another had long hair that hung down to his shoulders, but Aggie was sure that when the wind moved just right his ears were misshapen, almost elven if not quite that pointed. Each person in attendance had an odd characteristic that stood out to Aggie as they made their way from the casket to the space behind her chair.

When Aggie had stood to leave they were all gone. She never heard them leave or heard a car start to signal she was alone. Her heels had sunk into the damp soil underneath the lush grass as she walked back to her car. Just as she leaned down to climb into the driver's seat, a movement by the trees caught her eye. When she turned to see what it was, there was nothing there. She decided it must have been a squirrel or a bird that had been spooked by her approaching steps.

Now lying in bed, she wondered if she would ever sleep again. Aggie jolted in bed as she heard a creak of a floorboard that sounded like it came from downstairs. *What was that?* Usually, Aggie would talk aloud to herself, but she was startled and offhandedly worried someone would hear her. They didn't own any animals because her Gran was allergic. So, there should be nothing to cause that sound aside from herself. Aggie lowered her feet silently to the floor as she heard the sound again. *Seriously, what was that? Why on the first night I'm alone does the house have to make strange noises?* Part of her assumed it was just the house settling and nothing to be afraid of, so she scurried out of her room and downstairs quickly. Knowing the house as well as she did, Aggie didn't need to turn on a light to see around in the dark.

As she made her way to the downstairs hallway, Aggie froze. This was the second time in less than twenty-four hours it had happened. The door to the mysterious room that was filled with doorknobs was ajar again. She hadn't been back in there since the funeral because she was emotionally exhausted when she got home and went straight to bed. Now, the room was open and a light was glowing from under the crack in the door. The floorboards creaked again, accompanied by the sound of footsteps. Had that second sound just not reached her bedroom before? Forcing herself to move, Aggie made her way to the door. The closer she got she could see shadows bouncing around the room caused by the light that was now clearly visible. It wasn't a lightbulb more like it was a glow from a candle or many flickering candles. It was bright enough to see clearly into the room, but Aggie didn't recall seeing candles in that room or furniture for one to sit upon. This night was getting more and more strange the longer she was awake.

Placing her hand on the door, she tried to open it slowly to not draw attention to herself. Aggie peered inside; to her surprise there wasn't a candle anywhere in the room. The light seemed to be coming from a ball of light floating in the space. Captivated by this phenomenon, she was startled when she saw a man moving in the room. He was tall with dark hair, and a scowl that should have scared her. Instead, she was drawn to him in a way that she didn't understand. His hands were clasped behind his back as he paced the space. He looked like he was impatiently waiting for someone. Then, just as he was getting close enough to make out his individual features, a hum started from across the room. She followed the sound with her eyes, and she couldn't believe what she saw. A line was forming in the shape of a door on the wall. It flew open, and light poured from the empty space. Then, appearing out of the beam, another man stepped through.

This man was just as tall as the first, but his features stood out immediately due to the fact that he was bathed in light from the door. His hair was long and white and was pulled back into a low ponytail. Her breath caught as she took in his face. His angular features offset his lean body type perfectly, and if she were to describe him she would say he looked angelic. So perfect, words couldn't do him justice. Suddenly the door closed with a sound of suction, as though it were sealing as securely as possible.

The men met in the middle and shared a look, and shook arms in a way that seemed ancient. As the newest one turned his head to show his pointed ears, Aggie gasped and both men turned toward the door. She covered her mouth and flipped her body to the wall, hidden from the doorway. She hoped they would ignore it and not come looking for her. Those hopes were shattered as the door swung open and the dark-haired man stepped out with his arms crossed. He looked fierce and intimidating. Their eyes met and Aggie felt her entire body react. His nose twitched as he looked at her; it was as if he was inhaling her scent. Grasping her arm, he pulled her into the glowing room.

Realizing that both of these men were unarmed, or so it appeared, Aggie found her voice first. "Who are you and what are you doing in *my* house?"

# Chapter 2

The man with white hair stepped forward. He wore a serene look, and his lips were quirked up at the corners. "You must be Agatha Wasley; Blythe has told us so much about you. I am Liel and this is Mathius." Liel gestured toward the dark-haired brute of a man whose scowl was set firmly in place, as though with glue.

"Aggie. Please don't call me Agatha; I hate that name. My mother must have been envisioning me as a decrepit old woman when she named me. Wait, why would my grandmother tell you about me? How do you know my grandmother?"

"We both knew your grandmother very well. Her job kept us very well acquainted. We knew your mother for a time as well, but more by reputation than anything. Though we did meet from time to time in passing." Liel spoke again, leaving Mathius to represent the role of 'strong, silent type'.

"That doesn't actually answer all my questions. You still haven't told me what you're doing in my house. Not to mention, what happened to the wall over there when you came in?" Aggie just kept sweeping the room with her eyes, to make sure nothing else strange happened.

"While this might look like it is inside your house, you couldn't be more wrong." Mathius' rough voice startled her.

"You're crazy if you think this isn't my house. My grandmother just passed away, and with no other living relatives that makes the house mine. Although, I'm sure she left a will that I haven't received yet, stating the same. I might have never been inside this room before today, but that doesn't make it any less a part of *my* house." Aggie was ranting and she knew it, but she wasn't going to be told something so ridiculous, and actually believe it.

"What Mathius means is, you are in the Gateway. The other side of that door is *your* house, but this room is actually between the dimensions. You have likely only been granted to this space because Blythe has passed on. Her responsibilities now pass to you," Liel clarified, but really just made Aggie's brain hurt worse.

"Another dimension? Seriously? You expect me to believe that?" Aggie didn't believe it, but she did find it peculiar that the room just opened, on its own, the day they laid her grandmother to rest.

"I'm not one for telling lies, Agatha." Liel refrained from using her nickname as she requested, but it didn't grate on her nerves, as with everyone else. Actually, with his voice, the way it rolled off his tongue, it was the best she'd ever heard her full name sound. So, she opted to not say anything this time.

"Everyone lies at one time or another, but let's say I were to believe you. What responsibility am I now blessed with, besides upkeep on an old house that I can't possibly afford without a real job?" Aggie hadn't voiced these concerns to anyone since her grandmother's death, but it had been niggling at the back of her brain for days, and just sort of slipped out along with her rant.

"You are now the Gate Keeper. That was your grandmother's role for years. When the next in the family comes of age, the responsibilities pass on through the generations. Unfortunately, your mother passed before that time and your grandmother was forced to hold the job longer than any other in your family. It finally took its toll on her. It is not an easy task at times." Liel's voice carried a tone of remorse but it was only slight, as it seemed he didn't share emotions easily.

"What are you?" Aggie blurted without thinking. That was a bad habit of hers, but rather than take it back she squared her shoulders and waited expectantly for his answer.

Liel hesitated, but it was as though he was trying to figure out how to explain it. Just when she thought he wasn't going to answer, he reached out his hand to her. With his hand suspended in mid-air, palm facing up, Liel froze.

Without saying a word his eyes brightened, and it was as if they were glowing. His green eyes took on a hue she had never imagined before, but that wasn't all. His hand revealed an image as though a tattoo was being applied without anyone or anything touching him. A moment later, the picture became clear. It was a cross between a flattened lily and butterfly wings. The flower was pressed together in a teardrop and wrapped in a circle. As quickly as the image appeared, as soon as his eyes dimmed so did the mysterious tattoo.

"What was that? Why do I feel like, instead of answering my questions you're just creating more?" Aggie was flustered and becoming more confused by the second. Was she dreaming or was she losing her mind?

"My apologies, Agatha." Liel seemed to be stuck on her full name, unable to be swayed. "I decided, given your lack of previous knowledge, it would be easier to prove it to you rather than just tell you. My name, as I said, is Liel. What I didn't tell you, is that I'm head of the Elven army and the strongest warrior to live in thousands of years. My powers are quite vast and that is why I have been placed as the guardian of the Elven gateway. That is what you saw happen to the wall—as you so eloquently described it—when I entered this space." Liel had lowered his hand and crossed them behind his back when the image disappeared.

"Right, you're an elf." Aggie turned to Mathius. "I supposed that makes you an ogre?" Her tone boasted her disbelief and she began to pace the room, looking for hidden cameras or something to show she was being tricked for someone else's amusement.

"Absolutely not!" Mathius' chest puffed out and Aggie knew she had offended him unintentionally. He didn't offer up any further explanation. Aggie knew he would be a tough nut to crack.

"Then what are you supposed to be, since you are both standing in *my* house?" She wasn't ready to give up on the possession issue, and the idea of another dimension was still foreign and hard to believe.

"What I am is of no consequence to you. What matters is I'm here because things have gotten out of hand in my realm and I required some assistance. While I waited as long as I possibly could, I can't hold out any longer. I need the brotherhood to assemble again. So, what I am is of little importance when an entire race is under attack. I'm not here for you and therefore I don't owe you an explanation." Mathius' nostrils flared, showing his anger, not that Aggie needed a visual cue in order to decipher that.

"Well, if you say I'm the Gatekeeper, then I'd say you need me to some extent. While I'm not sure how much of this I believe, that magic show that Liel just put on was persuasive enough. So, unless he's the world's greatest illusionist-turned-cat-burglar, I'd say he has me leaning in his favor." Aggie was never one who needed to be told what she was supposed to do, and this was no different.

With a heavy sigh, Mathius began his explanation. "My home is under attack. It started out tame, but now it has reached a point beyond our control. We aren't completely sure who the source is, but their powers are unmatched by my people. It began with terrible storms, and we thought it was just a bad rainy season, but then they became more destructive and children started turning up missing.  One of whom is the Prince of Darkness himself. The king is furious that someone was able to breach the castle walls to take his son as he slept. The child is young and untrained. We must return him to his mother and father before anything unspeakable happens to him." That was the most Mathius had said since she met him, and Aggie's heart was breaking for this child who was now missing.

"Children? They're taking children? Oh, the mothers must be beside themselves." Aggie crooned her concern even though she didn't understand all the details. Instead, she picked up on what she believed to be the worst part.

"The timing is most peculiar," Liel spoke up, looking deep in thought. "How soon before Walpurgisnacht Roodmas Day did this start?"

"I'd say the first storm was about a month ago. What are you thinking?" Mathius questioned Liel's train of thought.

"If the culprit is taking children this close to the festival, I'd say they are siphoning the powers from the children but keeping them alive until the festival. So that means we have just a couple weeks left before they are sacrificed and the power transfer becomes permanent." Liel's tone never faltered, as though he was reading a textbook on Life's Most Disinteresting Facts.

"If someone is going to kill these children in just a couple weeks, how can you be so calm about it?" Aggie practically screeched.

"That is why I'm here, Aggie." This is the first time Mathius had used her name and his tone was a bit softer. She didn't know what caused the change, but she found herself drawn into his eyes. They were a clear blue, almost translucent, and the rarity of them drew her in more. "The Brotherhood is needed to bring down this force and rescue the children. If anyone is going to be able to handle this, it will take all of us."

"Who is this Brotherhood, and how do we reach them?" Aggie was desperate to do whatever was needed to help. She didn't understand anything that was going on, but at the mention of helpless children being in trouble all other thoughts were gone. She felt a pull to help these children she didn't know, as though it was what she was meant to do. Nothing else mattered, only the children.

The two men shared a smile between them and Aggie noticed their shoulders squared off a little more. "You're looking at two of the eight of us. The Brotherhood is made up of Guardians who protect the seven realms. The reason it's only Liel and me here now is that the other six are off on missions. We will have to send a message to their kingdoms and request a meeting of the minds." Mathius sounded very proud of his role and his team.

"Where will this meeting be held, and when? I want to make sure I'm available under any circumstances." Aggie still didn't know what Mathius was, but for some reason she was leaning more in the direction of believing them after the story he told and Liel's display of power.

"You aren't doing anything. We don't need you, and there isn't anything you can do." Mathius was back to his gruff tone, sounding final.

Liel placed a hand on Mathius' shoulder and said softly, "Mathius, you know that she needs to be there even in her current state. We can't expect her to rise to her potential if she isn't with us."

"You don't know for sure. Not all the gatekeepers embrace their destiny. They stay on this plane and manage the gateway, but most don't join the Brotherhood. Her grandmother didn't." Mathius sounded torn, and scowled in Aggie's general direction, as though she had done something personally.

"You know that Blythe was married by the time the torch was passed to her. They all have the choice and no one is told about the gateway until it is time to pass it on to the next generation. Unfortunately, the women of this family have been forced to hold the title longer and longer, as the years go on." Liel turned his attention back to Aggie. "My apologies for Mathius here; we have been without a complete team for many years. While most of us live for quite some time, it makes the Brotherhood a harder job at times without our ninth member. You are more than welcome to accompany us to the meeting. It will actually be held here in the gateway. You will see what magic this space holds the more you come here. I will send the messages right away and you will get your own invitation when the time has been set."

"This day has been beyond strange." Aggie sighed as the men spoke to each other to work out the details.

"The messages are on their way and I look forward to our next meeting." Liel bowed low to Aggie in farewell. Then he turned and headed towards the wall. Without stopping or giving Aggie a chance to speak again, Liel reached for the doorknob. Feeling the magic swell in the space, it was hard to believe she didn't notice this the first time when he arrived. Perhaps the magic was a one-directional feeling. She felt it because it was emanating from this room and not his realm. Looking through the door, she hoped to catch a glimpse of what his Elven country looked like, but was disappointed to find that all she saw was a bright light shining between the dimensions.

As the door closed behind Liel, Aggie turned to find Mathius was still standing in the center of the room. Not saying anything, he just stood there staring at her.

"Was there something else?" Aggie questioned as she fought the need to go to him. He was undoubtedly one of the most attractive men she had ever seen; another had just left the room. They each had different reasons her body pulled in their directions. Mathius looked like the kind of man who would protect her under any circumstance. His build was of one who would intimidate even the scariest of men. He wore a leather jacket, which added to the motorcycle club look he was emitting. She'd always had a thing for bad boys and Mathius seemed to be the worst of them all. Though, he also seemed to care genuinely about the problem happening amongst his people. The children were a soft spot for him as well.

Without another word, Mathius turned and headed for another spot on the opposite wall. He reached for a doorknob but she couldn't tell which one; there were just too many on the wall. How was she ever supposed to know how to operate a room when she couldn't even identify the points of entry? The magic filled the room again as he turned the handle. Yet, she couldn't see into the realm he entered, as it was blocked by another blinding light. Stepping in he disappeared, as did the light ball that was lighting the room.

# Chapter 3

Aggie woke the next morning a bit groggy and overly tired. "Man, I really need to get more sleep. I have the craziest dreams when I don't sleep enough." Aggie rubbed her eyes in an attempt to wake herself up a bit more. Looking around the room, everything looked normal. She shook her head to dislodge the dream she had. "Elves and gateways? Magical powers and untold dangers? I'm not eating that late, ever again." Chuckling under her breath at the insanity of it all, she crawled out of bed. Aggie didn't bother changing out of her pajamas. Not that she wasn't clothed wearing shorts and a t-shirt. The only thing she was missing was her bra.

Standing outside the strange room of doorknobs, Aggie remembered her dream. The two men had towered over her and the memory of them left her breathless. She couldn't understand what it was about them that had drawn her to them. Now she realized that she'd been dreaming and it made more sense. "All men in dreams are ten times hotter than in real life. It made sense that I would be caught up in them given the fact that they aren't real."

Making her way to the kitchen, she needed to get a cup of coffee in her to wake up the rest of the way. Without it, she would be walking around in a daze all day. Hesitating in the doorway, reality hit her like a ton of bricks. Never again would her grandmother be there, waiting for her in the kitchen. Coffee waiting and breakfast sizzling in the skillet. Inhaling deeply, she could almost smell the bacon that her grandmother always had frying to greet her and start her day. A single tear escaped before she broke from her thoughts.

She ran her hand across the old Formica table that had been in the house her entire life. The spindly legs were gold and had hidden a few scuffs from Aggie's teenage anger. She had a lot of memories at this old table. Her grandmother always insisted she be home for breakfast and dinner so they could eat together. Talking about her day as a teenager wasn't her favorite pastime. Wishing she could go hang out with her boyfriend and friends was her only priority. That didn't change her grandmother's rules. "One day you can make your own rules, but until then you will live by mine." Her grandmother preached this every single day of her life. Another tear trickled down her cheek and she swiped it away and walked over to the coffee pot. She needed to wake up and get her emotions in check.

The first thing on her agenda was to figure out what came next. She had received a packet from her grandmother's attorney a week before but refused to open it, given the fact that she didn't want to accept reality. Pouring some coffee into her favorite mug, she missed the lip slightly and some of the liquid hit the floor. Setting down her cup to grab a towel, Aggie turned to wipe up her mess. Confusion crossed her face, "Where did it go?" Looking everywhere she even got down on her knees, but it was as if the mess had magically disappeared.

Laughing at herself she grabbed her coffee and made her way to the old kitchen table. Taking a sip, she gasped, nearly spilling her entire cup. On the table that mere moments ago was completely clear, was an envelope perfectly centered on the table. It was a simple thing, but with no one else in the house it was a bit unnerving.

The envelope wasn't exceptional, just white and basic. Looking very much like an invitation. She chalked it up to being lost in her emotions and not seeing it, because the alternative would have been to freak out and potentially drop her coffee to the floor. "Maybe Gran left it here before she passed." Rationalizing was all

Aggie had left now. Picking it up she flipped it over and noticed a very faint golden line running around the perimeter, almost undetectable. The sunlight pouring in from the window above the sink caught the color on the envelope. Twisting it back and forth in her fingers, Aggie watched the line shimmer with amazement. When the light shadowed, the line disappeared completely. After playing with the elusive line, Aggie flipped it over one final time and slid her finger under the flap, breaking the seal.

Slowly, she pulled the cardstock-like paper out. The paper had the same shimmer as the envelope, as though it was part of a stationery set. "Who still uses stationery?" Aggie assumed it was as outdated as her grandmother's taste in furniture.

*Agatha Wasley, your presence is requested at the meeting of the Brotherhood. Please be in the Gateway at eight o'clock tonight.*

Aggie dropped the invitation as if it were on fire. It might as well have been, given what she was feeling. "Real? It couldn't have been real. Magic isn't real." Again, she found herself searching the room for evidence that someone was pranking her. Not that she had anyone in her personal life who would do that. Her grandmother never let her have friends over to the house.

*****

After fretting the day away, at just before eight Aggie stood outside the room of knobs. A part of her believed nothing was going to happen, and it was all still a dream and the invitation was a fluke. The other part of her knew she was about to experience something she couldn't fathom. Opening the door, the room was empty. Entering anyway, Aggie made her way to the center of the room. Taking a moment she examined the doorknob that Liel left from the night before, in what she thought was a dream.

It was delicate and golden with a strong vine that ran over it as though it were veined. Reaching out, she touched it lightly with just the tips of her fingers. Quickly she snatched her hand back as energy ran through her hand, causing it to feel a bit numb. Looking down at her hand the feeling lingered, so she rubbed her hand on her pant leg.

Taking in a few other knobs surrounding this one, she saw they all had minor details she hadn't taken in before. One had what looked to be daggers etched into the metal that seemed to be cast in bronze. The one below that looked like molten lava. "Mental note, don't touch that one, ever." Aggie was always one to talk to herself since she was usually alone when in the house, unless she was sitting in the kitchen with her grandmother.

Before she could take in another intricate piece of metal hanging on the wall, the room began to hum. Quickly she made her way back to the center of the room, running smack into a table with a full set of nine chairs. She rubbed the spot on her hip that took the greatest impact. "Where did this come from?" Aggie wondered. Not for long, though, because the room wasn't finished. Glowing light poured from several points of contact around the room. Looking around Aggie, realized that multiple doorways were breaking through the wall over several doorknobs. Before she could make it around to all the glowing lights, eight men filed into the space. All of them towered over her and were dressed in a variety of attire. One was dressed in a full suit and looked like he was attending a business meeting; another wore slacks and a dark shirt without a tie. Then she glanced at the faces of the next two, who appeared to have come from the same doorway. They were a mirror image of each other, but their faces were where the similarities stopped. One with dark hair and one with light, a smile and a scowl, they seemed to be more opposites of each other than typical twins. Dressed in jeans and t-shirts, these two were the most casual of anyone.

She couldn't tell you what the next man was wearing, because the moment she looked at his face the rest of the room disappeared. His smile was breathtaking and he was the most perfect specimen of a man she had ever encountered. The way his blonde hair looked as though it flowed and moved in non-existent wind. His curls were a bit unruly and resting across his broad shoulders. She could imagine hanging onto them in the throes of passion. His eyes were almost silver as the firelight reflected off of them and they captivated her entirely. As quickly as she was enraptured, it all cleared away as she noticed Mathius had walked up and smacked this gorgeous man on the back of the head. "That is enough, Ky. Let her at least meet everyone before you start working your wiles on her."

Not sure what had just happened, Aggie moved on to the last unknown man in the room. He was tall and willowy but looked as though he could scale any height with his bare hands. He wore a green button-up shirt paired with a light, airy pair of pants. They reminded Aggie of beachwear. Liel was the last man of the group and they all were now encircling her and gathered to the table.

"Good evening, Agatha." Liel was the first to speak, and he insisted on using her full name.

"I believe I asked you to call me Aggie. Care to introduce me to your friends?"

"Of course, it would be my pleasure." Liel turned toward Mathius first. "You know Mathius from last night." Continuing, he came to the twins. "I'd like you to meet Mitchell and Ren. Then we have Xavier," Liel indicated the man dressed all in black without a tie. "Next is Gryson." This was the man dressed to the nines. Next was the man who wore the green shirt, "This is Eldon, and last but not least is Kyrel." Liel finished with a flourish of his hand at each of them. Kyrel was the man who had entranced her from the beginning. She didn't let her gaze linger on him very long, for fear of being unable to tear it away. "Just for formalities, I would like to introduce you all to Agatha. She is Blythe's granddaughter and our newest Gatekeeper."

Most of their heads bobbed in acknowledgement, Aggie noticing that not all of the new faces bothered. She didn't know if she should take offense or ignore their potentially rude behavior. "I don't even know where to start. I'm sure we will have time to get to know each other better later, but for now let's just get to the problem at hand." Taking charge had never been a problem for Aggie, and now was no different. In a room full of drop-dead sexy men, it could be easy to get distracted by the way their shirts stretched over their bulk and left little to the imagination. Each of them was built in a way that gave her a better understanding of why they were chosen to be a part of the Brotherhood to begin with.

"Thank you for being considerate of our time and the reason we are all here. I know everyone will want to have a chance to speak with you, but we can save that for the end." Liel seemed to be the spokesperson of the group. Then Mathius took over and explained to the new portion of the group what he had told Liel and Aggie the previous night.

*****

"So, we have roughly two weeks to get to the bottom of this?" Kyrel, with his silken voice, spoke up first. He was holding his chin in his hand as he took in all the information, his finger pressed against his mouth in deep concentration.

"Yes, that is how it appears," Liel confirmed.

"Have you found any witnesses or evidence that we can trail?" one of the twins asked, but Aggie couldn't tell them apart yet.

"Which one are you again?" Aggie decided to ask rather than wait until after they finished their meeting. If she could get it straight now, then it would make the conversation easier to follow.

"Mitchell," the dark-haired twin answered gruffly, without another word. His twin, Ren, grinned at her and winked flirtatiously. Aggie just smiled in return; he was obviously going to be trouble of the sexy variety.

"There have been no witnesses and minimal evidence but perhaps you could sniff something out on-site, as the prince's room has been kept off-limits since the incident occurred." Mathius was nothing but a man of power, and when in the moment never to falter. He had information, and that was all he was going to give. Very little emotion sounded in his voice as he spoke, and Aggie wondered if that was his personality for when he had a job to do or if he was emotionally detaching himself from this case.

"You do realize we're good for more than just *sniffing out* your evidence, right?" Mitchell scoffed at Mathius' choice of words, leaving Aggie to theorize their meaning. In true Aggie form, she just asked.

"I suppose that there is a personal jab he's touched on there. So, I'm just going to ask, at the risk of sounding rude, what are you?"

Mitchell sneered at her question and didn't answer. Ren, on the other hand, had no qualms about being the source of information. "While there are proper ways to ask, we can let you off just this once, while you're still feeling out the ins and outs of all of this. Mitchell and I are the heads of the shifters. He's the Alpha, while I'm his Beta. I have nearly the same level of authority as he does, so we share the Guardian responsibilities."

"Shifters? Like, werewolves or something?" Aggie asked with a little hesitation. If these guys were werewolves, that meant the men in this room were far more dangerous than she let herself consider.

"We are not werewolves." Mitchell growled his words, slamming his hands firmly on the table as he rose from his seat. His reaction confirmed his possible heritage. "Shifters are a controlled species that aren't at the mercy of the cycle of the moon. Humans have ruined our honorable reputation." Clearly, she had stepped on his toes unintentionally.

"I'm sorry, I meant no offense. I'm less than twenty-four hours into learning about your worlds and I'm still trying to wrap my head around it all." Aggie hoped she could smooth things over with them all and not cause any more problems.

"Pay no attention to him; he's just grumpy by nature. You're welcome to ask any questions of us that you would like. If he's too grumpy to answer, just come find me and I'll help you." Ren was obviously the nicer of the twins and at least she could tell them apart. Ren's lighter hair fell in front of his face and he flipped it back, giving Aggie the impression that he would make a very dreamy surfer guy.

"Can we continue now?" Mathius cleared his throat to direct the attention back to him and the reason they were all there. Aggie nodded and the guys continued.

"I think we need to get on-site and start investigating so we can try and dig up some leads. This close to the festival, there is a good chance they will strike again." Eldon spoke up for the first time that night. His voice sounded like a melody, and Aggie knew right then that he would be one who could talk her out of or into anything.

"Do you have the rooms ready for us? I think it would be best to go ahead and leave tonight." Gryson's voice was smooth and commanding. Aggie assumed he was used to being in charge, and wondered what the actual dynamic of their little group was and who was considered the leader. Since they all were leaders in their own right, it was difficult to decide.

"The Brotherhood rooms were made ready when I came last night, so whenever you're ready we can start," Mathius was quick to answer, as though he expected the question.

The excitement Aggie felt overshadowed the remaining emotions storming through her. "We all get to go?"

With an eyeroll, Mathius nodded. "If you must tag along, a room will be prepared for you as well."

# Chapter 4

Aggie's palms were sweating as she approached the door to Mathius' world. She still didn't know what he was, and realized she had no clue what she was getting herself into.

"Mathius, before we go in—or out, or whatever—I think you should tell me what you are. I have no idea where we're going or what I should expect."

A smile broke out across his face, and she wished he would wear it more often. A glint of mischief shown in his eye, which should have worried her. Instead, it was like looking deeper into Mathius' soul. That one simple thing transformed him from the grumpy, unapproachable man to the tempting, handsome one standing before her. "I am a demon, Aggie." Her eyes widened at his words, mostly because his eyes flashed silver as he spoke. He continued before she could find the words to speak. "You are headed into the capital city of Ahael. You will see many of my kind, in more shapes and sizes than you could ever imagine." His tone was one of pride. He naturally expected her to react, so out of sheer stubbornness Aggie chose to just nod in understanding and remain silent. Mathius' smile dropped instantly at her lack of reaction, scowl firmly back in place.

He reached for a doorknob that she would never have touched; it was red with an orange glow in places and looked to have heat coursing through it like flames just below the surface. It reminded her of the lava one she saw earlier. "Do similar knobs lead to the same realms?" Aggie blurted out her thoughts, only half expecting it to be answered, since they were preparing to walk through Mathius' door.

"Just like on Earth, there are many magical portals in different areas and different countries. They act as a system to expedite travel. They all lead here, but one could travel from the United States to Ireland in a matter of minutes using the Gateway." Liel was always good for sharing information and doing it without a hint of annoyance in his voice. He seemed to be the only one who was able to keep his emotions hidden from the outside world.

"Can anyone use the Gateway? Could Joe Blow off the street stumble upon a door and end up in my house?" Aggie was panicking a little bit and she wasn't as good at concealing her emotions.

"Let's get through this door, and we will show you," Gryson chimed in, and placed a hand on her shoulder. He wasn't the one she thought would strive to comfort her first. Nodding, they all turned to Mathius who had paused in his intentions to open the door. Reaching for the handle, Aggie watched his face to see if there was a reaction to what she expected to be excruciating heat or pain from a burn. When he didn't react, she filed that information away for later questions, knowing if she didn't let them continue nothing would get done.

Mathius was the first to enter the door headed to Ahael. She assumed if anyone was on the other side guarding in his stead, he would need to be there to approve their entry. Xavier was the next one through, and his body was so rigid he almost looked like a piece of stone that floated over the threshold.

Eldon followed closely behind, as though he was afraid he might miss something if he waited too long. The twins walked up to the door side-by-side; for a moment Aggie thought they wouldn't separate and would brotherly fight through the doorway. At the last possible second, Ren let Mitchell take a step forward and enter the space only a moment before he joined him. They really were locked at the hip, Aggie observed silently.

"I'll meet you on the other side." Liel spoke right before he slid through the doorway, leaving Aggie with Gryson who still kept his hand resting on her shoulder. She didn't know why she hadn't shrugged him off. She was just too captivated by watching the rest of the guys disappear through this door to a land of mystery.

"Are you ready?" Gryson asked her and let his hand slide down her arm, clasping her hand gently. He never flinched or asked for forgiveness. She always did like a man who could take charge and not feel guilty for his every thought or movement.

Gripping his fingers tighter Aggie nodded, unable to think past her intrigue and excitement. She faintly felt a sensation that she assumed was from the door reacting with her senses. She wasn't a daredevil, but she loved a challenge. This was definitely a challenge that she wasn't going to back down from. Reaching down to grasp her overnight bag, Aggie let Gryson pull her through the doorway.

The light from that could be seen from the Gateway side of the door was nothing compared to the images flashing past her inside the door. Colors, known and unknown, flashed before her. She couldn't make out any specific shapes, not even the form of Gryson who she still felt clutching her hand. A gust of wind whooshed past her as she was pulled through this colorful world. If one could interpret the forms in this space, it would be a beautiful place to live. She listened past the wind now blowing the loose strands of her hair around her face. In the distance, she could hear what sounded like voices. She wondered if the group had already made their way through and were calling for her. Allowing the force to tug her through, when she opened her eyes next she was surprised by what she saw.

Ice was everywhere. Not just on the ground or on the trees, but the houses looked to be made out of ice or glass as they gleamed in the light of day. The trees weren't green or even winter-worn. They seemed to be made out of ice itself. The air was bitter cold, and none of this was what Aggie had expected from a demon realm. Glancing back, it looked as though the door was transparent and seen only when the light reflected just right. You would have to know what you were looking for in order to find it.

"Is this how it always looks?" Her voice was one of awe and wonder. As beautiful as this was, she had just come from a blistering summer at home to a winter wonderland, who knows how far away.

"No, this happened while I was away. When I left it was summer and everything was alive and well. Lush and vibrant, but it seems the weather has taken another turn for the worse. It's a good thing we are getting started. I fear this will just get progressively more complicated as we go along."

Their feet crunched on the ice-covered ground. Unlike snow, it was still very stiff beneath them as they walked. It was as though no one had even walked through the area for days. Aggie realized they were closer to town than she initially thought. The trees were just intermingled into the townscape. Rather than cutting the trees to accommodate the homes, the trees remained and the houses were structured around them. It made for some rather unique dwellings. This didn't inhibit the size of the homes, as Aggie noted one house in particular. This house was shaped in a way that actually wrapped around four different trees while still maintaining the structural integrity of the house.

"I can't imagine what this place looks like not covered in ice, but this is the most magnificent thing I've ever seen," Aggie breathed. Gryson, who hadn't released her hand upon crossing the threshold, gave her hand a squeeze.

"This has nothing on my home, *parum praesetes*." His words were spoken so close to her ear, she could feel his lips brush lightly on her lobe.

"What does that mean?" His words were spoken eloquently, as though the language could have been his first and more used than English.

"That is what you are in Latin, *little keeper.*" Gryson didn't elaborate, but his words sounded like a term of endearment and not just a flippant phrase off the tongue.

"It was beautiful. Have you spoken Latin long?" A smile tipped the corner of Gryson's mouth at her question.

"I suppose we haven't divulged everyone's lineage to you, have we?" Gryson's question was rhetorical, as he continued to speak instead of waiting for an answer. She glanced around at all the men now standing around, waiting on them. This didn't stop Gryson from speaking. "I am a Mage. That means I was taught Latin before any other language, as all of our casting is done in our primary tongue." Aggie's eyes widened. It was as though she had stepped into this dream world. She never before imagined that such places and people, or perhaps she should say races, could actually exist. Aggie couldn't formulate words to express all the ideas that had just entered her mind. Gryson reached forward and placed his hand under her chin, lifting slightly to close her gaping mouth. A shock hit her, like one would get as a child from running your feet across the carpet. The electric charge wasn't painful, but startling. Without another word, they both turned back to the group still waiting on them.

"If you two are finished, we need to head in to get all of you settled in your rooms. Then, if there is still light left after that, I'll show you the prince's quarters." Mathius seemed to have a one-track mind, and Aggie could appreciate that in this instance.

"By all means, Mathius, lead the way. I'll stop slowing us down." Aggie was slightly embarrassed that their conversation had made them fall behind.

"You aren't at fault. He is just not used to traveling with a human. He needs to allow for your need for knowledge of the things previously kept from you." Ren was quick to answer in her defense, resulting in a sound resembling a growl from Mathius. Ren smiled fully at that, as though it were his intention to get underneath the demon's skin. Just thinking about it made Aggie's brain run in eight different directions. She couldn't believe she was traveling in a demon realm with a demon, an elf, two shifters, a Mage, and who knew what else since the others had yet to reveal their natures. Aggie wasn't going to ask, since she had already made enough stupid moves that day. She did allow herself to speculate, and wondered how long it would take them to come clean.

*****

As Mathius led them through town, Aggie soaked it all in and got lost in the sights and smells. She didn't even realize when they all stopped in front of a massive gate, and ran smack into Mitchell's back. While she should have been embarrassed her first thought as her hand flew up to protect her face and landed on his shirt was, *Damn, what does he have under there, because I can feel every single ripple.* Thankfully, her mind and mouth were friends at that moment and she kept that very outspoken thought locked away for her personal time later. That made for a very vivid image. She quickly stepped back, putting some distance between them, but not before Mitchell turned and scowled at her. Darting her gaze away from his determined stare, Aggie took in the doors before them. They were the tallest she had ever encountered in her life and she couldn't tell if they were made of wood or not. The coloring said yes, but the texture made her believe they were actually a stone base. Intricate designs were woven into the very heart of each door. In the center were six boxes, three to each door. The completed picture was breathtaking.

"Where are we?" Aggie asked no one in particular.

"The demon castle; this is where the guardian rooms are reserved because it adds to the royal protective blanket when we are all here. There is a similar space in every realm. Those of us who live in the realm have a permanent room in the same wing." Mathius informed her in a way that made Aggie hope this man relaxed every once in a while. No way he could be this cold all the time.

Nodding her understanding, Aggie chose not to speak again for fear of a verbal reprimand. So far, it was mixed as to which of the guys were being nice to her, and three were still silent since the introductions. Kyrel had kept his distance after Mathius smacked him before. She didn't know if she should be thankful or take offense at his recoil. He had a particular allure that, even though they were separate, there was still a pull to him that was almost tangible.

Glancing toward the front of their group, a movement caught her eye. While they had stood there, she thought they were waiting for someone to open the doors. Instead, she realized Mathius was placing his right hand in the centermost square on the right door and the same with his left on the opposite door. Everyone waited without speaking through the process, and Aggie wondered what was happening. Then, out of nowhere, Mathius' hands began to glow red. She couldn't see his eyes but assumed they were glowing as well, given his display from before.

Just as she was leaning to whisper to Gryson to figure out what was happening, the doors shook and with a loud rumble to match their stature, split and opened slowly. Aggie started to walk toward the doors but stopped short. No one else had moved a step; Aggie looked around and hoped no one noticed her mistake. Each man looked at the slowly opening doors and then her eyes came to rest on Ren, who was looking at her with a grin and laughter in his eyes. Deciding to take a page from Mitchell and Mathius, Aggie scowled at Ren. Unfortunately, his shoulders bounced his mirth in return. She chose to ignore him until he forgot about this moment.

Soon the doors opened fully, and they all began their walk inside. The walls were made of stone, the palace resembling a fortress. The halls were lit with torch-light that seemed to be never-ending. She assumed it was the magical flame Mathius used in the room of doors the first night she met them. She watched as the fire danced, and the glow lit the hallways that looked more like tunnels. Even though the space could be used as a foothold, it was also extravagant. The tapestries on the wall painted pictures that were stories Aggie wished she knew. Perhaps one day, she could persuade Mathius to share one with her. The hallways sprouted in all directions from the main entrance, and Aggie was overwhelmed with everything she could see just from this vantage point.

"This way." Gryson nudged her toward the hallway on the right. She felt like the lone man out because she wasn't sure how she would remember how to get anywhere in this place, but everyone else seemed to have been here a time or two and had it covered. Each hallway looked basically the same. The only difference were the tapestries. Mentally recording a few that she passed when they made turns, Aggie decided they would be her virtual roadmap around this maze. At the left was a tapestry that depicted a woman on a hillside. Aggie read the nameplate at the base: 'The Wanderer'. A few more minutes they took another left and the first image she saw was something that resembled a dragon being crowned by some sort of flamed creature. Aggie was confused, reading the plate that clearly stated, 'The Flamed Dragon' in her mind, and continued.

After what felt like countless turns later, Mathius stopped in front of a dead-end hallway with nine multicolored doors branching off from it. Each of the men made their way to different doors. Xavier stepped through a red door. Mitchell and Ren disappeared behind matching golden doors. Eldon's door caught her attention because it wasn't so much a color as an iridescent shimmer as the torch lights flickered. Kyrel placed his hand on the knob of the door that appeared to be teal, and glanced back at her for the first time since they met. The pull intensified with the lingering look and nearly took her breath away. With a broad smile, Kyrel walked into his room and sealed the door again. Liel, Mathius, and Gryson stood in front of a white door. Aggie thought this was strange that they would share a room. "Well, I had no idea you boys swung that way." She giggled to herself at her own joke, but the guys all shared a confused look.

"This is your room. It is a space that hasn't been occupied for many years, but I made sure it was prepared for you," Mathius explained. Before stepping inside, she looked at the remaining doors in the hallway, assuming the silver, purple, and green doors would be for the remaining men. Not thinking any more of it, she turned the knob to her room and pressed her way inside. The men lingered at the entrance and let her take in the place.

It was the most extravagant room she had ever seen. A bed that looked custom-designed and larger than a king size was placed in the center of the room, not touching a single wall. She thought that was odd, but dismissed it as she was distracted by everything else. Walking around the room she ran her hand over the crown molding that adorned each wall. It was white with gold running through it, giving everything an elegant feel. There was a table in the room already set with what appeared to be a tea or coffee pot and a few treats, for which she was thankful, as she could really use a snack. The dresser was made of solid wood and had a built-in vanity. Aggie placed her bag on top of it and moved over to the wardrobe. When she opened it, her hand flew to her mouth and she gasped. It was filled with countless dresses that Aggie could only dream of wearing. Lowering her hand, she took in the soft textures, and noticed upon further investigation that each of the dresses were in the same shades of the doors she had just seen.

"Does everything meet with your approval?" Mathius' voice sounded directly behind her, softer than she had known he was capable of. She turned and noticed his brow was furrowed with worry. *Does he really think I wouldn't like—no, love—all of this?*

Quickly, in a hurry to reassure him, Aggie replied, "It's beyond my wildest dreams. Yes, it's perfect."

Sighing audibly, Mathius' shoulders squared and he was back to himself in mere seconds. "Good; I'll leave you to freshen up and I'll knock when we're ready to head to the prince's chambers." Without another word he turned and the three men left and shut her door firmly.

Being alone, Aggie squealed quietly and jumped up and down with excitement. This was her room for as long as they needed to stay. It was more beautiful than any hotel room, and came with clothes and a snack. She was in her own personal heaven.

# Chapter 5

Knocking startled Aggie from her silent reverie. Reluctantly she rose from the plush mattress. It was the most comfortable bed she had ever been in, and she immediately regretted standing. Grasping the ornate doorknob, she pulled the door open and was met by all the guys waiting in the hallway.

"Are you ready?" Gryson was the first to speak, and as she took in the other guys she noted mixed expressions. Mitchell stood with his arms crossed, leaning against the opposite wall. Mathius stood stoic, a scowl set firmly in place. Liel was impassive, just as she expected, with his arms crossed behind him. Ren smiled as her eyes ran past him, and she couldn't help but smile back. Xavier and Eldon were waiting expectantly for her answer. Aggie chose not to look in Kyrel's direction for fear of the pull retaking its hold. Rubbing her hand over her face to clear her thoughts, she then leaned down to slip her shoes back on.

"I suppose so. I wouldn't want to hold up the party." Closing the door behind herself, she hesitated. "Are my things going to be safe in here?" She had noticed she was the only one who had brought a bag with her. Did they know something she was unaware of?

"Your things will be fine. If there is anything else you require, simply let me know and I will have it brought to your room. I mean anything at all." Mathius was being kind to her and Aggie didn't know how to respond to that. His mood swings were giving her whiplash and she wasn't sure how to take them. Who was Mathius, and which version of him was a front?

"I'll keep that in mind. Now, let's get this show on the road." Aggie let Mathius take the lead but didn't wait for the rest of the guys. She stuck close to Mathius since he was currently being nice to her.

Before long, they stopped in front of a room. She was surprised not to see the door heavily guarded. "Where are the guards?" Aggie finally asked.

"They don't need guards. The room is magically locked," Liel supplied. Aggie then realized that Mathius' hand was on the handle and it was glowing silver to match his eyes.

"Are all the doors locked with magical keys?" Aggie was right behind Mathius, and he glanced over his shoulder and narrowed his eyes.

"When someone can merely dust themselves into any space, it makes it safer to magically lock down private areas." Mathius didn't elaborate beyond that and went back to unlocking the door.

"So, do you have to know the spell or is it a list of approved entry, like at a dance club?" Aggie's questions were obviously getting on Mathius' nerves because she could have sworn he actually growled, but he opted to remain silent and focused on the task at hand. Moments later, the latch clicked and the door swung open. Mathius grabbed Aggie's arm to stop her from entering. The rest of the guys filed into the room and got to work like a well-oiled machine.

"The locks are more like a list, as you so basically put it. Though it is released by magical fingerprint." Aggie was surprised that Mathius had been forthcoming and answered her question.

"If it's a fingerprint, why does it take so long to unlock everything?" She was pressing her luck, but Mathius had calmed slightly since unlocking the door.

"That is where the list comes into play. The magical fingerprint is sifting through the list one by one. If you break contact in any way, it starts over." Mathius pushed her into the room with the guys now that they had begun.

"That isn't very high-tech for a magical locking system. There are faster ways to do that with human technology, with actual fingerprints." Aggie was a little dumbfounded. She assumed that magic made life easier, but in this case it seemed like a harder process.

Mathius held his hand out flat toward her. Aggie looked at him, confused. "Magical beings don't have fingerprints." He left his hand there and Aggie couldn't help herself. Reaching for him she clasped his hand to examine it closer. Before she could get a good look, she realized her hands warmed under his touch and a feeling vibrated from her chest. Aggie gasped and dropped his hand, the feeling and the warmth disappearing in an instant.

Eyes wide with disbelief, she demanded, "What was that?" She was rubbing her hand against her chest, trying to understand.

"I think you and I need to have a chat. Now is neither the time or the place, though. Can I come to your room tonight so we can speak in private?" Aggie raised one eyebrow at Mathius. Had he gone from growling at her to asking to come to her bedroom in private?

"Are you sure that is a good idea?" Aggie feigned coyness and did everything she could to hold the face.

"I promise you will be perfectly safe in my care. There are just some things you need to know about your role as Gatekeeper that you might not want to discuss with all of us present. If you don't want to talk with me I'm sure I can convince Liel, or even Kyrel to take my place if you would prefer." There was a subtle hint of humor in his tone.

Aggie burst out laughing, drawing the attention of all the guys. "No, I think you'll do fine. If we're going to have an actual conversation, I'm not sure I can handle Liel's analytical tone for much longer. Don't even get me started on Kyrel." She covered her mouth to stifle her laugh and keep her tone lower. The rest of the guys moved back to their individual projects. Mathius smirked knowingly and Aggie found herself captivated by his smile.

The guys were working and she tried to stay out of their way. Walking over to the wardrobe, she realized upon closer examination that the prince was quite young. She was under the impression that he was a child, but not as young as the size of his clothes led her to believe. "What's the prince's name?" Aggie realized they had just been calling him 'the prince' and no one had referred to him by his given name.

"Rikan." Mathius' voice came from directly behind her. He hadn't let her get far away from him in the room. The closer he was to her she realized her body hummed in appreciation. *Was this a side effect of our touching?* The more she thought about it, the more she realized that was the first time any of the guys had touched her skin to skin. Then she remembered Gryson had touched her and she felt something then, too, but didn't know if it was the magic swirling from the gateway. Was that significant, or only her imagination running wild?

"I'm guessing he's about eight or nine, judging by these clothes." Mathius nodded once at her assumption. "How many other kids have been abducted? Are they all about the same age?" Aggie was slowly going through Rikan's clothes as she thought through her questions. Her heart was breaking for Rikan's parents, and all the other children's parents, as well.

"The children are all around the same age, seven to ten. None have come into their full powers yet, but the powers are there nonetheless. Something traumatic can force it out. We need to get to them before that happens." Mathius was very passionate about this, and it touched Aggie's heart.

"Did they only kidnap boys?" Aggie's brain was going a million miles an hour and it was hard to settle on one question at a time.

"No, they haven't been consistent with any particular gender." Mathius was the only one answering, and Aggie took in the rest of the room. Ren and Mitchell were wandering around the room, somewhat aimlessly. When she looked a little closer she could see their noses twitch. She watched them for a couple minutes, and they stayed longer in different areas than others.

"Are you getting anything?" The twins turned at the sound of her question. It was as though they knew it was directed at them. Ren raised an eyebrow at her, but to her surprise it was Mitchell who answered.

"There isn't any scent here that is out of place. It is all demon, aside from our own now that we are here. There is a latent scent of—" Mitchell hesitated, and scrunched up his face like he was trying to find the right words.

"Starting fluid," Ren supplied.

"Why would there be starting fluid in here? This is an eight-year-old's room. So, unless your olfactory makeup is similar to the human construction and your children have a propensity for getting high, there has to be another explanation." Aggie was wracking her brain for answers, but she wasn't an investigator or a scientist. All the things with that smell were likely endless.

"No, none of our chemical makeup is quite like a human's. We can't drink your alcohol and become intoxicated. Taking your kind of drugs doesn't put us under the influence. Our metabolism is significantly faster than yours. Some are more than others, but all are faster than humans." Liel gave her his usual overly-detailed response.

"You could have just said no," Aggie smarted off to Liel, and smiled to show she was only joking. "If Rikan wasn't using it for recreational purposes, then what else could it be?"

"Chloroform," Xavier intoned, and that one word had Aggie frozen. His voice was a rich, velvety baritone that sent goosebumps running down her spine.

"That makes sense; no one heard anything and a child would likely react or be upset to have a stranger removing them from their room at night." Mathius looked to be deep in thought as he revealed that small tidbit.

"If your bodies don't react the same way humans' do to drugs, why would chloroform do anything to any of you, let alone Rikan?" Aggie was doing her best to keep up, but now they were dealing with a completely different species of being and therefore outside her realm of knowledge.

"Just like human children have different tolerances, so do our children. While it wouldn't have knocked him out entirely it may have subdued him, not unlike a slow morphine drip used to subdue pain." Aggie rolled her eyes, of course Liel would answer her question.

"Is he the only one of you guys who knows these answers? No offense, Liel, but you make learning about your people very boring." Processing the information she received, Aggie started pacing the room. It seemed someone had abducted these kids and subdued them with chloroform. Sleeping children didn't panic or cause a ruckus. "How did they get out?"

A collective sigh rang through the room. Aggie glanced up just as Mathius came to stand beside her. Without saying a word, he gripped her by the shoulders and braced tightly. Aggie didn't get a chance to speak before the room started swimming. She felt like she had done a bad dose of acid or something equally as awful. When the room finally stopped moving, she was no longer standing in the same place. Instead, she was across the room, back in front of Rikan's wardrobe. Her stomach was in knots. "Breathe deeply; the feeling will pass in a moment."

After a couple of deep breaths, Aggie regained the ability to formulate words. "What the hell was that?"

"That, Aggie, was what I mentioned earlier about dusting. To everyone else in the room you merely disappeared, as though dust was blown from the mantel. In reality, you phased from one side of the room with me to another. It's the easiest way for us to travel. Anyone with demonic blood can do that." Mathius looked proud that he had caught her off guard with his demonstration.

"You're saying that all of you can do this?" Aggie's hand flew to her forehead. She was becoming overwhelmed with information and her little impromptu teleportation hadn't helped, only causing her to become dizzy.

"No, only those with demonic blood. Mitchell, Ren, Liel, Xavier, and Eldon weren't blessed with that privilege." Mathius' pride was reaching new heights. Aggie put all that together and something clicked.

"You're a demon as well?" She focused all of her attention on Kyrel and instantly regretted it. She was locked, and couldn't stop looking at him. Before she could stop it, she felt her feet begin to guide her straight toward him.

"Yes, well, I'm a kind of demon," Kyrel answered, and his voice was so captivating that Aggie just wanted to find a way to crawl inside and live in it. Her entire body was at ease, and there were no more threats or worries. All that was left was Kyrel and his charisma that had her lost to him. "I'm an incubus." His words were a story just for her. No one else existed, that is until Mathius smacked Kyrel in the head again and spun her around so she could realign her attention on anything or anyone else.

Aggie shook her head, instantly angry. "That's what you have been doing to me? You've been using your powers of seduction on me? Why would you do that to me? I should have known there was something magical at work. I never get dopey-eyed over men." Fuming, partly because she didn't want to become enraptured again, and partly because she wanted it to be natural attraction, Aggie refused to look at Kyrel.

"Not magical; my powers can be used to draw in the opposite sex, and occasionally not the opposite, but that only happens when I push out my powers. With you I haven't done anything of the sort. I would never do that to you. The only thing that I can figure is you're tapping into something more instinctual, more raw." Mathius cut him off again with another slap to the head. Kyrel never flinched once in the times that Mathius had done that.

"That is enough; we have other things to worry about and I will talk to her about that later." This piqued Aggie's interest but, given their current situation, she filed that away for later along with her other questions. "If there aren't any smells for you two to pick up and no one else is getting anything, let's all prepare for dinner and then tomorrow we can comb through the physical evidence collected the morning Rikan was discovered missing."

# Chapter 6

**D**inner was a quiet affair and Aggie was pleased to find out that, even though she was in a demonic realm, there was still normal food to be eaten.

"Was dinner to your liking?" Mathius was walking her back to her room, everyone else trailing behind.

"Yes, I honestly didn't know what to expect, but the steak was a pleasant surprise." Aggie hadn't seen a spread so large in any buffet on Earth. She felt bad that she couldn't eat more.

"They knew to prepare for you but didn't know what you would like." He hadn't reverted to his bristly self all day, and for that Aggie was grateful.

"I'm not picky; however, while I'm willing to try new things, I'm glad it wasn't anything outside of my comfort zone for my first night. They don't have to go to any trouble for me. In the future, I'm happy to make do with whatever is provided." They stopped outside her room and the rest of the men walked straight to their own, most without so much as a glance. She still didn't know how to feel about most of them, but she wanted to get along with everyone since she was going to be spending more time with them. At first, it was a bit intimidating and farfetched, but now having lived it for a day she realized how real everything was. The thought of these kids in an unfamiliar place held captive by a strange demon was unthinkable. More than anything she wanted to help get them back where they belonged without anything else happening to them.

"Are you still up for that discussion?" Mathius wedged his shoulder between her and the door, to prevent her getting past him alone.

"I guess, but I'm getting tired, so let's make it quick." She hoped that she sounded convincing, as she didn't know that she had a lengthy discussion in her after her day.

"I will try to be quick and concise. If you have any questions you can ask them or wait until tomorrow. I'm afraid, though, that the details I need to reveal to you can't be put off for long." Reaching for the doorknob, Aggie noticed it glowed softly under his hand. It was so fast it was nearly imperceptible.

"Are these rooms locked like Rikan's?" She stopped before entering because she was intrigued. Mathius nodded and pushed the door open further. "Then why doesn't it glow when I touch it?"

"That will be answered before the night has come to an end. Please head inside, as the information I have to give you is sensitive and I fear you won't want anyone hearing it until you are more prepared." Mathius waved her inside and she followed his encouraging. He shut the door behind them.

Aggie sat on the bed and pulled her legs up and crossed them. If this was going to be a sensitive conversation, she was going to be comfortable.

"Aggie, you come from a very special family. The Wasley family is descended from the first Gatekeepers. It has passed through the bloodlines to each female child. It will pass through the male children as a carrier to keep the family line intact." Mathius was starting to sound like Liel. If it weren't for the facial expression and tonal changes, she would have questioned him.

"There is a part of being the Gatekeeper that is a choice for each to uphold. It doesn't eliminate the position or the importance at all, but the choice is a difference of power. Your ancestors, including your grandmother, chose not to take on every role, and just chose to maintain the doors in the Gateway. If you so choose, you could ultimately be the ninth Guardian." Aggie was glad she was sitting down, but Mathius wasn't finished.

"In order for you to accept your role as the ninth Guardian and full Gatekeeper of the realms, you must consummate your bond with the Guardians individually. With that, you will take on your complementing powers to each one of the Guardians." Mathius stopped. Aggie wasn't sure if he was finished or if she even understood him correctly. She didn't know if she could straighten her thoughts into questions or if she was destined to be lost in the chaos forever. Since she wasn't speaking, Mathius reached over and took her hand. The warmth spread instantly and the buzzing in her chest, that felt like home and everything she could ever want, was like it had never left her. Aggie found herself leaning into his touch, but before she could connect any other body parts to his he spoke again.

"That is why we feel this connection when we touch." Aggie's eyes flew open and felt her mouth drop open again. He gently closed it before pulling both hands back to his own lap.

"You feel it, too? I'm not crazy then." She breathed a sigh of relief, but then his words fell into place. "You're saying I'm meant to have sex with all of the Guardians? Did you guys have sex to form your bond?" She felt silly for even asking, but the way he worded it that was exactly how it sounded to her, not that she would fault them if that was the case.

Mathius scoffed at her. "Of course not; our powers are natural. You are human and must be gifted powers when you accept your full role as Gatekeeper and ninth and final Guardian. Yours is most important, and strengthens the internal bond between all of us. We will not only be stronger, but nothing will be able to defeat us as a completed unit."

"You only answered one of my questions. I'm supposed to have sex with *all* of you?" Aggie wasn't put off by the idea but just wanted to get clarification. She found each of the men attractive in their own way, but she hoped she had time to get to know them all individually before being asked to *consummate* anything.

"It isn't only about the sex; it is about the bond. You must choose to mate with each of us. There is one true mate for everyone, and ours is the Gatekeeper. While we can mate with anyone we please, it will become more intimate and complete with the one truly meant for us. In our case, it is you." Mathius' eyes darkened at his own words and he drew a bit closer, as though the idea of mating with her was the only thing he ever wanted to do.

Aggie's thoughts caught up with her like a scratch across a record player, "Wait! You're saying I'm supposed to have sex with all of you. So, all I am to you is the power equivalent to a broodmare? Without me, you all don't come into your full power?"

"You're overthinking this. You get powers as well. So, it is what you humans would call a win-win situation." Mathius' words had Aggie fuming.

Before she could say anything that she might later regret, Aggie simply pointed to the door. "I think it's time you left me to sleep. I'm not sure I can rationally speak to you anymore without a good night's rest and some coffee tomorrow morning."

"Now, Aggie—" Before Mathius could continue, she opened the door and shoved him toward the hallway. While he was stronger and heavier than her, she was determined to rid her personal space of him.

When she couldn't budge him, her voice rose louder and echoed down the hallway, "Mathius, if you don't walk out of here on your own, I will march my happy butt all the way down to your room and lock your ass out!"

"You can't lock me out of my own room," he said with a devilish smirk. "Did I not prove to you earlier that people coded to the room can just phase in? It is my room, even if you could figure out how to get in there before me and shut the door. I could get in purely because it is *my* room."

"Don't attempt to cloud my opinion with logic, that up until today wouldn't have been even remotely considered logic, mind you. I want you out of here so I can get some sleep." She was practically shouting at this point and she was pretty sure she heard at least one door latch click, meaning someone had come out into the hall to enjoy the show. "Whoever is out there, come get this goon out of my room this instant."

Moments later Kyrel came into view; not who Aggie was expecting at all. "What seems to be the problem?" Aggie avoided looking directly at him for fear of his hypnotic entrapment. The idea that he was an incubus was a teasing thought. One she might consider pondering once alone, and allowed to consider all this new information.

"He dropped a bomb on me and expected me to react better than I did. Now I need him to leave while I digest everything that I've learned today." Aggie thought she did a good job of reining in her temper, since she wasn't angry with Kyrel, even if she couldn't actually look at the demon.

"A bomb?" Kyrel's face was a mix of emotions and Aggie realized, while these men looked like men, they weren't human. So, she needed to watch the human phrases and slang around them.

"I made her aware of her options and possible destiny," Mathius relayed, with little remorse for upsetting her. His words were matter-of-fact, as though they had been discussing the weather. Aggie watched as Kyrel's eyes darkened.

"Oh no, you don't. Not you, too. I'm taking the rest of the night for me and letting myself have a much-needed break. If you would be so kind as to help me remove this bastard from my room, I'll get the rest of my plans started." With a slight nod, Kyrel gripped Mathius' arm and tugged lightly. Aggie rolled her eyes; of course he would move easily for Kyrel. As soon as they were across the threshold, she slammed the door. To her surprise, it didn't bang as she had hoped. It was as though the door had been pressed closed slowly. So instead, she kicked the door just for good measure, to release her frustration.

Breathing out a heavy sigh, Aggie decided to take a shower. Thankfully, her room had an en-suite. She had yet to explore it, but what better time than when she needed to relax. Stepping through the doorway, Aggie gasped suddenly, walking into a glass room. She remembered that the homes in the ice-covered wonderland that was Ahael looked like glass. What she didn't realize was that it wasn't just the ice. Luckily the lower half of the glass was frosted, but the upper portion was clear and she could take in the winter landscape by the light of the moon.

Her eyes glanced around the space. She realized that, in addition to a shower, she was blessed with a full-size tub. Upon further inspection it even had modern accessories, like jets. Without much delay Aggie quickly changed her plans in favor of a hot bath and beautiful scenery.

*****

Lost in thought, Aggie found herself thinking of the guys. She would have to be dead to not notice they all were more than attractive. Now that she knew about her future options if she so chose, Aggie couldn't help her thoughts from roaming the possibilities. She didn't know if it was her thoughts or the jets flowing through the water, but she couldn't stop the tingling between her legs. Given the fact that she was alone in the bathroom, she gave in to temptation. *After all the men I've dealt with today and the news I was just given, I'm allowed to take care of me now.* Aggie figured her train of thought was permission enough. Her fingers trailed down her body, stopping at her nipples and tugging lightly. A moan escaped her lips as her other hand extended farther to her center. As her fingers ran over her sensitive nub, her body thrummed in response. Before long she had worked herself into a rhythm, tweaking her aching nipples and caressing her clit just the way she knew would have her climaxing quickly.

Just as she suspected with the images of the men fresh in her mind, Aggie was tipped over the edge with the strongest orgasm she had ever experienced. It wracked her body with such an explosion she didn't know if she would ever come back down to earth. When her muscles finally relaxed, Aggie was breathless. If these men caused such a reaction just from the pictures in her mind, what would happen if she had one of them in real life?

A crash sounded from the bedroom side of the door. On instinct she covered her body and watched the door for a second. Then she remembered that only those granted access could enter her room. Leaping from the tub, she haphazardly threw a towel around herself and yanked the door open. Scanning the room, she nearly screamed when she realized what had made the sound.

There, standing near the door to the hallway, was Kyrel. He at least had the decency to look sheepish. "What are you doing in here? I thought I told you guys I wanted to be alone." Aggie was practically screaming and out of breath due to the heart attack he nearly gave her.

"My apologies, Aggie. I couldn't help myself. Usually in this wing I have no issues, but I sensed your activities and was drawn here almost like a drug." Kyrel's eyes remained glued to the floor and for that Aggie was grateful.

"What do you mean, sensed my activities?" She scowled at the top of his head, as though it were his eyes.

"It is my nature to feed off of the energies of sexual desires. You basically sent out a homing beacon and I followed it." Kyrel glanced up slightly but didn't meet her eyes. Aggie wasn't sure what would happen if he did. She wanted to hang on to her anger a little longer and not have it taken away at the whim of another creature.

"So, you felt me when I was touching myself?" Her words were hesitant as her anger faded into embarrassment. She was alone in the bathroom. Never would she have gone that far had she known there was an audience a few feet away.

"Your sexual desire was what brought me into the room, but once I was here I might have helped you along a bit." Gone was his timid, shameful act and his smirk rested firmly on his face.

"What do you mean you helped me along? Did you come into the bathroom at some point?" Aggie was confused and a bit worried what all this meant.

"I don't have to be in the same physical space to use my powers on you. I knew you needed to relax, and since your mind had already drifted there on its own I decided to help you be as relaxed as possible." His grin firmly planted on his face showed Aggie that whatever he had done was more than just standing at the door and listening.

"You're saying you stood there and magicked your mojo somehow, and caused me to climax harder than I ever have in my life?" Aggie wanted him to deny it, because the thought of it was both terrifying that he could do that without touching her and intriguing for the same reason. What would happen if they actually touched? Their eyes met and Aggie felt drawn to him just as before. Only this time she didn't stop herself, and when they were only inches apart he answered her.

"It is how I sustain the beast inside. I hope I didn't offend you, but you seemed to have needed some kind of release and, given the fact that you threw us out, you weren't going to be letting any of us help you directly. My powers allow me a certain amount of leeway and, since I was already here, I figured I should lend a hand in some way." His hands came to rest on her arms just under her shoulders and locked her away from him, but that didn't stop her. Since they were touching and she was clutching her towel tightly, their skin was in direct contact. The buzzing feeling she felt with Mathius was there with Kyrel, too. Though with Kyrel it seemed more like a cat's purr vibrating her. No pain, only something representing sheer relaxation. Not in a state to resist, Aggie rose up on her toes and leaned in. Kyrel didn't need any instruction and lowered his head to meet hers. Their lips met and Aggie felt sparks. She wondered if they were physically shooting sparks since the feeling was so real.

His lips were plump and soft and moved across hers, like they had done this a thousand times. Her hands lifted of their own accord and wrapped around his neck to give herself more leverage. Fingers curling into his hair, Aggie dragged her nails across his scalp, eliciting a moan from him. She licked across his seam and he opened to her. Their tongues met and fought for dominance. Kyrel won and he deepened the kiss. His arms wrapped around her, pulling her closer. Only then did she realize the fabric of his sweater was rough against her skin. Against her nipples, her very naked nipples. Gasping in his mouth, Aggie broke the kiss. Glancing down quickly she realized that, while lost in the moment, she had completely dropped her towel. Before she could hurriedly reach for it and hold it in front of her, she glanced up with flushed cheeks and swollen lips from Kyrel's assault. Only to find Kyrel's disheveled clothes and a very appreciative look in his eyes. "So much for modesty," Aggie muttered under her breath. Brushing her damp hair over her shoulders she wrapped the towel more securely around herself, keeping herself covered as best she could.

"You have nothing to hide, my dearest Aggie. I would be happy to continue this further and explore the rest of your body with my mouth. I'm hungry and ready to taste every inch of you." Aggie didn't know how to interpret his words since he said he was feeding off her energy before. The idea of literally being his meal was a bit off-putting.

"I think you've had enough tasting for one night. I think I'll go drain the tub and turn off the jets. Then I'll try and get some sleep before I have to face everyone tomorrow with my new-found knowledge." Kyrel nodded and bowed his head, backing toward the door.

"As you wish, my dearest. I hope you have pleasant dreams, and I shall see you in the morning. I know I'll sleep better with your taste still on my lips." Without another word, he slipped out the door.

Aggie closed it behind him and leaned her back against it. She reached up to feel her kiss-swollen lips and sighed. "Why do they have to be so alluring? I couldn't get a bunch of ugly, meat-headed guardians whose only saving grace was that they were good at their jobs?" Chuckling at the thought, she got ready for bed.

# Chapter 7

The next day, Aggie made her way down to breakfast. Luckily it was easy enough to find since no one had bothered to give her a tour the day before. Walking in, she wasn't surprised that all the guys had beat her there.

"Thanks for getting me this morning. I'm just glad this place isn't hard to navigate." Sarcasm was her best defense, and today she needed shields at full strength. She was already at a deficit because her sleeping habits weren't what they should have been. Between her conversation with Mathius and her impromptu make-out session with Kyrel, her REM cycle was definitely damaged.

"We weren't sure when you'd be ready to see any of us, and didn't want to press you." Mathius spoke up first, and everyone else simply glanced up or nodded. Kyrel chose not to look up.

Deciding coffee was needed more than conversation, Aggie made her way to the breakfast bar. The amount of food set up was a dream. Anything she could have dreamed up, and a few unidentified things as well, were on display. It was as though she had died and gone to food heaven. The first to draw her attention was the pyramid of coffee cups, and her hands wrapped around the top one before she could take another breath. Coffee was a lifestyle and part of her morning must-haves. That morning would be no different. Pulling the lever on the carafe, the liquid that came out was lighter than she expected. Turning to face the guys, a scowl marred her face as she sniffed the offending liquid. "WHAT. IS. THIS?" Each word was punctuated and the last letter practically spat at them.

"Tea," Mitchell responded, smirking slightly at her obvious distaste.

"Are you serious? Haven't you guys heard of a little something called coffee? If we're going to be spending time together, I'm going to need coffee. Is that going to be possible, or am I going to have to make a quick jaunt through the gateway every morning to get what I need in order to function?"

"That stuff isn't worth drinking, it is disgusting, and I don't know how you drink that drivel. Can't you just drink what is provided, or are you too much of a princess to be a gracious guest?" Mitchell was on a roll and wasn't backing down, but little did he know Aggie was more than capable in her current coffee-less state to keep up.

"I'll have you know that coffee is considered a delicacy in many countries. If I can't have a caffeine boost in the morning, my brain isn't going to fire on all cylinders. I didn't ask for any special treatment. Honestly, the only thing I need in order to cope is coffee. Everything else is an afterthought, and while I'm very grateful for them they're just not necessary. Coffee is necessary!" Aggie was practically screaming by the time she finished her rant.

"Calm down, woman!" Xavier stood and made his way toward her. "Even if they didn't have coffee, which they do, Gryson can conjure anything we need on a whim. Mitchell is just being an ass because he could smell your personal activities last night. He's likely just fighting a case of blue balls, and is none too happy about it." Xavier's face looked bored, but Mitchell's face was red with anger. Aggie was pleased with the turn of events. While she should have been embarrassed by the comment about her activities, he flipped it back and made Mitchell the butt of the joke. Then she thought harder about the words he used.

"What do you mean, smell?" She turned her attention to Kyrel. "I thought you were the only one who could sense such things."

"I didn't say he sensed you. I said he *smelled* you. I imagine, given that you are our mate, it was even harder for him to resist, but especially for the shifters who have an exceptional sense of smell, it was like you were upwind and teasing them." Xavier sat ramrod straight and hardly moved as he spoke. He took a sip from his goblet, and Aggie could only assume as to its contents.

"Isn't it a little early for day drinking? We have a lot to do and, given your word vomit now and the fact that I haven't heard you speak much at all, I'd say you've had enough." Xavier smiled; then, without question, passed her the vessel. Aggie wrapped her fingers around the stem and cupped the bottom and tipped it toward her mouth. The liquid didn't move like alcohol. It was thicker than anything she had ever drunk before but was still too dark to make out the exact color. Raising the goblet to her nose, Aggie inhaled and instantly her nose curled at the metallic smell.

Sticking her finger into the mysterious drink, her finger emerged coated with a reddish substance. "What is this?" Holding her finger to Xavier's face, to her surprise he simply leaned forward and wrapped his lips around her finger, sucking the substance off. Her lip curled in disgust. "That doesn't answer my question, but now I have so many more."

"Are you sure you want to know?" Xavier's rich voice caressed her skin, and made her wish it was more than just his voice. The power of the timbre left her feeling in want and need of him.

"I wouldn't have asked if I didn't want to know. I tend to be very direct and to the point most days. I don't like to beat around the bush for anything." Aggie leaned back, but Xavier still held her hand in his grasp. She noticed that his touch was different from that of Mathius or Kyrel. His touch was cool, as though he had been outside this morning without gloves. The buzzing that raged through her with Mathius was more of a flutter of thousands of bees buzzing around her heart with Xavier. Jerking her hand back, the sensations stopped instantly. It was getting hard to fathom all the changes that had been happening the past couple days. With her Gran's passing, and now the discovery of this new world, Aggie didn't know how much stranger this could get.

Xavier's eyes narrowed at her abrupt change and Aggie was sure his eyes took on a reddish glow. Now she wasn't sure what to think as he licked his lips and inhaled the air around her, as though he were tasting, but appeared to be more like a snake smelling the air. Blinking quickly, he came back to the present. Xavier shook his head slightly as though clearing his thoughts. Aggie wondered where he had gone for that split second.

"O Negative; it is my preference for breakfast. It tends to blend well with anything that I might still have in my stomach from the night before. Lunchtime I go for something a little richer, perhaps an AB Negative. Then, for dinner, I prefer something more refined and rare, like an RH Null. I have a pristine palate and I don't let much stop my cravings for the finer things in life." Aggie felt her jaw fall open at his words, but had a hard time formulating a sensible sentence.

Glancing back and forth between the other guys at the table, she gathered her thoughts. Ren seemed to be holding back his laughter at their exchange, but his brother Mitchell seemed to be more interested in consuming as many calories as humanly possible. *How many calories does a shifter need to consume on a regular basis?* Aggie's passing thought was a minor distraction from the current brain dilemma. Xavier had really thrown her for a loop with his description of his dietary needs. The rest of the guys were distracted by this or that, only sparing her and Xavier a passing glance between bites.

"Are you telling me that you're drinking blood right now?" Aggie finally found her words and dared ask what seemed like an insane question, but with everything she had recently experienced in the past day or so it was becoming easier to grasp. Xavier simply sipped from his chalice, closing his eyes. His head bobbed in a subtle nod that Aggie would have missed had she not been completely locked on his actions. "What does that make you, some kind of vampire or something?" Her tone gave a hint to her scoffing that she only partially believed the words that she spoke. Surely vampires were still a myth, even though she had been told that shifters, elves, and demons existed. There was still minimal evidence that couldn't be explained away if someone tried hard enough. Unfortunately, Aggie didn't have the knowledge or wherewithal to explain things away with any sort of skill. That left her with the most obvious explanations, and hoping against hope that she was wrong.

"What else would I be? Do you know of another being who survives on this particular elixir?" Xavier sounded like he was speaking down to her. Aggie was starting to get the impression that Xavier thought he was better than anyone else. So, instead of answering him she ignored his question.

Turning her attention to Mathius, she queried, "Since I don't know that I can grow accustomed to hot tea in lieu of coffee in one day would it be possible to get a cup of coffee, or would that be too much trouble?" Her eyes were pleading and she hoped he would take pity on her.

However, it wasn't Mathius who responded. With a flick of his wrist, Gryson caused a steaming cup of her favorite morning brew to appear in front of her. Hesitantly, she reached out and gingerly touched the rim. As her fingers connected she jerked her hand back, startled by the connection with an actual coffee cup. The heat of the steam wafted over her and Aggie caressed her fingers across each other. Tentatively, she lifted the cup in her hands and raised it to her lips. As the liquid sluiced down her throat, she stifled a moan. "Thank you, Gryson, this is perfect! It's the same coffee I have at home. How did you know that?

"I asked the brownies," Gryson answered simply. Aggie looked over her shoulder. Running her eyes back and forth, she searched for any desserts.

"Brownies? Why are you having conversations with the desserts? Also, if there are desserts, why didn't I get chocolate added to *my* breakfast menu?" Aggie had no clue what he was talking about, but now that he mentioned chocolate she really wished he had conjured up some of that as well.

"No, the brownies in your house that handle all the cleaning up. Who knows why, but they actually enjoy it." Ren thought he was actually clarifying, but Aggie was pushed so much farther into a state of uncertainty that it didn't help in the least.

To her surprise, it was Eldon who took pity on her and clarified, "A brownie is a being similar to a sprite. They move very quickly and usually in between planes. This allows them to stay hidden from most, almost as one would stay in the shadows. They have a knack for helping, but can cause their own chaos when they deem it necessary. They can help or hinder on a whim; you never want to upset one or your life could go from easy and blissful to crazy and panicked in a matter of moments." His voice lulled her into a state of complacency because of its lyrical, story-like grace. Aggie knew she could listen to him speak on the most boring topic and she would be captivated.

Aggie was so caught up in his words she didn't realize he had stopped, and she sat there with a look of adoration plastered on her face. Ren, in usual form, snickered, and that brought her back to the present. Quickly Aggie shook off her entranced spell from Eldon's voice and attempted to save face, realizing that everyone was looking at her and waiting for her response. "So, you're saying my Gran hasn't kept house for as long as I've been there, and the entire time I was growing up I didn't have to actually keep my room clean?" Aggie was full of mixed emotions. First, she was still upset that her Gran was gone forever, but now a secondary emotion was brewing. She was livid that, as a child, she was grounded a time or two for not keeping her room clean, when her own Gran didn't actually clean any part of the rest of the house.

"I'm sure she was just trying to do her job. It was her responsibility to keep the Gateway hidden from the real world. It was also her job to keep it from you until the time came for you to fulfill your role. Unfortunately, she passed before she could tell you about it," Gryson supplied, only putting a small damper on the flames of her temper that they had stoked by sharing this information. She knew it wasn't logical for her to be mad at her Gran, but there was so much she didn't know, and it would have been easier to take the news from someone she knew and trusted than eight strangers who just appeared in a magic room one day.

Latching on to this new information, Aggie's thought drifted to a time many years ago when she was still just a whiny teenager with life challenges of another nature.

*"Gran, I have to be there in fifteen minutes. If I don't leave now, I'll be late." Aggie stomped her foot to emphasize her frustration.*

*"Then I guess you should have cleaned up that mess before it got this late. Now you're just going to have to settle for being late and clean it up quickly, or be much later than necessary and risk missing the time with your friends." Gran was always calm and never raised her voice to Aggie, but her tone left no room for argument. With a huff, Aggie turned toward the kitchen to clean up the dishes and the mess from her baking earlier. If only she hadn't promised her friends she would bring her famous chocolate chip cookies and sugar cookies for movie night. She should have just waited for it to be her turn to host. Stepping into the kitchen, Aggie was startled to find that everything was back where it needed to be and there was even a shine on the counters and the stove. Each of her cookies was placed neatly in the*

*Tupperware container and sealed tight, ready to be transported. Her jaw went slack and she blinked in disbelief. She didn't know why Gran had played it off that she would be late if Gran herself had already done the work. Instead of overthinking it, she ran to the sitting room and threw her arms around her precious Gran.*

*"Thank you so much!" Aggie squeezed her one last time and noticed Gran's confused face, but she didn't say a word. Aggie grabbed her cookies and ran out the back door.*

Understanding dawned on Aggie's face as she came back to the present. That mess, all those years ago, wasn't cleaned up by Gran, but by these elusive brownies. Taking another drink of her coffee, Aggie allowed her mind to settle. She wasn't actually angry with her Gran, but it was an easier emotion than questioning all the new things she was being introduced to recently.

"So, an elf, a demon, two shifters, a mage, an incubus demon, and now a vampire. Does anyone else want to enlighten me as to their history of origin before we discuss my newest piece of information and how I've decided to handle it?" Aggie lifted an eyebrow in Eldon's direction and her coffee to her lips, and took a long sip and relished the familiar flavor. For a moment she thought he was going to ignore her in favor of the silent reverie he had kept. Up until last night, Eldon hadn't said much of anything. He and Xavier had kept their voices minimal, only speaking when things were of the utmost importance. Xavier's conversation this morning while enlightening her was the most he had spoken since she was introduced to him. Then when she was about to give up hope that he would be forthcoming and willingly offer up the information she had asked for, Eldon cleared his throat and spoke softly. His lyrical voice bounced through the room even with that minimal sound.

"You might have a hard time understanding what I am." His musical notes were almost inaudible as he chose to give up his self-imposed vow of silence.

"I can't imagine it would be any worse than anyone else in this room. Seeing as how two of you can literally change shape, one of you drinks blood for sustenance, and one of you, maybe two, can actually transport themselves by mere use of thought." Aggie fought an eyeroll and waited for Eldon to continue.

"Not so much that you wouldn't believe me, but you might have a misconstrued idea of what I am. I am of Fae descent, and that means different things to modern people than what is factual." Aggie's eyes grew large as she took in this information. Her fingers itched to see his power take shape.

"Fae? As in fairy? Oh, do you have wings? Can I see them? Do you live in a tree?" Eldon gave her a withering look that instantly muted her interrogation. It was so instant that she feared his powers included the ability to take someone's voice. The look that was still pasted on his face kept her in fear of testing her theory just yet.

"This is what I meant—humans have ruined the reputation of the Fae. Making us more like pixies, flitting from tree branch to flower, bringing in the seasons." His words were laced with such disdain that Aggie glanced up at him, expecting an eyeroll; then again, she couldn't see someone like him stooping so low. "I am Fae, born of magic interlaced in the earth. While I'm connected to the trees and plants, I am in no way controlling them. My powers are connected and drawn from the power of the earth. I do have wings, but they are more glorious than any miniscule pixie's wings." Aggie halfheartedly hoped that he would show her, but after a moment she realized that wasn't going to happen.

"I'm sure you're a sight to behold in all your glory." Aggie's words held a hint of awe as she envisioned this creature in a new light. Moving on quickly, she addressed the elephant in the room. "Now, as for this discussion about my potential within this group of misfits." Her choice of words got a couple snarls and some laughter. She didn't pinpoint the exact owners of each sound—but she was sure Mitchell was one of those who didn't like being referred to as a misfit, given his Alpha status within his own circle.

"Do you have questions?" Mathius piped up, reiterating what he had started the night before.

"Not necessarily questions, as much as some ground rules. After the new discoveries I've now been made aware of," Aggie let her attention fall on Kyrel for a split second before continuing, "I think there need to be some stipulations and boundaries. I completely understand that you have been incomplete for many years, and I'm more than happy to help where I can to get these kids back, but I'm not just going to fall into bed with eight men just because you say I'm supposed to. "

"No one ever expected you to do that, Agatha," Liel chimed in, and Aggie fought her natural sarcastic reaction. He was always so methodical and, in this, while she knew he spoke the truth, what else could they have expected? They had found their ninth link, and after so long they surely wouldn't want to prolong it further, would they?

"Of course not, Liel. I just wanted to say it out loud, making it clear for everyone. While I don't know the best way to go about this, as it was just sprung on me last night, I just want you all to be aware that I'm willing to try. However, I'd like to take the time to get to know each of you, rather than just create a schedule of sex to complete some bond that isn't even apparent naturally. I would like to make sure we have a connection before we start discussing the horizontal tango or the meetings between the sheets." Of course, Ren started laughing at that with a boisterous enthusiasm. Aggie paused, wondering if he was going to be able to regain control of himself. After a minute or so, he finally calmed and Aggie realized she needed to ask a very pointed question. "Come to think of it, am I at risk of getting pregnant by any of you? I'm on regular birth control but, given that none of you are exactly *regular* yourselves, I'm going to bet I'm going to need to make new arrangements." Rubbing her belly absentmindedly, not that she didn't want kids, she definitely didn't want them right now. Halting her maternal distractions, Aggie looked around in hopes someone had an answer for her. Gryson was at her side before she made the full sweep of the room with her eyes.

"You have nothing to worry about. I can give you something that will ward off pregnancy until you take the, let's call it a counter-potion. That is easier to explain in your current understanding, but is getting ahead of ourselves and won't be needed right away." His words could have been offensive, but the way he said them and the look in his eye was one of compassion and understanding. Placing a hand on her shoulder, Gryson pulled her against him. Now that she didn't have the conflicting feelings of a gateway door pulling at her, she realized that his touch was electric. Stronger than the buzzing she felt with Mathius. She felt like the synapses of her brain were vibrating. His touch was different, as she noticed they all were. Since she knew what was causing the sensation, she didn't pull away. Aggie let him linger, and closed her eyes to the feeling to see where it would go. Unfortunately, or under different circumstances would be more like fortunately, it shot from her brain straight to her core. With a gasp, Aggie jerked her body away from his touch. Eyes wide, she turned to face him. His brown eyes were glowing almost a lavender color that simmered back to his brown as soon as they met Aggie's hazel ones.

"Did you feel that? Do any of you feel that?" Aggie started the question directed at Gryson, but quickly expanded it to the rest of them. Even though she had only come in contact with a few of them, the question was still open to them all.

Gryson leaned down, but didn't make direct contact with her. However, she felt the words as he spoke and his breath caught across her ear. "I feel your touch to my very soul, dearest Aggie." A chill ran through her, and goosebumps ran down her arm as his breath carried down farther than she could actually feel it. She resisted the urge to rub the feeling away.

# Chapter 8

Shaking her head in an attempt to clear the fog created by the shift in the conversation, she went on. "Okay, well then, I guess we have that all sorted. Should we talk about where we're at with this case of disappearing kids and the shift in the weather?" Aggie looked out the glass wall and took in the winter wonderland. Beautiful beyond words, and the ice glistened in the sunlight that didn't seem to warm. The architecture of this castle was phenomenal. Humans didn't see things the same way as these architects seemed to. They saw a home as more than just a shelter. They seemed to see the beauty underneath. Rather than destroying it or covering it up, they built the trees into the structure and added full glass walls. They weren't just panels, so one could take in that which was inspiring outside as well. She had seen the glowing lights the previous night from the bathroom but this was something one would only have seen in pictures, and it took her breath away.

"We determined with our search last night that there had been no one inside the room who wasn't allowed. The locks hadn't been broken, but it will take a while to ascertain who has been through there." Mathius started the debriefing, and Aggie took in his words but didn't detour her attention from the lightly frosted window, that when she looked closely could make out the tiny snowflakes frozen to the glass. That took her back to her childhood, when Gran would let her run through the freshly fallen snow and catch snowflakes on her tongue. Gran would sit on the porch on her swing and watch her with laughter in her eyes. A tear escaped Aggie's eye and, before she realized and could catch it, a finger ran across her cheek. Glancing up, she saw

Ren was standing beside her now; he took the tear he had just caught on his finger and slipped it into his mouth, never once taking his clear blue eyes off of hers. Their wordless exchange was the most powerful conversation she had had with any of the guys. It was as though he knew what she was feeling, and he silently comforted her in his own way.

Turning her attention back to Mathius, she said, "Nothing in the space stood out, so we assume that whoever abducted Prince Rikan must have dusted him out to avoid detection, as well as any signs of a struggle. Even though we have decided that he was probably drugged in some way." The recap wasn't completely necessary, but it was nice to hear all the details lined out to better identify any gaps they might be overlooking.

"How many children have been taken, and what is the understanding of their given or expected powers?" Aggie was running on a theory, but she wasn't sure if anyone had considered some kind of correlation if gender wasn't the draw.

Mathius thought for a moment, but then went to the sidebar and pressed a button. "I know there are five children missing. I'm not sure what their prolific choice of magic is, but I will in a moment." Just then a petite young girl came into the room, but she was more than that. Her eyes flared a deep hunter green, a shade Aggie had never seen in someone's eyes before. Then when she and Mathius spoke Aggie was sure she saw a fork in her tongue like that of a snake. As quickly as this girl came, she left. "I've requested the information and we will have it shortly." The look on Aggie's face must have been clear. "What is wrong?" Mathius' face was painted in confusion.

"Who was that and what was she?" There wasn't any emotion behind her words, but a slight breathy tone gave way to astonishment.

Raising an eyebrow at her, Mathius pointed in the direction of the girl. "Her name is Delia, and she is a handmaiden who works in the castle. She is an Apep demon."

Aggie mentally recalled her school history classes, cataloging the useless facts that she'd learned and filed away for a rainy day or random trivia night. "Egyptian, serpent-like demon?" Aggie was beyond actual sentences and was stating facts to make sure she was on the right track.

Smiling a little, Mathius seemed to realize what she was trying to say. "Yes, in your world the Egyptians were the ones who saw the Apep demons. I believe the most well-known was Apophis. When he was in his prime they worshiped him with the reverence due to a god. I think if the lowly humans hadn't decided they were better than us, and continued their worship, we would have remained on Earth a few more centuries. Those were some *memorable* times." He looked as though he were reliving them himself, and not just the stories of the Apep demons shared with their youth.

"How many different kinds of demons might I encounter on my visit here?" Aggie wasn't as lost now that she realized that there would be physical characteristics that she might be seeing as they manifested themselves in human-like form.

"Thousands." Mathius didn't elaborate, and his one-word answer made her think of Xavier. The stoic vampire reclined in his chair, looking more bored than interested in their current conversation. *Thousands of different demon species that could be encountered on a moment's notice. Am I ready for this? The guys were a lot to handle in the beginning but I pushed through because it seemed like the best course of action at the time, but thousands?* Aggie's thoughts streamed as if on a film reel in her mind. So many things to consider, yet she had no real understanding to know where to start.

A moment later, Delia made her way back into the room with a file folder. *How very human of her.* Aggie's thoughts had trailed back to someplace close to her usual sarcasm and snark. It seemed like she was getting back to feeling more like herself on this rollercoaster she had been on the past few weeks.

Without so much as a word to Delia, Mathius flipped through the file. Aggie wondered if servants were seen and not heard even in the demon world. While she and her Gran never had the means for servants, to Aggie's knowledge, mentally ruling out the Brownies there were others in their smaller town whose finances allowed for such luxuries.

"It appears that Rikan had the gift of fire. Though his full powers hadn't manifested, he did have minimal abilities that he was beginning to hone slowly through daily training." Mathius flipped to the next page. "The first one taken was a young girl in her early teens. She seemed to have come into her powers of water. She could manipulate it and was already proficient in her skill, but at her age there are still things she would be working on to perfect." Flipping the page again, he continued, "The second child was a boy, close in age to the first. His skills lay in air manipulation." Aggie was starting to notice a trend, but waited to hear the other two children's skills. "The next two hadn't come into their powers, but one is an earth wielder and the last one is an amplifier. They will come into other powers that complement their own, but these are their specialties."

Everyone else took in the information silently, but Aggie didn't wait any longer. She was a part of this team and was determined to pull her own weight and show her own worth. She wasn't just a pretty face that was here to polish their *knobs*. She was here to help. "Am I the only one who thinks the fact that you're suffering from weather-related challenges in this realm and these kids seem to have gifts that revolve around nature isn't just a coincidence?" Mathius and Liel shared a look, but neither spoke.

Xavier leaned up from his lounging position and placed his feet on the floor. Drinking the last of his goblet he placed it on the table and placed his hand beneath his chin, deep in thought. Aggie thought he looked a bit like 'The Thinker' statue by Auguste Rodin, and remembered the movie that animated him. Biting her tongue, because this wasn't the time or the place, she thought, *I'm thinking. I'm thinking.* All the while, stifling a snicker. The twins growled in unison and Mitchell began to pace the room. Eldon's eyebrows perked up and it made Aggie realized that he might be the most connected person to this case, because he also sourced his powers from the earth. Gryson crossed his arms but didn't speak. Kyrel stared out the window, but she could see that he was frustrated in the way his shoulders slumped forward in defeat. They were all thinking in their own way.

"If that is indeed the common denominator, then we can stop wondering if the children's powers are being siphoned. That can be added to the surety column." Mathius spoke his thoughts out loud and everyone shared their agreement. Aggie was proud to say she had helped in the process, even if it was a small step in the right direction, but at least they had a lead and something more to go on than speculation.

Moments before, it was bright and sunshiny. Now the sky was blackened with storm clouds, and a flash of lightning streaked across the sky. That was followed quickly by a crack of thunder resounding across the sky, so loud the walls of the castle shook. Aggie shrieked involuntarily in her surprise at the sudden switch she wasn't prepared for in the least. "Where did that come from?" she asked no one in particular. She'd hated thunderstorms ever since she was a child. Her mother used to wrap her up in her arms and calm her down. When her mother passed unexpectedly, nothing seemed to work in the same way. So, instead, she suffered in silence and just tried her best to hide from violent storms like what was happening outside the castle walls.

"These are the weather changes I spoke of yesterday. They come in silently and without warning, changing quicker than any natural storm could and much more violently. Hence the winter ice in a season that should bring on unfathomable heat." Mathius' words gave her pause, but she was too busy cowering from the second rumble of thunder to put her thoughts in any sense of order.

"Unless Gryson can block that sound from my head or one of you can make that stop, I'm going to be useless to you until this storm passes. I can't think at all over that chaos." Aggie opted for half-truths and didn't share with them how terrified she really was.

A moment later warm hands rested on Aggie's shoulders from behind. She didn't know who it was because her eyes were closed, but they started kneading her tense muscles and she slowly relaxed, but not completely. Soon lips trailed her neck, joining the hands that didn't quit, light pecks that gave her goosebumps. Her skin tingled where he had trailed kisses, but Aggie refused to open her eyes as she was still hiding from the raging storm on the other side of the glass. The water pelted the glass, like it was carrying sand along with it. The sound grew louder as the winds increased. Aggie curled up again as another earth-shaking boom sounded, and she involuntarily jumped. The mystery hands never ceased their manipulations and the kisses traveled all around, never breaking contact with her skin. The effect was intoxicating, and Aggie wished she wasn't so terrified that she could actually open her eyes.

Then, before Aggie could consider what was happening, a second set of hands cupped her face, drawing her out of the cocoon of safety she had imagined around herself with her arms and legs. The sensation across her skin was nearly overwhelming. A vibration encompassed her entire body in a mold of safety. Never ceasing their ministrations the mystery touches didn't make it to every inch of her skin, but the feeling did. She had only ever touched one of the guys at a time. This was new, but not unpleasant or painful, and she now knew what the word 'overstimulated' meant. Pulling her close but not away from the first set of hands, lips gently brushed hers and a slight scruff swept along her chin and cheeks. Surprised by this Aggie's eyes flew open, and looked right into grey eyes that held a turbulent storm of emotions. Eyes that belonged to Mitchell.

"What are you doing?" Aggie pulled away from Mitchell and glanced over her shoulder, to find Ren's hands still connected with her shoulders. The tingling and chills had stopped radiating through her and the goosebumps settled into a more common reaction.

Mitchell stood and took a step back, but his eyes never left hers. "I was trying to calm you down. It worked for a moment, but you're too stubborn and emotional. Are you sure you aren't bipolar?" Mitchell's temper flared, but he settled it with a touch of sarcasm that surprised Aggie a bit. Her fingers went to touch her lips that still buzzed with the touch of Mitchell's. Ren's hands were ever-vigilant and never ceased their movements. They were to the point of distraction. Reaching up, she stilled his movement with her hand. It was then and only then that she realized that the twins' quick thinking had indeed taken her mind off the storm, in a way nothing had since her mother's death.

"Thank you," Aggie started softly. "Both of you." The look on Mitchell's face was priceless. It was as though he expected Aggie to react as he did and not with gratitude.

Ren leaned forward and his words caressed her, without physically connecting with her. "I'm happy to help in any way you ever need me to." The chills returned even without direct contact, like the promise was enough for her body to remember.

"I'll keep that in mind. The fact of the matter is I haven't been able to calm down during a storm since my mother died. That was the first time someone has been able to help. You really have no idea how grateful I am." Getting to her feet, Aggie made her way to the group of men. Now with a renewed focus, she could contribute and know that her opinions were valid and not stunted or broken.  "Now that I'm no longer caught up in that nonsense, where were we?"

Before anyone could answer her the door to the parlor flew open and a woman waltzed in, carrying herself with an air of superiority. Aggie immediately homed in on her elegant black dress that looked more like raven feathers stitched together into a never-ending seam, then draped over her and wrapped to fit her body perfectly. She abruptly stopped at the center of the space and the clack of her heels instantly silenced without a misstep. She appeared to be in her early twenties. Her coal-black hair matched her dress perfectly as though they dyed it to match, and not a single hair was out of place in her pristine coif. Just being in her presence was intimidating, and Aggie found herself taking a small step back. So she didn't have to be so close and perhaps judged against this beauty of a woman.

"Yavari, to what do we owe the pleasure of this visit?" Mathius said formally, with a slight bow. The rest of the guys followed suit, but none were very low. This woman was some sort of royalty but, judging by her lack of headgear, Aggie deduced that she was likely not the queen.

"Mathius," Yavari purred, and took a few steps to run her hand over his jaw in an affectionate way that hinted at a familiarity that made Aggie want to fly across the room and tear her hands from his face and off her body. A sharp pain radiated in Aggie's face as she realized she'd been clenching her jaw far too tightly. "I heard you boys had arrived last night. I wanted to come and see you upon your arrival, but unfortunately a prior engagement kept me ensnared for too long." Yavari never put any distance between herself and Mathius, and she looked at him as though she could eat him whole. Digging her nails into the palms of her hands, Aggie remained firmly planted in her place slightly behind Xavier. Not that she was scared of this woman, but more like this reaction to the situation was making her nervous.

"We were quite busy and got an early start on the matter at hand. We are back at it again this morning. Do you have anything new to share with us that will help us resolve this any faster?" Mathius took a step back, turning his body to face the rest of the room. In his own way this included everyone, and he pointedly looked at Aggie. Then Mathius nodded his head almost imperceptibly, but she saw it and for that she was thankful and surprised. That tiny gesture settled her nerves, his obvious effort to separate Yavari from himself allowing some much-needed space between the two.

"I wasn't even home at the time when poor little Rikan was taken. It was so devastating for all of us. His sweet mother is simply a wreck." Yavari placed her hand on her heart and her brow furrowed in a compassionate gesture. Something about her words was off to Aggie. She couldn't quite put her finger on it, but it was there.

"I hope if you hear anything that could help us you will pass it along." Mathius held his composure, but Aggie noticed a hint of frustration in his eyes. She hadn't known these guys long, but her connection to them was strong and she had a way of reading them in a way she could only read close friends.

"Of course I will, Mathius," Yavari crooned again and made Aggie want to hurl. This woman was clearly delusional and had a thing for Mathius. After realizing Mathius didn't share her attraction Aggie felt herself relax, but she didn't move. Drawing attention to herself was the last thing she wanted to do at this point. It seemed Yavari only had eyes for Mathius at this point anyway. With that, she flipped the train on her dress that Aggie hadn't noticed before, and sashayed out of the room just as dramatically as she came in.

# Chapter 9

nce again alone, the room seemed to breathe a sigh of relief. Aggie was the first to speak up. "Who the hell was that?"

"That was the king's sister, Yavari. She is a bit of a handful and quite the character. We have to tolerate her because she is still royalty, no matter how we feel about her." A visible shudder ran through Mathius and Aggie knew there was a larger story to tell there.

"Did you two have a thing, once upon a time?" Aggie blurted without a hint of jealousy and something more akin to taunting.

"I would rather not discuss it," Mathius grumbled, and turned away from the group to pour himself another cup of tea.

"Oh, come on, I know so little about you guys, and I'd rather not start off with a long list of secrets to unravel, but time is already against us," Aggie pleaded and even batted her eyelashes a little for good measure. Just before she broke out her signature pout, Mathius sighed and his shoulders drooped.

"She has had a thing for me our entire lives. She was second in line for the crown, and I was always to be head of the royal guard. We grew up in the same circles and she was always there. I never returned her affections, but that didn't once stop her from pressing her luck. I've been telling her no for years."

"I figured as much." Aggie knew her words would catch him off guard, but the speed at which he grabbed her made her breath catch. Quickly she realized he had dusted her to the other side of the room and pressed her back against the wall. His lips were on hers faster than she could get herself under control from the magical transportation, and was quickly lost in the feel of his touch and his lips moving with hers. Nothing else mattered; the room fell away as did the remaining inhabitants. It wasn't until they were startled by someone clearing their throat that Aggie felt guilty. She had been kissing Mitchell minutes before and now Mathius, all while everyone was in the room and watching. This wasn't who she was. Aggie never cheated on boyfriends, and never really paid attention to other guys if she was in a relationship. *Is that what this is? A relationship? Nothing has been defined, and, if that's the case, then who's to say I can't kiss or hug or touch any of them if I decide to?* Aggie let her brain wander for a moment, attempting to justify what had just taken place.

Without another word about it, Mathius went back to all business. "Now that we are all on the same page, where do you want to start today?"

"Ren and I will walk the castle and see if any scents from the room become clear or more defined. Perhaps we will find a lead." *It must be the Alpha in him that makes Mitchell so much of a dictator. I wonder if he's always in control or if he lets his guard down for, 'special activities'.* After their brief moment, Aggie had a few new ideas about this macho man standing before her.

"I would like to go outside the castle walls and visit with any of the townsfolk to see if they have any new information. While I know the previous crime scenes have grown cold now, I'm hoping someone has a tiny piece of information that will give us something to go on." Xavier was as stoic as ever, and so rigid. Aggie wondered if he ever let loose.

"Do you have the power of compulsion?" Aggie was making it a habit of blurting her thoughts out of the blue at them, as though they had been friends forever and wouldn't be offended. She heard Ren chuckle. Aggie remembered that he said her method wasn't the politest way to ask them about their powers. This seemed to only be a formality, and none of them seemed to be taking offense by her method of getting information out of them.

Xavier's smiled spread slowly across his face, Aggie made a note not to meet him in a dark alley where he might be upset or hungry, showing her that devilish grin. "I have the power over the weak-minded." He was always so straightforward when he spoke. Never mincing words, but also never fully explaining. Aggie knew they had more important tasks at hand, so she filed that away on her ever-growing list for a better time.

"I will go with you." Liel spoke as though he knew Xavier wasn't going to share anything else with Aggie.  Aggie scrunched up her face at him in a childish way, but he wasn't even fazed.

"As will I. I'm sure I can persuade one or two to share some stories," Kyrel added quickly.

"I'm not sure those stories are the kind we are trying to uncover," Ren chimed in with a smirk. Everyone just shook their heads at his train of thought. He really was the troublemaker of the bunch.

"That leaves the rest of us to go through the mail." Mathius finished his tea and made to leave the room.

"Mail? You guys have a mail system here?" Aggie thought she was confused before, but now she was off the scale.

"Not in a sense that you would think, but more of a magical sending system. It isn't as easy to maintain, but we can send messages through magical means directly to a person we have a connection with. I want to check and see if I recognize any signatures or if Gryson can break them down for any trace." Mathius spoke as though this was perfectly normal and not the most insane things someone might have ever heard. The rest of the guys never questioned, so she had to assume this was a normal thing. Trying to go with the flow, she merely nodded and followed them out. Everyone went their separate ways, when a hand clutched hers and a new sensation ran through her. It felt like a thousand butterflies were flapping across her skin and inside her stomach. Aggie slowly looked up and saw Eldon keeping pace with her. Though he wasn't looking at her she could feel him throughout her body, and the draw was unbelievable. *This must be what people mean when they say fate.* Aggie walked silently as her thoughts drifted. Eldon never let go of her hand and she never pulled hers away. She was content to feel him and how her body reacted to him.

Soon they stopped in front of a simple-looking door and Aggie was puzzled. "What is this place?" All the other places she had seen in the castle were overdone and ornate, to draw attention. This room seemed to blend into the wall. The only real reason she knew it was a door was the knob that materialized the closer they stood to it. *Does this place exude magic all the time? Is everything imbued with spells in order to make this castle function?* Rubbing her temples, Aggie realized all of this was giving her a headache. Perhaps humans shouldn't spend too much time in the other realms, just to prevent mental overload. Again, this was placed in her mental file.

"This is our security room. It's not on any maps and is intended to be inconspicuous." Mathius' hushed tones weren't completely a whisper, but they were obviously an attempt to keep from drawing attention to them.

Stepping into the room, Aggie was in awe of the tactical space. Everything one could possibly need was here. Weapons, ones Aggie could recognize like swords, ax-like blades, and daggers, combined with ones Aggie couldn't dream of explaining or describing. There looked to be a meeting space in the center. She could picture the guys all sitting around the table, exchanging ideas, like a great meeting of the minds. Without asking, she made her way toward the table and ran her fingers over the worn wood. Many conversations and heated debates had taken place at this table. She could feel it, as though the wood was radiating the feelings through her hand and telling her all about it. She smoothed the aging boards in small circles, almost as though she were reassuring a small child. Aggie didn't know why she was drawn like this, but she had to assume it was because it was a connected piece of furniture to all the guys.

"We are going to start over here." Gryson cupped her elbow and guided her to the far corner of the room. It had a blank wall on it that looked like a projector screen was embedded in it. With a wave of Mathius' hand, it came to life with an ethereal glow. That was quickly replaced by mixtures of rainbows swirling on, and a fog lightly poured over the surface. Nothing was tangible and Aggie felt as though she was watching the opening scenes of a movie before the credits began to roll. Quickly, shapes started swirling around on the screen, leaving her imagination to take each shape into consideration. She didn't know what was happening.

"Don't you want to see Prince Rikan? He will be disappointed if you leave before he gets to see you." A woman's voice filtered through the space, causing Aggie to whip her head left and right to determine the source.

"I haven't the time, dear sister. I'm late for a meeting now as it is." That voice Aggie recognized, and wondered who Yavari could be speaking to. The guys didn't mention another sister.

"If you must, then." The mystery woman's voice was disappointed but strong. "Please don't stay away too long or he may forget what you look like. He always did adore you." Aggie was beginning to put the pieces together. The picture faded out, back to the faint light from nowhere. Aggie told her mind there was a hidden projector in the room, just trying to ease the throbbing in her head.

"That was Queen Annare speaking to Yavari," Mathius supplied when he thought he knew what caused Aggie's confused look. Aggie just went with it to not bring up how hard this magic concept was for her to handle.

"It was the night of the kidnapping," Gryson added as they all continued to stare at the blank screen. Aggie decided to call things what they looked like and not overthink it.

"Do any of you have a piece of paper and a pen?" The three men looked at her as though they were asked to produce a unicorn. "You know, so the non-magical here can take notes. My brain might miss details, but if I write things down I can be helpful." With a flourish of his fingers and a smile, Gryson created her request from thin air. The best part was she noted that he had procured another bit of information from her life at home somehow. He had supplied her favorite pen. Something with gel ink always wrote better than the traditional ballpoint or stick pen. So now she could take these notes and feel a little more at home. As a reward, Aggie stretched up on her tiptoes and kissed him on the cheek. Technically, the first kiss she had initiated, but she was taking things slow. He had saved her twice today with his magical abilities, and for that she was grateful. It was the least she could do to show her appreciation. Gryson took the opportunity to wrap his arms around her and hold her, for just a second, before he released her back to the floor. Only then did she realize he had lifted her off the floor to assist her in her task at hand. She really was a midget in comparison to these guys, but she would make up for it with her big personality.

Using her new pen and paper, Aggie noted that the queen and her sister-in-law had a conversation about the prince on the day of his disappearance.

"Well, at least she was telling the truth about not being home when he was taken," Eldon piped up, and his lyrical voice caught Aggie in a spell that ended the moment he stopped speaking. She really wanted to get to know him, but he was the quietest of all the guys. At least Xavier spoke up more often than Eldon, even if he was vague in his comments and not forthcoming with information. She knew more about Xavier, the second quietest of the bunch, than she did about Eldon. Their moment in the hallway had been nothing short of a surprise, but she wasn't going to look a gift horse in the mouth, as they say.

"To be honest, and I know I'm new and don't know anyone, I didn't think her statement was completely truthful. I'm not sure what it was, but it felt off to me or forced in some way." Aggie didn't want to upset anyone or step on toes, but maybe they were too close to the situation to have seen it. Perhaps an outsider was just what they needed. "Am I the only one who noticed that?"

"She seemed perfectly in character to me." Mathius confirmed her suspicions that he was blinded by something. He said he had no attraction for her. So, maybe it was the fact that he was avoiding her and couldn't see everything clearly because he wasn't looking at her under a microscope, and more like trying not to touch her with a ten-foot pole. Gryson nodded his agreement, and this frustrated Aggie because she needed them to trust and value her opinion, just as they would any of the other guys.

"I sensed something as well." That beautifully captivating voice cut through Aggie's frustration like a knife. "I'm unable to say exactly what it was, but her story didn't sound genuine to me either." With a small, shy smile in Aggie's direction, he finished his statement. Back to his silent, reflective self, Eldon had captured her interest better than any of them could have ever dreamed of doing.

"We have no evidence against her, and this," Mathius gestured at the screen, "gives nothing but proof in her favor."

"I didn't mean to insinuate that you were wrong, but she might not be as innocent as she appears. Instead of jumping to conclusions, let's just make a note to keep her in mind and not write her off." Aggie made a show of writing down this on her paper but didn't say another word.

Another wave of Mathius' hand and the screen came to life again with rainbows and fog.

"Trust me—they don't know anything," a familiar voice once again trilled over the airways.

"How can you be so sure? They can't find out about us." This was a mysterious male voice, and Aggie wasn't sure if any of the guys knew who it was.

"I told them I had a meeting; as you know, I have many official meetings at all hours of the day or night. I don't operate on a daytime schedule like my *brother*." Yavari's tone was dripping with disdain and that concerned Aggie. She had never had any siblings but knew that some, even as adults, didn't see eye-to-eye all the time.

"Yes, but our meetings have nothing to do with court and the pomp and circumstance that you like to flit here and there, pretending to go on about this and that." His voice was a deep and rich, like someone who might have been noble. Though Aggie snickered at her thought. Who was she to say what a noble did or didn't sound like?

"I don't pretend anything of the sort. If I did, you'd think I wasn't with you of my own choice and purely for social standings." Yavari purred her words like the seductress that she was. Aggie heard that tone just a short while ago directed at Mathius. Without another word, the screen faded yet again.

"That didn't sound suspicious at all," Aggie deadpanned in hopes of getting a couple laughs. She was disappointed, as stoic frowns met her smiling face as she scanned the room. "Damn you all, Ren would have laughed at that. Next time I'll endure Mitchell's brooding and go with them." Crossing her arms, she openly pouted at her lackluster crew.

"I don't recognize the other voice." Gryson didn't acknowledge any of what Aggie said and just began addressing the mail. Now that Aggie thought about it, they were more like phone calls between places than mail. She would mention that when she was with a crowd that listened to her opinions, not just placating her by letting her tag along.

"It's familiar, but I can't place it either. Almost like it was a voice I heard once in passing rather than from someone I might actually know or have been introduced to. I'm usually pretty good with voices and names." Mathius' tone was prideful, and directed at Aggie with the last statement. She didn't give him the time of day and glanced over at Eldon, who was still deep in thought. She was sure that Mathius growled or grumbled under his breath at her response or lack thereof, and she beamed.

"It seems we need to speak to Yavari again, but I don't want to spook her. Is there anyone who might be close to this situation and have some insight into her day-to-day?" Eldon's eyes never broke from the screen that had faded to the haze and swirls of colors. It reminded Aggie in some way of the colorful aspect of the knobs inside the secret room. She didn't know how to refer to it yet. The guys called it the Gateway, but to her it was just another room in her Gran's house, no matter what they told her. To change that thought process would be like rebranding her brain.

"What if we spoke to the servants? Delia seemed helpful enough this morning. I'm sure they hear things that we don't and wouldn't be able to uncover. People of this stature have a tendency to think of those beneath them as invisible. Did you notice Yavari didn't even notice me this morning or question who

I was? That could've been because all she cared about was to get Mathius in the sack or because I'm right." Aggie didn't bother to look at Mathius, she could hear his snarl plainly.

"That idea has sound reasoning. Do we know who her chambermaid is?" Eldon acknowledged her, disregarding what Mathius was grumbling about. "If we can find out when she's out on her next meeting, we may be able to get an appointment or a few moments with her, at the least."

Never ceasing in voicing his displeasure at Aggie's jab, Mathius spoke with a hint of frustration in his tone. "I'll look into it and persuade her to hold court with us." Aggie struggled not to laugh at his old language. She was going to have to get these guys to lighten up and teach them some modern speaking skills if she was going to be around them this much. She made a mental note and refocused her attention on the matter at hand.

"Don't you think all of us rushing in to speak to a servant is going to draw some attention?" Aggie spoke up, expecting to be ignored once again.

"Why would that be of consequence to us?" Mathius was on the rougher side of life, Aggie had noticed. He was more of a 'take and ask for forgiveness later' kind of person than a person who thinks about someone's feelings. He was the definition of caveman thinking. She wasn't saying he wasn't smart, because the cavemen invented some pretty handy technology in their time, but he had a very one-track mind. If he had a goal, that was all that mattered. Simple things, like perception, didn't matter as long as the goal was accomplished. He was rather transparent like that, and Aggie had picked up on this characteristic rather quickly.

"I don't know how much of our business you want to travel down the grapevine. If not the servants, I'm sure the nobles will whisper." Aggie was sure he couldn't be that dense to not realize that people were going to talk.

"We do not have grapes here or any vined fruit. There is no need for concern." Aggie groaned in frustration at Mathius' words.

Taking a deep breath and then releasing it, she said, "No, 'to travel down the grapevine' just means to gossip." Aggie was just getting a small dose and could see what was to come. This was going to be beyond trying, and hard to get through with any sort of grace. They were going to be a challenge, but if anyone could step up to the plate it was her.

Mathius considered her words in silence for a moment. Aggie watched as emotions traveled across his face. First confusion, then that quickly moved into shock, and then finally into understanding. She was thankful his emotions were so easy to read. "I believe you might be correct. I will go alone and report back."

"Do you think that's the best idea?" Aggie pressed her luck, hoping he wouldn't get growly again.

"What do you mean? Of course, I'm the best person for the job. These are my people and they will be more comfortable speaking with me." His voice was raised slightly, but not seemingly from anger or because she questioned him. It was more like he was astonished that she would suggest otherwise.

"Not to disagree with you, but perhaps I could throw out another scenario. What if, say, I were to go with one of the other guys, whoever has the most experience with your people. We might be a bit less intimidating for a lowly servant than the head of the guard. If you were to go, don't you think they might think they were in some kind of trouble?"

"You're saying I might scare them? Are you saying that I'm an imposing figure and I can't relate to the common people? You make me sound like a pompous ass who carries himself as royalty." Mathius laughed at the thought even though she hadn't confirmed or denied anything. The other two were silently watching the exchange, enthralled as though they were watching a sporting event on television.

"Have you seen yourself? You have been a bit of an ass to me since we met, and your hulking form," Aggie gestured at, well, all of him, "isn't exactly one to lend itself to endearment upon first glance." With a huff, Mathius turned away and crossed his arms like a petulant child.

Breathing heavily, he took a few moments to compose his thoughts. From his profile stance, Aggie could see his nostrils flaring open and closed, then without warning he whipped back around and got right in her face. His eyes were cold and flat. The life in them was missing. Aggie wondered how he could turn it on and off with the flick of a switch. "I'll have you know I'm more than capable of handling this job, but instead of trying to stand here and convince you I will send Eldon with you. He is the second-most qualified person for this job in this room. He may not know my people, but the way of his own will help him through this task." Aggie didn't know what that meant, but the heat in his words wasn't lost on her. "Mark my words, I will prove to you my worth in due time." Aggie also realized they were no longer talking about the task at hand.

With her mouth agape, Aggie stood frozen at the display she had just witnessed. She didn't know what to say. *I didn't mean to upset him, but I needed to convey my point and opinion about the next step. We could have easily lost all headway if we didn't plan this properly. Thinking with our heads and not egos would play a huge part in all of this. I guess that's my role, to rein in the crazy from time to time. I'll be needed to put things into perspective since obviously no one else is going to step up for the job.* She added the last thought with a touch of snark as she looked up at the two silent observers still standing in the wings.

Unable to stand it any longer, she said, "Neither of you gaping fish thought it helpful to jump in and help at all?"

"We didn't think it was prudent to choose sides in this particular situation." Eldon shared his thoughts honestly.

"Not to mention, it was pretty exciting and attractive to watch you hold your own," Gryson added with a grin in her direction.

Rolling her eyes and sighing in frustration, she said, "This job is going to be harder than I thought." The words were spoken under her breath and not for the ears of the three men standing in the space with her. "I guess we should make arrangements with the maid."

"Why don't we just speak to Delia and see if she can get a message to the girl we need to speak with, instead of tracking her down on our own? She can report back to us and let us know when and where to meet." Gryson's idea had merit, and at least she knew he was thinking like a strategist and not a man with something to prove.

"That makes sense. At least we know that we can trust her. Mathius, would you make the request?" Aggie was trying to mend the bridge at least a little for now, even though he hadn't had time to cool off completely. She wanted him to know he was still needed.

Mathius didn't look up right away, as though he was considering her request. Then he looked at her with a touch of fire in his eyes. "I'll make the arrangements for you, but you will debrief with me immediately after the meeting, in your chambers." Aggie wasn't sure what he was getting at, but the blaze was growing in his eyes and Aggie wondered if it meant what she thought. A chill ran through her body as she thought about all the reasons he would want to meet with her. None of them had anything to do with a rundown of the evening's events.

# Chapter 10

They all left the space and made their way to the common room that they'd had breakfast in. It was only then that Aggie realized they had been in the security room for hours and she was feeling a bit hungry. That must have been the guys' intention because when they arrived a full buffet was laid out again and Aggie's mouth watered.

"If this is how every meal is going to go, then I'm going to need bigger pants." Aggie wasn't a big eater, but she did love her snacks. If she wasn't getting her snacks here, this was going to have to be the next best thing. Her eyes roved over the food, everything from deli sandwiches to full steak, and every side in between. "What happens to the leftovers?" Aggie's thought came from nowhere, but it was a viable question.

"Leftover what?" Liel looked at her with confusion painted on his face. He reminded her of a robot or a dog with his head cocked to the side, and though his facial features were relatively blank Aggie feared that she would never figure out who he was through this stony exterior. Surely, he had some sort of personality and was just not showing it. Aggie wondered what it would take to find the real Liel.

"The food, of course. I know we aren't going to eat all the food. It seems a bit excessive. What do they do with the leftover food?" Her arms were spread wide to encompass the tables of food, that now, taking in all of it in this context, she realized covered three of the four walls of the room. "Who in their right mind thought we could eat all this food, or would even consider it?"

At that Ren started laughing and Aggie shot him a look, stopping him instantly. Clearing his throat to regain his composure, he explained, "It's not real."

"That's the craziest thing I've ever heard. We ate it this morning." She walked over and picked up a roll and promptly threw it at his head, which of course he dodged, making her even more upset at him. She did hear a couple snickers at the exchange, though, so she felt better that they thought it was funny she was attacking Ren. "Well, had that hit you I suppose it might have knocked some sense into your dense head. They're real enough to bounce off the floor, the way it should have bounced off your head."

Gryson appeared beside her and the closeness was nearly enough to feel him, but he didn't touch her. "What he means is this food is magic. There is a demon skilled in creating the image of food. Her spell, for lack of a better word, is designed to be a figment or an idea of what is available, and upon touching it then it completes the design and it becomes just as real as it looks. So, there are no leftovers, as you called it. This food isn't really here."

Aggie took a moment to consider this. For everything she had seen, this wasn't too much of a stretch of her imagination. It was more of a story brought to life. She reached down slowly, not quite touching an avocado. It could have been her brain compensating for what it knew, but she could feel the weight of it against her fingers and the slight chill from the refrigerator that it may or may not have been sitting in prior to being set out for display. It was unreal. On instinct, she pressed forward to touch it and the sensations only increased upon actual contact.

"How is that possible? I can feel it before I actually touch it, as though it's real. I'm not saying I don't believe you, I'm just trying to wrap my head around this, as my brain is overpowering my senses."

"Allow me to demonstrate." Eldon surprised her, as she didn't hear him step over or notice his approach. "Please close your eyes."

"Close my eyes? What are you planning to do, shove this avocado in my face?" As expected, Ren chuckled at her question.

"No, I'm merely attempting to draw a correlation between the magic and your body's natural instincts. So, if you will bear with me and close your eyes, I believe you will understand in just a moment." With a sigh Aggie complied, and before she knew it she felt a pressure between her eyes, pressing on her head. It was on the edge of bringing on a headache.

Unable to control herself, Aggie pulled away from the weight. "What are you doing?" Her eyes flew open and there stood Eldon, with his finger hovering right between her eyes. "I don't understand."

"Your subconscious felt the pressure of my finger just by bringing it close to your face. Never once did I have to touch you in order for you to feel its impression. Some of that is from the shadows crossing your closed eyes. While you can't see them, the light in the room changes and you 'feel' my finger. The same is true for the food. You can feel its presence just because, subliminally, you know what it should feel like. Even something you might have never encountered would feel of some substance, merely because you know it should feel like something." Aggie was thankful that Eldon was the one who performed that demonstration. If anyone else had done it, she would have been more concerned she would have ended up pranked. Also, if Liel had done it he would have been so caught up in the scientific explanation that she would have been more than lost.

"Can we please get back to business, or are we going to spend the entire day coddling this girl?" Of course, it had to be Mitchell who ended the magic lesson. Aggie didn't grace him with an indignant look.

"Yes, how did your trail-*sniffing* go, today?" Aggie wasn't in the mood for Mitchell's personal brand of jerk. Instead, she wouldn't let him be in control of this situation. If he wanted to be an ass, then no one was going to stop her from retaliating or at least holding her own. His lip curled up and a deep growl rolled out of him from the pit of his stomach. "Easy, Fido; with that lip curl I'm going to think you're The King, but not in the Alpha sense." Aggie was throwing her A game.

Ren didn't hold back, but burst out laughing at their antics. "Would you two just make out already? As funny as this tension is between you, I don't think we are going to get much accomplished until you figure out how to get past it."

"I believe we already tried that, or something close. While it was a great distraction, it did nothing for the lasting effect of, well, him as a whole." Aggie wasn't going to hold back. This was her moment and, while she didn't know them all well enough yet, they might as well realize she wasn't going to hold back just because it was the polite thing to do.

"Enough, I'm not discussing this anymore. Our *sniffing*, as you so ineloquently worded it, wasn't very effective. While we got a few traces of familiar scents, the trails were, as expected, cold. I think we are going to have to compare a more recent space." Mitchell wasn't growling anymore, but he wasn't happy either. Answering her questions was more of a duty than something he wanted to do. That much was obvious to Aggie.

"Are you saying you want another kid to be kidnapped, so we can take advantage of the evidence?" Aggie was appalled at the thought of this, and her opinion wasn't going to go unvoiced. "You can't possibly want to wish this pain on another family or ruin another child's life. It's bad enough they're taking children to begin with, but what you're suggesting is inhumane."

"It's a good thing we aren't human, then." Mitchell's words were flat and unemotional.

"As much as you might dislike it, Mitchell's words are very valid. It would be better for us to catalog the children who have powers that seem to be of interest to the people responsible for the heinous actions. Then perhaps we can better predict their next moves. If we are already on top of that front, perhaps they won't have the upper hand after all." Liel, the robotic voice of reason. For some reason, Aggie wasn't as upset with his thought process. She didn't know if it was because he was thinking practically or the fact that he didn't have an actual emotional reaction in any way. So, it wasn't like it was strangely absent in this case.

"Okay, let's table this for now. Xavier, what did you guys dig up?" Aggie couldn't process what was happening. Perhaps it was her human side blocking her from seeing their side of things. It went against everything she knew. The only thing that she thought of as an option would be to move on.

"The townspeople are scared." Xavier smiled, and Aggie was surprised because his demeanor was always one of sophisticated suave but not friendly. His affinity for suits didn't help in that either. He wasn't very approachable, and for that she was thankful that Kyrel had gone along for the ride. Since she was sure Liel wasn't of much help outside of reading people.

"Kyrel, do you have any words of wisdom that will make your trip seem a bit less useless, like the Bobbsey Twins?" Aggie was growing tired of the runaround.

"I found a nice maiden who was very forthcoming. She spoke of hidden corridors and secret meetings with cloaked figures. Hushed voices carrying on an echo into mere murmurs." His words were like a caress on her skin. His powers were overwhelming, and it took all of Aggie's focus and willpower to not give into it.

"Did you leave this girl in the same condition you found her?" Aggie wasn't worried about the girl's life, but she needed to know he hadn't harmed her with any of his wiles.

"Now, what kind of demon doesn't reciprocate when a female is so helpful? Of course, I relieved her of her tension. As you recall, I'm quite skilled in that department." The timbre of his voice dropped an octave and he was speaking lower for her ears only. Unfortunately for Aggie, most of the men in the room had nearly superhuman hearing, among other special skills. While none voiced any concern or discomfort at the shift in conversation, she heard a few groans and shifting of feet. Aggie thought a few were sounds of desperation rather than that of displeasure.

"I'll have Mathius recall the findings of our little escapade and then we can regroup with all that we know." Aggie turned to have Mathius take over, and she noticed his stance had drastically changed. She wondered if the shuffling of feet was the men adjusting their stances so they were more comfortable after Kyrel's passing words.

It didn't take but a moment for Mathius to take the proverbial torch and run with it. He quickly regaled the tale of their calls and the concerns about Yavari and her mystery caller. Quickly, the group pulled in tight to hear all the details. It was obvious that only one of their paths had resulted in juicy information, and the men were acting as though they were getting some hot piece of gossip.

"I bet you guys are the biggest talkers in your realms. You probably sit around gabbing like a bunch of hens." Aggie's words were actually heard that time, and Liel looked at her with his typical confused face.

"Chickens don't talk in your world." The way he said those words make Aggie wonder if they did elsewhere, but before she could clarify someone beat her to the punch.

"She means telling stories and spreading rumors." To her surprise it was Mitchell who responded. Now Aggie wore a matching face to Liel.

"How did you know that?" Aggie's eyes were as wide as saucers. She had spent most of her time, so it felt, explaining slang and human phrases to these men and Mitchell was, in some way, just playing stupid. This made no sense to her at all.

"The shifters are required to spend five years of our early adult life on earth, before we can take our rightful place in the pack. It helps the animal in us tame a bit, so they realize they have to share their time with our human selves. Since the children can't go alone, we wait until they are the human adult age to take this journey. After that we can rejoin the pack or stay in the human realm if we so choose." It was Mitchell's mirror, Ren, who responded, and for once not in a joking way. For that, Aggie was grateful.

"So, you two actually have experience with human terms and basic language outside of textbook communication. The ins and outs have been practiced and not just observed." Aggie was overjoyed. That gave her help in explaining to the others, as well as two fewer to teach.

"Of course, we do." Mitchell's lip curled at his snarl, and he sounded offended. As though it was absurd for her to think otherwise.

"No offense to any of you," Aggie looked around the room at each guy, "but how was I supposed to know? It seems the rest of these guys were born in the Dark Ages with their concept of modern human language. I have been struggling from the very beginning." The guys all shared a look and everyone, including

Liel, started to laugh. The look of a smile on his face was the best thing she had ever seen. His face practically glowed and the tips of his ears turned slightly pink with the exertion of the emotion. "Did I miss the joke?" Aggie hesitated, but after a second realized what was happening. "Wait! Are you saying you were all playing me the entire time? Every time you questioned my words or choice of phrasing, you were just trying to see how long you could keep it up?" Aggie would be upset, except it was rather perfect. Something she would have had fun doing herself if the situation had shown itself. Quickly, she joined them in the laugh, and she was thankful that it meant they all had a terrific sense of humor.

Their amusement settled into a low murmur and the group grew quiet. "Now that we have that sorted, Eldon and I have a mission to prep for. Mathius, have you sent word with the girl who was here before? Delia, wasn't that her name?" Aggie scanned the room, looking for Mathius. She found him leaning against the far wall, looking more like a bad ass biker than anything else. If she had seen him on the street looking like this, she wouldn't have had any doubt of what he was capable of, even if the demon bit would still be hard to swallow.

"Yes. Delia. I sent word to her when we arrived to eat. She will be here shortly to get an exact message. I didn't want to risk anyone intercepting the message and throwing a kink in our plans before we got started." Mathius' use of a modern phrase made Aggie smile, allowing the extra reinforcement to sink into her brain and wash away any doubt that this might have been the actual joke. Knowing she could speak to them normally made this a little less stressful and a bit more exciting.

"Good plan; I'd hate for her to get into any trouble because of something we caused. Now for the plan. I don't like the idea of baiting children, but if we plan to protect any others from meeting the same fate then I suppose we should know who we're protecting. Since I'm new here, who would like to or be best at doing this job? I'm still learning your strengths." Aggie didn't care that no one had formally put her in charge. It seemed that since they weren't complete without her, her role was likely to be the middle ground. If she could lead them and be the neutral party, then perhaps she would best serve her ultimate purpose. Not to mention, none of the guys were complaining at her choice to take command of the situation. Though she wouldn't allow them to bench her through the process.

"That would be Liel and Mathius, in this situation. Mostly because Liel has an eye for detail and Mathius knows the community. He can get the records and help filter them best by age and skill level." Eldon's lyrical voice startled Aggie slightly as he came up silently behind her. Would she ever tire of hearing him speak?

Catching herself as she began to lean into the sound of Eldon's words, she continued, "Mathius, after you get word to Delia on what we need, can you and Liel get to work on that list for us?" She wasn't one to dictate. So even as a self-imposed leader of this little misfit brigade, Aggie would be sure everyone was happy in their individual role before setting it in stone.

"I don't like leaving you to your meeting alone without being available." Mathius wasn't going to let it go.

"We've discussed this. I don't want you to get all bent out of shape. By your request, I'm taking Eldon with me and if anything goes awry it's not like there aren't five other guys who could jump in to help. Isn't there some kind of demonic or magical earpiece I could wear? Something that would allow us all to communicate, or at least for someone or all of you to hear if something goes wrong. We have that technology in the human realm; surely you have something." Aggie was grasping at straws, but hoped she was on the right track.

Mathius looked confused, but just as Aggie had hoped there was an alternative. "I believe I can put together something, but I'd have to spell us all and it wouldn't last a long, but it should be long enough to get through the meeting." Gryson was deep in thought, his thumb and forefinger caressing his chin and jaw. He wasn't speaking to anyone in particular, and went silent soon after as he backed away from the group. Aggie assumed he was putting his plan together.

"As long as whatever it is will be undetectable to the demons." Mathius was adding stipulations, still reluctant to give in easily.

"I can cast it on you last to see if you can detect it, even knowing that we are using it." Gryson didn't sound as though he was happy with Mathius' level of trust in his magical abilities. Aggie could only picture these two talking about football plays or racing cars. She was slightly distracted with that visual and missed Mathius' response. Ren's quick movement caught her eye as he moved between Mathius and Gryson when they each took a fast step closer together.

"Now, boys, I think we can be adults and trust that if someone says they can do something, then likely they will be able to safely pull it off. I would imagine that if Gryson wasn't fully confident in his abilities, he would speak up before we all put one hundred percent of our faith in him. I would expect that from any of you and not just because of this insane importance you have placed on my shoulders, but in order to protect each other as well. You have been a brotherhood longer than I've been in this picture. I expect you to continue to trust each other and not question that unless someone gives you cause." Aggie wasn't going to let them turn on each other. She couldn't figure out how they possibly got along without her before now.

Mathius and Gryson grunted their agreement, but Aggie didn't let it stop there. She moved and her gaze met each of the men individually, even though that was extra difficult when she connected to Kyrel. "Do you have any way of toning that down, even just a little bit?"

Kyrel's eyes lit up at her question; all the guys had nodded their acknowledgment to her request, but Kyrel still hadn't. Now she had thrown him a bone and wondered if she was suffering from a lady boner due to the aftershocks from Kyrel's powerful gaze. "That's a loaded question. The best thing I can do is tell you that there are times of the month that I am more, shall we say, potent than others. Also, my soul mate will be more affected by me than others, but over time you will build up a level of immunity by exposure. Similar to a drug that isn't as effective from prolonged use."

Fighting an eyeroll, Aggie gritted her teeth and decided she didn't care what anyone else thought or Kyrel's feelings. "So, you're saying you have demon PMS? Not to mention you're my personal drug of choice, if what you all have been telling me is true, that is. Is there a way to speed up the immunity effects?"

Kyrel's face scrunched up at her description, but Eldon and Ren shared a laugh over the sentiment. She didn't mean to be crass, but there was no other way for her to explain it so precisely. Reality sucks, but sometimes the truth just needed to be said.

"I'm not sure that is how I would have phrased it, but I suppose you're fairly accurate in your description. I'm not sure there is an accelerant outside of perhaps a bond-mate. Though it has been many years since one has pursued that course of action, it could be the answer." Kyrel's eyes lit with hope at his own words. She didn't know if he was hoping for her to agree or for that to be the solution to their seeming problem.

Aggie groaned at his timing and choice of words. "Here we go again. You guys are trying to force my hand. Slow down and let me make my choices as they come to be. I don't want to make any decisions without having proper time to consider my options." She wasn't too upset, but more put out that all of their conversations seemed to run full circle back to this point. "Now back on track, again. Eldon, you and I have to get ready for our little excursion this evening. Gryson, you have a spell or whatever to prepare for as well." She waved her hand around as though she were swishing a magic wand. She hadn't seen him do so but, given her limited knowledge of magic, that was the best hand signal she could come up with on short notice. His potential offense was little to be concerned with at the moment.

A knock sounded on the door, and since Mathius was closest he greeted their guest. In walked Delia with a pleasant smile on her face. "I was told you needed to see me."

"Yes, we were hoping you could tell us who Yavari's handmaiden is, if it isn't too much trouble." Mathius' words were spoken roughly, but with a high level of respect. Aggie appreciated that he didn't speak down to her even a little, given their difference in status.

"That would be me. I've only become useful in other things since my services aren't as required for Yavari's needs, given she is so frequently away from the castle." Delia spoke clearly, but Aggie noticed a hint of sadness in her tone. She wondered what could have caused that.

"We would love to speak to you at length about that, but this isn't the time or the place." Mathius stood with his arms crossed behind his back and Delia stayed right in front of him.

"I agree; how about this evening? I would say later after the servants have gone to bed. They tend to talk, you know, and security traipsing the halls would lead to suspicion. I'm not sure what you wish to speak of but I'd rather do it in private. Also, could you not send everyone? That much traffic even after hours is bound to cause alarm." She was direct and to the point. Aggie appreciated that trait and knew they would get along great.

"Actually, we only planned to send two of our crew; Eldon and Aggie, our newest addition to the team." A swell of pride filled Aggie's heart at Mathius' words. That was the first time she had been included outside of a meeting or two. This felt like more of an official context. Nodding, Delia turned and left, so as to not attract any unwanted attention.

After a quick bite to eat, they all made their way out of the dining room and on to their own individual tasks. Eldon trailed along with Aggie and they made their way back to the bedroom wing. Aggie stopped in front of her white door. White, the color of purity, reminded her of a snowy day, not unlike the storm that had passed through this village. Washing away all the dirt and grime, or at least erasing it from view. Was this color symbolic to her role, and what she would embark on as the final link of the Brotherhood of Guardians? Would she be washing clean her life before, and starting new and fresh like the pure white door in front of her?

The clearing of a throat broke her from her wandering thoughts. Eldon stood with his hands behind his back, waiting patiently for her to open the door. "Oh, I'm sorry. I was lost there for a moment. So much has happened since my Gran's passing, I'm not sure how to sort it all out in my head. If I stay silent too long and allow my mind to wander, it all comes to a head in an attempt to find a proper place to file itself away. Unfortunately, there are no categories that fit any of this outside of fiction." Reaching for her door handle without pause, she didn't wait for Eldon to respond. As though it wasn't locked, the door clicked open and allowed them entry.

"Wait." Eldon's word gave her pause and she turned to face him, not sparing her room a second glance. Without another word, his liquid blue eyes began to change. They were almost without color, forcing Aggie to look closer to see that they were actually iridescent like the wings of a fairy. They shimmered and almost looked as though the color actually moved. Just as she began to speak to convey their beauty, his hands which were folded began to glow. Her attention was now captivated by this new image before her. As he separated his hands ever so slowly Aggie could see lush green, like the leaves of a plant. The glowing subsided and he lowered the hand that kept this green item covered, to reveal three red roses. Glancing back at his eyes, she saw that Eldon's blue had returned as though it had never actually left. That gave Aggie pause; she glanced around the hallway, and without much effort they landed on Eldon's chamber door. A perfect match to his eye color Eldon's door stood closed, and Aggie had a new appreciation for what she was seeing. The magic that displayed itself so clearly in each of their eyes, and while she hadn't seen them all perform their own skills, she guessed each would match the color that was imbued in their bedrooms.

"These are beautiful, but why are you giving me flowers?" Aggie had hoped it didn't mean he was apologizing for something he'd done, or in advance of something he was about to do.

"I wanted to cheer you up. While I'm not sure what it would be like to be in your shoes and so unaware of the many worlds that have surrounded you your entire life, I want you to know I'm willing to try to understand." Aggie wasn't sure, but that might have been the kindest thing any of the guys had said to her yet. Eldon was quickly becoming a favorite in her eyes. He seemed quiet at first and she couldn't get a read on him, but now things were changing and, while she didn't know when or why, it was for the better.

"Thank you, that was a wonderful idea. Let me get these inside and in water. Then I'll need to find a spot for them where I can see them almost anywhere in the room." With a smile of pure happiness, Aggie turned and pushed the door open wider so they could both enter. Upon entry she gasped, dropping the flowers where she stood. Instead of the exceptional space that had been here when she left that morning, Aggie now stood facing a disaster beyond compare. The room was more than trashed, it was destroyed. The curtains were ripped from the windows and the rods were snapped in two. The table that held her snack and tea when she first arrived was scorched and still smoldering, the heat radiating from the smoke as though this was all still quite fresh. Her bed was snapped in two and the covers were torn and sat beside the burning table, or that's what Aggie assumed they were, as they were nearly unrecognizable. This was horrific, but when Aggie reached the far side of the room she screamed as she saw the word INTRUDER burned into the wood of the wall panel above the closet, and her clothes were still on fire. "How did this happen, and how did we not smell the smoke outside? We could have prevented this or slowed the progression if someone had smelled the fire." Aggie touched her face and her fingers came back wet. The trials of the past few days were catching up with her. Not only had she lost her Gran but now a space that was once her own, even if only for a short time? It was devastating.

Eldon wrapped his arms around her and turned her to face him. He gingerly wiped away the tears, causing the butterflies to zing to life around her faster than ever, as though she was wrapped in a tornado. Aggie didn't care, though. This closeness was just what she needed, and she was going to take all she could get. Leaning into his touch Aggie let Eldon take the burden of supporting her, if only for a moment. Eldon began to shake and Aggie glanced up at him with concern. His face was taut with concentration bordering on painful.

"What are you doing?" Aggie reached up and placed her hand gently on his cheek and his trembling ceased, though he didn't open his eyes even a crack. She chose not to move her hand, instead believing she was helping him in some way.

"I'm reaching out to the twins." His reply was rushed and through clenched teeth. Aggie's heart broke for him and kept her hand fixed in place, but brought her other hand up to mirror the first on the opposite side. She didn't know what he was talking about, but let him finish before pelting him with questions.

Since they were wrapped around each other, she felt when his body relaxed and his face went back to normal. Looking up to meet his eyes, she saw they were still their brilliant blue, "Did you just use part of your magic? I've no idea what all you are capable of, and now I can't help but be curious. Though my first priority is to be sure you're okay."

Eldon placed his finger over her lips to silence her. "Be still; I'm perfectly fine. That is just one of my powers that I don't use very often because it takes so much out of me. Unfortunately, this was one of the times I decided the alternative was much less pleasant. I couldn't bear to leave you alone, and I didn't think it would be wise to leave this room to anyone else who would seek to destroy it further, or you for that matter." Embracing her tighter, he placed his chin on top of her head.

Aggie absorbed what he was saying before having a dawning moment. "Are you saying Gryson doesn't need to put his spell together and you could just talk to the guys in your head if something were to go wrong?"

Eldon chuckled softly and she felt the vibration from his throat pressed against her skull. "No, I can't call on that power so easily. As you saw, I don't exactly hide it as well as Gryson's spell will. If we were standing in a hallway and I started to shake like that, I would think it would draw some unwanted attention. That is why I didn't say anything about it before. It wasn't the best course of action at the time." Aggie thought about this and nodded quietly. "You are the one who said we should trust our strengths, and if someone says they can handle something we should believe in them. I knew Gryson was the best one for the job, and I allowed him to be in charge of that situation. I, on the other hand, have another job to do and that is to keep you as safe as I can while we get any information we can. I can't do that by drawing attention to us and taking mine off of you."

With that there was a commotion in the hallway, and Aggie's hackles rose. She grew stiff in Eldon's grasp, and then in ran Mitchell and Ren. Aggie visibly relaxed in Eldon's arms and she audibly sighed. The twins stopped as quickly as they ran in and took in the space. "What the hell happened in here? Did you leave a curling iron on?" Ren's hands were on his hips, and though his words were full of humor it didn't reach his eyes. Aggie realized immediately he was trying to defuse the situation with his usual comedic relief, and for that she was grateful.

"This is a bit more damage than my tiny haircare products would have caused, but thank you for assuming my incompetence. I haven't set anything on fire in my life." Aggie wasn't angry, but it took her mind off of the horror that was her room by playing along.

"Well, you're what, twenty-two? You've got time. I can work with you one-on-one and we can up your game. There is always time to learn a new skill. We can even talk to Gryson or Mathius and get them in on it. They have fire-wielding skills. You could screw up one of their spells and, best-case scenario, blow something up." With a wink, he joined his brother who was already working his way around the room. They took in every aspect of the disaster and Aggie wasn't sure what all they were doing, since Mitchell said they were more than just *sniffers*. Aggie silently observed as they made quick work of the space.

"Looks like the majority of the wreckage is concentrated in the closet area." Mitchell pointed at the angry message on the wall. "Not just because that is written up there, either. I'm sure that is what you were thinking, but it is actually the darkest part of the burn pattern, as though they used an accelerant of some kind. Anyone with any magic at all would have circumvented that and just cast or used their powers on this, and it would have been much more efficient." Mitchell squinted at the smoldering clothes still inside the closet. "Looks like someone has a bone to pick with you."

"How would anyone have a problem with me? I haven't spoken to anyone with the exception of the eight of you. Who would have done this?" Aggie was grateful for Eldon's supportive hand still placed protectively on her lower back. She could almost close her eyes and imagine better circumstances for him having felt the need to place his hands on her. Instead, life was getting in the way with yet another problem. Would she ever have a calm moment in her life again? First, it was missing children, then weather attacks, and now attacks on Aggie herself. Squaring her shoulders, she silently resolved to get through this as unscathed as possible.

"Well, based on what I can pick up, your attacker was female. So, she is likely threatened by your presence. Perhaps she once fancied herself at one of our sides and is now disappointed by your appearance among us. It is no secret how the Brotherhood of Guardians mate. For us, it is all or nothing, and we take that oath upon accepting the role laid before us." Aggie had never heard them voice this to such an extent, which got her thinking.

"How old were each of you when you were asked to accept your role?" She almost didn't want to hear the answer.

"It was a different age for each of us. Our cultures are different and society standards vary. For example," Eldon had pulled her attention away from the twins as they went back to searching the room for clues, "I was a prodigy and I knew I was next in line for the guardian succession. I was only eleven at the time of my choice to accept my destiny."

"ELEVEN?" Aggie practically screeched her question. "You're saying that you weren't even fighting your voice change and learning about who you were, and yet you were expected to make a life-changing choice that you wouldn't be able to change back?"

"I wouldn't change a thing. My waiting to settle down until I met my one true equal was the best choice of my life." Eldon's chest puffed out to show his honorable choice and how he truly believed he was doing the right thing.

"Are you saying you've never…" Aggie didn't finish her thought because, even though they all swore they were in this as a group, the idea of talking about sex in mixed company still bothered her.

Figuring out her train of thought, Eldon proceeded to answer her, "I assure you I'm no virgin. I have had my share of women." The thought of any of them with another woman burned painfully inside her chest. She had no rights to feel anything about them before she met them, but that didn't change her reaction. Eldon reached down and took her clenched fist in his hands. Slowly he released each finger one by one. "There is something you should know about us. When we accept our roles in the Brotherhood, we agree to have a spell cast upon us. We aren't required to be celibate, but we are unable to procreate."

"That's your safety precaution? A magical condom?" Aggie was trying to put his words in a way she could actually understand.

"No, this is more than a condom," Ren joined their conversation. Aggie was so caught up in this she didn't even care anymore that they were openly discussing sexual relations with each other as a group. "The spell isn't broken until we are bonded to our one true mate. In our case, we all know who that is intended to be, so it isn't a guessing game or even a game of Where's Waldo, or Wendy, in this case. So, if we have sex to scratch an itch, then we aren't worried about possible ties to her when it is all said and done."

"What if you were to fall in love with one of these placeholders, in the meantime?" Aggie didn't want to hear the answer but that was becoming a recurring trend. Steeling herself, she prepared for the answer that was bound to crush her.

"While that hasn't been an issue, if it were to have happened then we could have chosen to live out our life sterile and give up our place in the Brotherhood." Mitchell decided to add his two cents' worth and Aggie was thankful it was he who answered that. While she didn't hate him, they weren't anywhere near as close as any of the other guys. They had shared one very sexually-charged kiss earlier, but that didn't mean she was ready to stake her claim and give up the fact that they hadn't seen eye to eye from the get-go. He always had a comment or some sort of attitude for everything she said or did. That wasn't any way to start a relationship if they were ever going to do so. They would have to find some common ground. This conversation wasn't her favorite one, and if anyone was going to deliver bad news it should come from her least favorite guy.

"I can respect that. I'll admit this conversation leaves me feeling raw and frustrated, but it's better to know you all weren't forced to give up happiness in a crap shoot of whether some girl accepts her role as your Ninth and one true mate. As we've established, it hasn't exactly been a short wait for you." She nodded in Mitchell's direction and placed a hand on Ren and Eldon's arms. For the moment, she was thankful the storm had brought on cooler temps and they were wearing long sleeves. No mixed sensations to mess with her already-blurred feelings.

"Actually, time in the other realms runs differently than on Earth. As you can see, we are all not much older than you. While your grandmother has known us for many years on Earth, it hasn't been but a few months in our separate times." A jolt of panic ran through Aggie as she realized what Ren was saying.

"Are you saying years will have passed before we get back to my house? I'm the last living relative. If the house is presumed to be empty, won't someone try to buy it or take it from me?" That was a reasonable question since the world she knew was always out for something that someone else had or the next big thing.

"There is nothing to worry about. The rest of the world thinks that you have taken an extended vacation, and the Brownies are keeping the house in a suspended state. No one will think anything or be the wiser." Eldon spoke softly to calm her panic, and for that she was grateful yet again.

# Chapter 11

itchell, as expected, brought everyone's focus back to the matter at hand. "Are either of you going to tell us what happened in here?" Aggie didn't know what to tell him, but she knew shying away from it wasn't an option.

"I'm not entirely sure. We just came back in here and this is what we found. Had we come in any sooner it seems we might have seen some of this still ablaze." Aggie shuddered at the thought of coming that close to open fire.

"Somehow we didn't smell any of the fire, either. The door was cracked before we walked in for a moment as we finished our conversation in the hall. No smoke came out into the hallway. It was contained by some unknown power. The only problem is I can't sense the magic. We might need Gryson or Liel to try to see what they can pick up. Did you guys get anything?" Eldon seemed on edge about all of this. Aggie didn't know if it was a self-conscious issue about not being able to protect her from an unknown threat or something else.

"Why did you only call them, and why them first?" Aggie didn't understand completely how his power worked, but the best approach was usually the direct one.

"I told you it was a power drain. I hoped between their power to locate clues most of us can't see and their strength, we could elude anything or anyone that might still be lingering nearby." Aggie hadn't thought about them being jumped if they looked too closely at what was going on.

"Oh, I guess I didn't consider that the firestarter might have stayed in the room or hadn't made it out yet. Thank you for being proactive and not leaving me alone. Come to think of it, if I'm going to be hanging around and staying in this gig, perhaps we should look into training in some way. I'm not the biggest or the strongest person. I haven't been formally trained in any way. I talk a big game, but nothing really comes of it." That was a hard thing for her to admit. She'd always liked to think of herself as a bit of a scrapper or a badass, but really, she only spoke up in the times she knew she would win. With what they were currently dealing with, it seemed she was the underdog and likely to come out on the bottom in any fight.

"We can arrange for training in any downtime we have during the investigation. I'm sure my brother and I can lead that for now." Ren was always so forthcoming, and everything he said or did was always graced with a perfect smile that made Aggie weak in the knees. Although, she would never admit that.

"I love when you volunteer me for projects." Mitchell's dry, sarcastic tone was without feeling, but Aggie knew he wasn't genuinely happy for this new addition to his schedule. "No, all we can smell is smoke, but I did find this beside what is left of the table. Do you recognize it?" He held a scrap of fabric that seemed smudged with some kind of sticky substance. It wasn't familiar, but as Aggie looked closer she noticed it had a faint print. The dark color of the fabric was impossible to decipher after it was smudged, but the design was a rusted gold color and looked a lot like filigree.

"I don't recognize it, but it looks like it could have been part of a curtain at one point in time. Look at the design and the texture of it. It's too thick to be worn, unless someone in the castle favors very heavy dresses that would slow even the fastest runner down. The filigree that's stitched into it shouldn't ever be on a dress design like that. Maybe in a simpler pattern, but this is all over it as though it went from the top of the piece to the very bottom systematically." Aggie tried to be as detailed as possible, not sure how designer-friendly the boys were. Mitchell cocked his head to the side, examining the scrap of fabric. Then he glanced at the curtains still covering the windows. Ren followed his brother's line of sight. It was as though they were having a conversation in their minds. "Can you speak telepathically with each other?" Aggie blurted.

Mitchell just scoffed at her, but made no effort to answer.

"No, it's a twin thing," Ren offered, but went back to working through the puzzle with his brother. "It looks like these aren't the same as the ones in this room, but I wonder what room might have this pattern. I guess we could always ask Mathius for guidance on that matter." The twins were making their way around the room for a final check to make sure they didn't miss anything.

"I think, if you'd like to stay with them, I could go and get the others. Were they in the same room as you?" Eldon's question was directed at the twins.

"No, we had already split up to work on our separate projects again. I'm not sure exactly where everyone is, but they will probably be heading toward their rooms for a little while to prepare. So, you might check there first." Mitchell graced him with a response and Aggie considered the fact that she wasn't the one who asked and therefore he got an answer directly.

"That sounds logical. Aggie, you can come with me if you'd rather." Eldon sounded meek and not himself. She didn't know the best answer.

*What does he want me to say? Does he want me to say yes? If I do, would it boost his spirits? Is he just asking to be polite?* Aggie decided to go with her gut, and answer the way she was feeling and not just to make him feel better. "I think I'd rather stay here.

I'm still a bit shaken up from this encounter, and while this is the place it happened at least I don't have to keep my guard up." Eldon's face visibly relaxed. She guessed she answered the way he had hoped and mentally patted herself on the back, filing away that information for later. *Go with your gut, Aggie. Things seem to go better when you do.*

Eldon turned to leave, but before he did he turned back and placed a sweet kiss on the edge of Aggie's hairline. It was a simple gesture, but Aggie now knew she was his priority and leaving was secondary.

Turning back to the brothers, she saw Ren wore a knowing grin. Unable to help herself, she stuck her tongue out at him. She realized he brought out a juvenile side of her that she hadn't seen in years. "Is there any way I can help, Wolfie?" She was feeling brave and, since she was talking to Ren, it was better odds that he wouldn't literally bite her head off. That didn't stop Mitchell from growling audibly. "Easy, boy; I was just joking." Gasping, she covered her mouth quickly, realizing what she had just said and how it likely sounded. "I'm so sorry! That isn't what I meant at all."

"I'll bet." Mitchell mumbled, but then immediately turned back to what he was working on. Ironically, Ren thought this exchange was hilarious and was doubled over, laughing silently. He had obviously moved past audible and straight on to the silent, can't breathe variety.

"Are you enjoying this? He could have eaten me for all I know. His wolf probably didn't appreciate any of that conversation and is probably not liking me at all right now." After saying it out loud, Aggie was truly nervous and worried for her safety. "Maybe I should have left with Eldon. At least I know there isn't a beast inside of him, clawing to get out and destroy me."

"Let me let you in on a little secret, *Princess.*" The last word was filled with disdain, which hurt Aggie just a bit. "The last thing my wolf wants is to eat you. Well, not in the normal sense of the word." Aggie stood staring at him and she realized her jaw had dropped open in shock. With great difficulty, she forced her mouth closed and her brain to work again.

"Wow. Uh. I guess I was wrong." She stammered through that and realized her brain hadn't fully rebooted from its abrupt halt. Then, without warning, Ren added his two cents' worth but wasn't near as subdued as Mitchell.

"I think my wolf and my *head* have plenty of ideas of what we would like to do with you." A low growl came from Ren's throat, so deep it sounded like it came from someone else. "See, my wolf likes this way of thinking." He trailed kisses up her neck and she felt that familiar chill run over her and a subtle version of the vibration she felt when they both touched her. His tongue dragged slowly along the vein in her neck and the vibration moved lower in her body, making her knees weaken. His eyes flashed gold and the growl was stronger this time. Aggie noticed his hair was lengthening while his actions became more intense. His kiss moved to her jaw and quickly found her mouth as his hand fisted in her hair at the nape of her neck. Rough wasn't necessarily something she would have ever considered, but with Ren it was definitely working for her.

A moan escaped her as she lost herself to the sensations Ren was creating. His free hand found her breasts through her shirt and kneaded them a bit forcefully, but it wasn't painful. She felt herself lean into his touch, silently pleading for more. Grasping at his clothes, she shoved her hands beneath his shirt and could have died at the feel of the rippling muscles covering every inch of his body. Running her nails down the exposed skin, his wolf rumbled his acceptance and pleasure. Unsatisfied with that reaction, Aggie repeated the process but dug her nails in deeper, knowing full well she would have left a trail of marks, but no blood, this time. Ren's reaction was perfect; while his wolf snarled getting more excited, Ren jerked her head back where his hand was still tangled in her hair, kissing her soundly, and their tongues battled for dominance. He lifted her from the floor, causing a gush of wetness to soak her panties. She responded immediately, wrapping her legs tightly around his hips. Ren's hands settled perfectly under her ass and gripped each cheek tightly, digging his own fingers into her flesh through the fabric of her pants. Arching her hips, she ground into him and his obvious arousal. She could only imagine how endowed he would prove to be once she rid him of his clothes.

The door burst open with a loud bang, startling Ren and Aggie out of their bubble. Aggie squeaked and quickly tried to muffle it. Ren didn't even flinch or come close to losing his grip on her, for which she was thankful. "I thought this was a crime scene, but now I'm starting to wonder what we just walked in on." Gryson was smiling and Aggie's cheeks flushed. She could feel the heat traveling to her face and away from the area that it previously resided, saddening her at the loss.

Embarrassed, she scrambled out of Ren's arms and he lowered her slowly to the floor. Sneaking a glance back at Mitchell, Aggie noticed the glow was slowly leaving his eyes. The tightness in his pants was unmistakable. Aggie wondered if he would have joined in had they not been interrupted so suddenly. That was another thought she filed away for later, only slightly ashamed that it reignited the fire that was boiling moments before.

"Um, we got sidetracked." Aggie saw Gryson was accompanied by everyone else. They all seemed to be riding in like white knights to save her from unknown danger. "Did everyone need to come? I feel like you all had other things to be working on. Gryson, did you finish the spell?"

"Not yet; I heard what happened and wanted to be sure you were all right. It seems, though, that these two had it well in hand." Gryson didn't look angry, but he did look a bit envious. That made Aggie feel desirable and wanted. Her heated face lessened slightly.

"Mathius, Liel, did you guys get the list finished about the kids who might be next on the list of targets?" Still breathless, Aggie tried to rein in control of the situation. This was proving difficult because they were all staring at her, obviously aware of her aroused state.

"We were pulled away before we finished. This was more important," Liel said, and Aggie was touched at his concern, but needing to take her mind of her fear she dug deep for control.

"Well, now that you're here perhaps you can help us figure out what happened in here. We've figured out that the fire wasn't magical, and that some sort of curtain was used to start the blaze. Perhaps it was partially soaked in the chemical or substance used to ignite everything." Aggie's flustered state faded, quickly getting back to work. Realizing something for the first time since all this had happened, she said, "I have no clothes. What am I going to wear and where will I sleep?"

"You will stay with us." Mitchell's flat statement was unexpected. This man was full of surprises. For always acting like he had a stick up his ass when she was around, he was being very generous.

"That makes the most sense. We have an adjoining room and the most space, for our wolves when needed. We can bunk together if needed, unless you want me to stay with you," Ren added suggestively. The chill returned and she wasn't even touching him. The draw to him had grown, and something had changed after their encounter.

"That is not the reason I suggested it; well, not the last part." Mitchell gave his brother an annoyed look only a brother could give accurately. "I was betting that if someone is on the hunt for her, as this message suggests, we are the first round of defense for her. Even while we are sleeping, our wolves are on alert and will identify any danger."

"Oh, that too. I was just hoping for some added benefit of her being so close. I've had a taste and I'm not sure I want to wait for the main course." Ren wasn't shy about his intentions, and that turned Aggie on all over again. Shaking her head, she made a futile attempt to shake their encounter out of her system. If this was her reaction to just one of them, and the pull was getting stronger, how was she ever going to resist them all?

"I honestly don't care where I sleep. I'd be happy with the floor, but I do want to be safe. Constantly looking over my shoulder or waiting for the next shoe to drop isn't my idea of fun. Now, Mathius, have you seen these curtains anywhere?" Taking the scrap from Mitchell, she handed it to Mathius to examine.

His face scrunched up and his head tilted from side to side, like someone trying to figure out a puzzle. "This is impossible," Mathius muttered under his breath, but Aggie was standing close enough that she heard him plainly.

"Impossible? That doesn't sound like a start to a good story." Aggie took a step closer and the other guys mirrored her actions, waiting for Mathius to explain.

"Many years ago, there was a woman who lusted after King Talogar. It was a time before he had married Queen Annare. The king acknowledged her as a potential mate, but had made no commitments. He knew, as king, he would need to be mated to carry on the line, should anything happen to him, though he hadn't found her yet. This woman was almost crowned, when she began to show her true colors. She treated the servants like lesser beings and that was something King Talogar never wanted. He knew the castle wouldn't keep itself and that people were necessary to make that happen. They weren't better than anyone as royalty. That is one thing that has always made him a well-respected king. Those around him were always considered before all else. She thought as the queen that would make her the most powerful woman alive and everyone should treat her as such. Over a short time, the servants began to talk and word got back to Talogar. He was appalled, but trusted their words and never doubted his people.

"He confronted her and she lashed out, trying to hurt Talogar, and the guards had to intervene. There was a struggle and threats thrown out against the king and his entire family. The change was so abrupt, and she screamed and screeched her words. The guards lifted her from the floor, and she was dragged kicking and screaming to the dungeons.

"Her threats and anger never ceased, and they kept her locked up for a month. After that time, she was brought before Talogar. He asked if she admitted her wrongs and if she was ready to pay the penance for her crimes. Instead, she cursed him and a lightning bolt shot from the ceiling, aimed straight for the king. I dove in front of the king and took the bulk of the energy. Had it not been for my armor and magical spells protecting it, I would have been dead. For that, I was promoted and she was stripped of her powers and banished to the outer lands that are uninhabited for the remainder of her life. She is now only known as *The Wanderer*." Mathius absently rubbed at a place above his heart, trapped in the memory.

Aggie came close and placed her hand over his, stilling his movement. She recalled the tapestry on her way in and grieved for the woman and for Mathius. The sayings about women scorned were no joke, but there was a level of pity one should have for the woman. Sickness or misbelief were no excuse, but there was still a level of reality for the woman and their own choices reflected that. Their belief in these false realities was their downfall.

"I don't understand what that has to do with this piece of fabric." Aggie softly rubbed her hand over his, never separating and enjoying the sensation his touch gave her. No longer scared by the reactions they produced, just relishing their differences.

"This isn't a curtain, it is the fabric she wore as a cloak and cowl. It is her family crest, of which she was very proud. She was never seen in public without it. She felt like, if seen at a distance, those who saw her would know the respect she was due. It was sent with her to the void. All remaining pieces were destroyed with her things." Mathius was very solemn, and his words were spoken with much grief. His memories of this woman and the incident were still fresh, as though they might have happened the day before and not years previous. "I was promoted to head of the guard after I recovered."

"So, why is my room on fire and not yours?" Aggie knew the question was inconsiderate and rude, but she couldn't be the only one thinking it.

"Perhaps one attempt on my life taught her I'm hard to kill. Attacking you is her way of hurting me by default." Mathius shrugged, not one hundred percent certain of his answer.

"That makes sense, if she was stripped of her powers, why the room wasn't magically burned. The fabric may have been left intentionally so we would come looking for her. Maybe she is looking for a fight and one last shot at you, Mathius." Eldon's theory was valid and worth considering. The thought that someone was picking a fight with Mathius out of revenge and attacking her to get at one of the guys brought out a protective side of Aggie.

"If she wants a fight, I'll give it to her. She can't do any of this and just get away with it." Then it dawned on Aggie. "Did you say she hit you with lightning?" Mathius nodded. His face was stricken with remorse Aggie didn't fully understand. "The children who have been taken have weather-related powers and the weather is what is changing to disrupt life here."

As though he had been hit with a stack of bricks, Mathius stumbled back. "That's it! She's back and by taking King Talogar's son, she is drawing the lines of battle. She wants him to come to her." Mathius began storming around the room, knocking over anything that was still standing. Aggie dodged a few things that came a little too close.

"Enough! Losing control isn't the answer here!" Xavier boomed through the chaos. "We need a plan of action and someplace to start looking. Obviously, she has found her way back from the void. She could be anywhere. We need to start narrowing down options of where she would hide."

"Now that I have an idea of who it is, I can scry for possible power spikes along with this scrap of fabric." Gryson was ever helpful and full of ideas, and for that Aggie was grateful.

"Do we still need to meet with Delia if we know who's behind all of this?" Aggie didn't want to be left out of the action and she worried that if she left to go on a mission of lesser importance, the guys would leave without her.

"I think we should still see what she has to say. Those messages were more than enough to make me uncomfortable about Yavari's intentions around the castle. It is possible she has a connection to this after all." Eldon was the voice of reason, and Aggie was forced to agree. She had heard those messages in the Security Room with her own ears. Yavari was capable of anything.

# Chapter 12

alking down the hallway, Aggie was ready to get this meeting over with. They were meeting in Delia's chambers to avoid any prying ears. Gryson had finished the spell and she now had to control her thoughts. The only way he could make it work was to tie everyone into actual emotions. It was the best way to avoid them being found out, by making them alert for help audibly.

"This corridor is darker than I expected," Aggie muttered to herself. She slowed her steps to avoid tripping on a loose stone, even though she knew that the likelihood of that was slim.

"Are you afraid of the dark, wee one?" Xavier's voice sounded in her head and she cringed at the thought. It was a strange feeling to have someone speak to her and not actually be there. The only forgiving factor was that they were all connected, as though they were in a room having a conversation. That didn't take away the unease of knowing everyone could hear her, no matter what.

"Now, Xavier, don't toy with the girl. It isn't her fault you are attracted to dark corners everywhere you go." Kyrel's words made Aggie stifle a laugh. Nothing made a person look crazier than talking to yourself and laughing at silent jokes.

"I love to do unspeakable things in dark corners. It is my nature." Aggie didn't know if Xavier meant his choice of meal or other more tantalizing activities, but she was happy to imagine them.

"Oh, my dear. I like the way you think," Xavier purred in her mind. Eldon never once acknowledged the conversation happening in her head, but she knew he could hear. Glancing up at him as they passed one of the few lights in the hallway she caught a glimpse of his resolute face, but his slightly pointed ears were tipped in red. He shared that trait with Liel, but his ears were shorter and slightly rounded on the edges, and then pointed at the very tips that were now crimson. Liel's were elongated and pointed as though they had been stretched as a child.

"Are you okay, Eldon?" She paused in the hallway and reached up to touch his ears, but hesitated at the last minute as he tensed. She felt his apprehension as though it were her own. She couldn't hear his thoughts. "Why can't I hear what you're thinking?" She blurted the last part, as was her norm when she wanted to know something badly enough.

"I'm blocking them. It takes years to learn, but even though we're connected I'm only transmitting what I want to be heard." Matter-of-factly and with little emotion, she was reminded of Liel yet again. "It takes a great deal of concentration." That made sense now. He must have been focusing so hard to block, his regular intonation was lost in the process.

"I can feel you, though." Then she realized how that sounded as the rest of the crew laughed in her mind.

"That is the cost of blocking all else. Strong emotions break through."

"Why did you tense when I reached for you?" They had both stopped walking during this exchange.

"We should get moving or we'll be late, and that wouldn't look very good since we requested the meeting." Eldon deflected her answer, frustrating her. She shoved her hands into the pockets of her jeans, but Eldon ignored her obvious tantrum. They picked up their pace again and Aggie stewed in her thoughts, not caring that everyone must know how angry she was for being ignored.

"For our kind, the ears are an erogenous zone. Fae and Elves share that between our species. It isn't considered polite to touch them in mixed company or amongst strangers, any more than if someone were to grab your breasts in public." Liel, as ever the voice of reason and information, must have taken some sort of pity on her and shared that little bit of information. Eldon, on the other hand, flared again with his reddened tips. Aggie realized he didn't want her to know that and was embarrassed again. First, it was the silent conversation between the guys, and her shy little Fae was now embarrassed to have been turned on by her in a hallway.

"I'm not going to say I'm sorry, Eldon. I will say I will never knowingly make you uncomfortable in public again. I do want you to know I'm flattered more than you know. The thought of how you see me is beyond words and I'm sure at this point you can all figure out my reaction to any and all of you individually. It doesn't take much for you to get my blood pumping.  Hey, and what girl doesn't want to spend time with a guy who can literally create flowers for her on a whim?" That got him out of his shell, because a beautiful smile crept onto his face. She felt satisfied that he was back and out of his funk.

"Oh, man! You broke out the flower wild card? How are the rest of us supposed to compete with such chivalry?" Ren's words made Aggie laugh out loud, but she quickly covered her mouth because the outburst echoed through the walls of the hallway. *This castle really needs some sound dampeners,* Aggie thought, her hand still clamped over her mouth.

"That it does; thankfully our bedrooms are damped magically, so certain sounds won't escape into the hallways," Ren added suggestively.

"Well, then, it's a good thing you aren't competing with each other, or so you say." Aggie said her words audibly because to everyone else she and Eldon could have been having a passing conversation. That, and the idea of telekinetic conversations creeped her out. It was bad enough the rest of the guys were in her head; she didn't have to join them.

A short walk later, they arrived at Delia's room. Knocking quietly so as not to have it echo down the hall, Eldon stepped back to stand beside Aggie while they waited. When the door cracked open, Delia's face appeared in the crack. Aggie felt more like this meeting was clandestine and not just a passing conversation.

"Hello, I'm Aggie, and I'm sure you know Eldon. May we come in so we can chat?" Aggie pulled her hands from her pants pockets and held them facing out, to show they were there under friendly circumstances. Delia hesitated and then nodded while opening the door a little wider so Aggie and Eldon could pass through. Quickly shutting it behind them, she waved her hand over the knob and it was quickly covered in a golden serpent moving across and embedding its teeth in the doorframe. Immediately it hardened into solid gold as though it had never once moved. Aggie didn't know what to think, but was definitely impressed by the show of power. While to everyone else it was probably just a little display, to Aggie it was amazing.

"That should keep out any unwanted visitors, or at least slow them down long enough for us to get out of here." Delia seemed rather paranoid. Was there more to this meeting than even they knew?

"Well, then, I guess we should get started." Eldon took charge and for that Aggie was thankful, even though Delia didn't seem bothered by Aggie's presence. "What can you tell us about your dealings with Yavari?"

"Yavari." Delia chuckled sardonically. "She used to be great. I've known her since I was a kid, you see. I grew up in the castle. My parents have worked here and I always played at their feet as a child. This is the only home I've ever known. When I was old enough, I started working as a lady's maid in the court. I loved my job, as I got to hang out with girls relatively my own age.

"Yavari requested me when I was eighteen. She and I got along great, and because she was the daughter of the king there wasn't much she was allowed to do, for fear of her safety. She would send me with notes to boys she saw in the market on her guided outings that she thought were cute. She was like any other teenager, hormone-driven and sweet. She resented her father for keeping her from the lifestyle she wanted, but tell me a child that doesn't apply to." Delia was very open and honest. She sat comfortably as she told her story across from Aggie and Eldon in the sitting area of her quarters. The space was a little bigger than Aggie expected, but as the lady's maid to the king's sister, she would probably have a bit more rank.

"Something changed when she reached her mid-twenties. Her brother had taken the throne and she was still restricted for her safety. She felt that as an adult she should have more freedom since she wasn't actually wearing a crown any longer. She became angry and plotted opportunities to leave the castle after dark. I wasn't privy to the places she was going or who she was meeting. When she would return I could feel the emotions radiating off of her. She felt different and the happy young girl was gone. We no longer stayed up at night to talk about love interests or life problems. The day the Prince Rikan was born it was like a switch was flipped. She went from a pleasant person to be around to being volatile and hard to predict. She would go from regal to vicious in seconds and without warning. The planned excursions increased and became more secretive. I found spells cast over her room for privacy when I would come to check on her. I'm might be her lady's maid, but my privileges to her room for cleaning or preparation have been limited and at times revoked." She flipped her hand to reveal scars running over her palm. "I've learned to knock, rather than press my luck. It's like a game to her and the spell on the room prevents me from healing them." Delia stared at the puckered skin on her hand. Her face winced as though reliving the pain that must have accompanied the wounds the first time she received them.

"I'm so sorry; she sounds truly evil." Aggie wanted to befriend this girl and not just because of the physical pain she had endured. She just looked like she was lost and needed someone to talk to. Pressing her luck, Aggie rose from her seat and moved over to sit beside the girl. In the light of what she had gone through, this Apep demon seemed small and beat down from years of abuse. Resting her hand on Delia's leg, Aggie attempted to convey her sympathy but not pity. No one wanted to be pitied. Aggie didn't pity her; she was in awe of her strength. Delia was badass in her own right, but had just misplaced her spirit. Aggie wanted to help her find it.

"Is there any chance that you have since figured out who she is meeting in the secret getaways?" Eldon leaned forward with his elbows resting on his knees. The conversation had gone from uncertain to comfortable very quickly. Delia was a very likable girl.

Delia hesitated, "I... well... once I followed her when she went through town. I was so nervous that she would know what I had done, but she had changed so much over such a short period of time I was worried someone was influencing her actions." Chewing on a nail of her good hand, Delia stopped and grew quiet.

"Where did she go?" Eldon pressed her, but his lyrical voice made everything seem okay and took the stress out of his words.

"I'm not entirely sure. She passed through town, wearing a hooded cloak. That made it easier to follow her, as no one wears those anymore. While it hid her face from onlookers, I knew it was her. She walked for a while after we left town and I thought she was just taking a cleansing walk, but then we reached a field and she stopped abruptly. It was so unexpected I was worried I had gotten too close while tailing her. Then out of nowhere she just disappeared. I imagine she sifted, but I have no idea why she walked so far just to phase to a new location." Delia had drawn her feet up underneath her and was still nervously chewing on her nail. This conversation wasn't one that made her relaxed anymore. The initial part was easy because she spoke of the happier times. It was obvious she was scared of Yavari and didn't know the extent of her powers to find her and know she was ratting Yavari out.

"Thank you." Aggie reached over and grasped Delia's hand, squeezing lightly as it was her injured hand. Aggie wanted her to know that it didn't define her or scare Aggie away because she had scars. Everyone had scars, some just weren't visible to the naked eye. "We won't keep you any longer. You're welcome to find me if you need anything or just want to talk. I don't just mean about this, but if you remember anything else feel free to reach out. I'm happy to be a sounding board or just a friendly ear." Giving the hand one last squeeze Aggie released it. Delia just stared at her in shock. Slowly a smile crept up on her face, one of appreciation and understanding. Delia looked as though a huge weight was lifted off of her.

"Thank you again, for everything. We won't be in touch unless something pressing changes things. We don't want you to get into any trouble for associating with us."

They all made their way to the door and Aggie reached for the handle but at the last second hesitated, realizing that the door was still sealed. Not wanting to risk what might happen if she touched it, Aggie backed away. Delia laughed. "Oh, silly me. Let me get him off there for you. Stanley, come!" The serpent quickly unraveled and faded into glittery dust. Then the golden sparkling dust floated across the room and landed in the palm of Delia's hand.

"Stanley?" Aggie's left eyebrow shot up in question. Delia just beamed at her. "Cute name. Does he do any other tricks?"

Delia placed her finger beside her nose. "Only time will tell; I have to keep a few secrets to myself." The girls burst into a fit of giggles and Aggie felt wonderful with the release of endorphins. It had been a while since she spent some quality girl time.

She and Eldon made their way back to the hallway of their rooms, where the rest of the guys were waiting. That didn't stop them from chiming in once Eldon and Aggie were out of earshot of the room.

"Anyone have any thoughts on all that?" Mitchell's gruff tone was the first to address the elephant in the room. Though his voice in Aggie's head grated on her nerves, it also reminded her of what he mentioned about his wolf earlier, setting her afire all over again. Her sex drive was in overdrive and she had to get a handle on it.

"Princess, you are beyond out of control. Rein it in, for the sake of the rest of us if nothing else." Mitchell groaned in her mind as did a couple others she couldn't pinpoint, as they were muffled.

"I'm sorry, I'm having a hard time controlling things." *Kyrel, you aren't the cause of this over the link, are you?* Since she was speaking directly to someone not in the space, she chose to think it to him, and the fact that he responded seconds later made it feel just as strange as she had anticipated.

"Nope that isn't me. It is all you. I might be connected to you mentally, but I can't physically hear you with my ears. It is with my mind. I can't smell you or sense you outside of this mental link." She could hear the humor in his voice as though he was smiling and laughing at her for asking, but she felt justified given his propensity for *leaking*.

"All right, I'll try and control my urges in the future. I thought I was doing all right but perhaps I'm not doing my best." Aggie reached out and clasped Eldon's hand as they walked, and a smug feeling came off of him.

"What is that for?" Ren was the one who asked. They couldn't see what was happening and Aggie chose not to inform them, as did Eldon.

"Does anyone know if there are any estates that are out past the city? Anything that might have been abandoned or inhabited by an elderly family without any children to pass it on to when they passed?" Xavier was thinking rationally and had moved past the sexual tension, leaving Aggie to wonder if he had blocked it as Eldon had done.

"I will have to check the maps and see; perhaps it will show something on the perimeter of the city limits. Though it sounds like Delia had to walk for a while before coming across it. That might mean it isn't going to show on the maps." Mathius paused and Aggie thought it sounded like he was humming or somehow deep in thought. The fact that they could block this really bothered her. She would speak with Gryson about this. Perhaps there was something he could do in the future. "We might want to pull the census for the past few years and see if any families have drastically changed, warranting an empty house."

"That sounds like a plan. I assume my room is on lockdown. When we get back, should I head straight to the twins' rooms?" Aggie was growing more and more exhausted by the moment. The day had taken its toll. They were gaining ground but the days until Walpurgisnacht Roodmas were drawing closer with each passing sun cycle. There were only about eight days until they were out of time. The realization was draining. She didn't have much left and she wasn't used to this lifestyle. The thought of the kids being left any longer in the hands of a madwoman, trying to find a loophole to get her powers back and hurting how many families in the process, made Aggie sick. Aggie knew life wasn't fair, but children were off limits.

"We will be waiting for you. Given the fact that you sound exhausted, I'll have the bed ready for you. We can take shifts to guard you while you sleep." Ren was being extra sweet and Aggie wondered what changed. "Or we could take turns making you more tired." There it was, the Ren she was expecting. He had just held out for added effect.

"Don't put your cart before the horse. She might hit the bed and pass out. I'm not into necrophilia. I save that for the creepers, like Xavier." Mitchell sounded archaic with his choice of analogy. Although the jab at Xavier made Aggie laugh, it was surprising to her. He was joking. He wasn't snarky. What had changed?

"I don't enjoy my women dead; I prefer to partake of their living essence while I pleasure them. Trust me, it is worth it, for us both." Xavier's rich baritone and his choice of words gave her warm chills at the visual he had created.

"We'll be back in a few minutes. Gryson, is there a way to turn off this link? I'd like to enjoy my dreams without wondering if you guys are seeing them as well." Eldon gripped her hand a little tighter. She didn't know if it was compassion or fear for them running into trouble without the link.

"I have a manual deactivation for you to drink when you get here; we all have to do it together or we will stay connected by the tether holding anyone who hasn't cut the cord. What are you planning on dreaming of, little keeper? Perhaps we should stay linked so we can all encounter what Aggie's dreams are like." Gryson knew he would only encourage the bad ones in the group with his words, and he succeeded.

"I'm on board for that, unless she wants me to give her something to dream about before she falls asleep. Then I'd prefer you all to stay out of her head so she can keep her focus on the important things at hand." Ren didn't block his thoughts and his ideas were very vivid, including a few things Aggie had never tried or considered before. He would definitely be a bad, or perhaps good, influence on her in the sex department.

"Enough both of you. I'll be back shortly and until then I'd like to call for silence. Since it seems you can all block your thoughts, let me walk the last few feet in peace." She was thankful for the quiet that met her. She knew the tether hadn't broken, but they were respectful enough to grant her request.

"Do you have anything to share to make the walk less daunting?" Aggie looked at Eldon expectantly, but the look on his face was one of surprise. His eyebrows shot up so fast she'd have thought she asked him to strip naked in the hall. "What?"

"I assumed you wanted to walk in silence. I wasn't expecting you to ask me to share my thoughts." Eldon stammered a bit, and the more time she spent with him she realized that this beautiful Fae was naturally shy. While he wasn't meek in any way and could hold his own given the right situation, shy was his go-to safe place.

"I wanted the buzzing in my head to cease. I had no idea how weird that would feel, but it was beyond intrusive. While I know they can still hear us, I'd like to pretend for a few minutes it's just us walking through these halls alone." Sighing, she snuggled in closer to Eldon's rigid body. He took a moment to relax, then wrapped his arm around her and she never released his hand. Now it rested beside her own shoulder still clasped in his hand. It was almost romantic, walking through the castle wrapped up in each other.

When they arrived at the twins' door, Eldon pulled his arm from her shoulders and clasped her other hand. They stood like that for a moment before Eldon leaned forward, pressing his lips against hers. Always the sweetest kiss from the sweetest one of her men. Wondering for a moment, Aggie pressed forward and licked the seam of his lips in hopes of sparking something in him. It worked, because he opened to her and thrust his tongue in to meet hers. Aggie's body was on fire and she threw her arms around his neck, standing on her toes to reach and not break the connection. She adored the feel of him pressed against her and she let her thoughts drift. Rubbing her body along the length of him, she felt him grow harder. Her nipples puckered against his chest and the fabric of her bra rubbed them roughly, causing friction. Aggie let her fingers trail up into Eldon's hair and she gripped it lightly, unsure of how much he preferred.

Eldon's hand dropped to her lower back and pressed her hard into his length, groaning at the contact. She let one hand fall and ran it up the back of his shirt. Aggie was surprised to find taut muscles running the length of his back. Without another thought she tore his shirt from his body right there in the hall. Neither was thinking clearly and the hall was empty. Nothing to interfere with where they were headed. Her eyes roved over his bare skin with awe. Without another thought she lowered her head and ran her tongue over his puckered nipple and sucked it into her mouth, letting her teeth lightly graze as it released with a soft pop. Her nails grazed the other nipple and he shuddered. She let her tongue flatten on it, creating a much-needed balance. Lifting her from the floor he smashed his mouth down to hers while gripping her cheeks tightly, on the verge of pain. The delicious feeling was the perfect amount of pleasure mixed with the sting of his fingers pressing into the skin. He backed her against the wall and his hands breached the fabric, sliding down the crack of her ass, quickly finding her wet slit. Smiling at what he found, he plunged his finger inside and met no resistance. Curling it, he dragged it back out and hit her sweet spot deep inside her. His fingers were so long there was no effort or challenge in hitting her hidden pleasure points. After a couple times, he turned his hand and ran it the opposite way, creating friction she had never felt before.

She pressed against him, rubbing her clit into his engorged cock just enough to almost push her over the edge. She scrambled to free the button on his pants. As tight as he was against the zipper, he had to be in pain. Just before she had gotten her hand around him to completely free his manhood, a door opened nearby.

"Well, this is quite the sight. Would you two like to come in and we will pick this back up in privacy?" Kyrel was standing across the hall in his own teal doorway, beaming. Aggie was so close to taking him up on his offer, as worked up as she was, but modesty took over. She slid down the wall and smiled at Eldon.

"Can we pick this back up in a little while? I definitely want to finish what we just started," she whispered as she refastened his pants back to their former restriction, and for that she felt horrible.

"Let's get these guys out of our head and then we can head to my room before the twins steal you." One last peck on her lips made her sad they had to stop.

"I apologize for interrupting you; we held off as long as possible. The thoughts you two were sending were pushing even my limits. The rest of the guys might have been taking matters into their own hands and couldn't come out here to take the head of the snake, so to speak." Kyrel didn't look sorry, but Aggie assumed that was because he fed off their energy and his coffers were probably pretty close to full.

Rolling her eyes at his antics she asked, "Where are we meeting? I'd like to get you guys out of my head sooner rather than later."

"They're all in there." He was pointing at Ren and Mitchell's door. "We wanted to be all in one place to make the separation easier. Only then you two started in and easier wasn't what I would say was happening. So, in an effort to give them some privacy to finish up what you caused, I sifted to my room to put an end to your hormones." Kyrel proceeded to open the door without knocking and Aggie got an eyeful of what she'd missed. There were no words. Xavier was refastening his buttons on his trousers, Gryson had just pulled his zipper up, and Mathius was tucking in his shirt. Everyone else was still out in all their glory, as though finishing wasn't anything to rush. Liel was laid out in his afterglow, and even limp he was still something to write home about. It took an effort to not rush over and get him going again to see him in his prime. Ren and Mitchell weren't quite finished and their dicks were straining in their own grasp. They were pumping away, and when they noticed her looking at them it only fired them up more. On impulse, she licked her lips at the idea of her looking turning them on more. They both groaned simultaneously and exploded with massive orgasms, leaving them spent and relaxed on their sofa. Aggie felt herself grow wet again at the sight she just took in.

"Well, now that that is out of the way, can we get this other problem taken care of that caused all of this?" Kyrel brought them all back to reality.

# Chapter 13

Aggie didn't know what to say about all of this. It was hard to fathom that all of this was caused by her reaction to Eldon. Though she did have to remember that they were men after all, and ultimately think with their dicks most of the time. They all finally cleaned up and composed themselves, and none of them apologized for the display, not that Aggie wanted them to at all.

"Let's get this over with. I would like to get back to my evening. Unlike the rest of you, I keep getting interrupted and I have whatever the girl version of blue balls is." After the display she just saw, the band-aid had been ripped off and the filter removed. There was no need to hide behind propriety or formalities. Judging by the mixed responses she was receiving through the link, they were shocked and some were becoming turned on once again. She wasn't sure how to react other than to speed up the process. "Gryson?"

"I have the antidote right here." Gryson made his way to the twins' fridge.

"Wow, you make it sound like we've been infected by a disease, which is so reassuring." Aggie rubbed her hands up and down her arms to tame the hormonal goosebumps radiating through her.

"Well, I wouldn't call it a disease in the traditional sense of the word, but you have been infected. Part of what I used to implement it was kind of like a tapeworm." Gryson said the words with clinical coldness.

"I knew something was off about this thing. My wolf has been practically crawling up the walls of my insides, trying to get out. I'm going to have to let him out for a bit after we take this, if I can keep him contained that long." Mitchell rubbed the back of his neck, trying to soothe the itching of his wolf scratching to get out. Aggie was so shocked by the news she ran to meet Gryson on the other side of the room, and grabbed the first vial she could get her hands on and urged the others to do the same.

"So how do we do this, one, two, three, drink or does it just have to be close together?" Aggie had a new sense of urgency and wanted this over with if there was something living in her to keep the link connected.

"As long as it is close, that is all that matters. We each contain a piece of the same creature, so once it is incapacitated it will reconnect as one inside the last vial that is drunk." Gryson still didn't seem to see how wrong it was to keep this from everyone.

Without another word Aggie drank hers in one gulp, followed quickly by Mathius and Ren. The rest followed suit and Gryson was the last one. They all waited with bated breath, watching Gryson's vial. Then a moment later, just as Gryson described, the small creature appeared inside his vial. Aggie refused to look any closer when she realized it was furry, rather than slimy, as she had assumed it would be. "Get rid of it! That magical creature isn't going anywhere else inside of me if I can keep from it." Aggie turned her back on Gryson and the magical little creature until she heard the door click. Assuming it was safe to turn around, she was surprised to find he wasn't the only one. Liel, Mathius, and Xavier had gone along with him. The remaining men stood still, waiting for her to speak. Mitchell and Ren didn't last, though, and began pacing the room.

"You can all stay and have a pow wow in here, but you're going to do it with a couple furry beasts prowling around. This space was made to include them and they haven't been let out today."

Without another word, the air began to sizzle and a deep growl came from Mitchell. He barely got turned around before his back bowed and the hairs on his body elongated. The muscles in his legs stretched and tore through his pants, leaving the sight of Mitchell's tight ass to admire. Aggie couldn't turn away from the image before her.

Soon the same thing started with Ren, but he didn't turn around. Shedding his pants quickly, Aggie was blessed to see his cock in all its glory. Apparently, this entire process was a huge turn-on or the thought that she was watching it unfold had him aroused. Aggie licked her lips without thought, wondering what it would be like to have him enter her. In the blink of an eye, there were two oversized wolves pacing where the boys were previously standing.

Mitchell's wolf was a gorgeous black beast with flecks of silver catching the light. He stood taller than any wolf she had ever seen before, and with the stature one would expect from an Alpha. He was almost regal.

Ren's wolf was a beautiful chestnut color and his fur was a bit shaggy. The expression on his face was comical; his mouth was open and his tongue lolled to the side. Both wolves were muscular and looked to be able to handle a load of any size if asked. Without warning, Ren's wolf bounded over to her and lapped at her face happily. Giggling at his antics, she pushed him off and her fingers laced into his fur. Unsure of proper etiquette with a shifted wolf, she hesitantly scratched his neck and up toward his ears. He leaned into it and her touch and a rumble vibrated from his throat. "You're not a cat. So, stop purring, Wolfie." His wolf's rumbles shorted out in tiny bursts almost as though he was laughing at her joke. "I guess you needed to stretch your legs, too. It's nice to meet you finally. I'm in awe of both of you. Words won't do your beauty justice." His fur was softer than expected. Aggie thought it would be course, but its thickness was gentle under her touch and she could almost curl up and cuddle him for hours.

Just then, something bumped into her leg. Glancing down she saw a ball of black and knew it was Mitchell's wolf. "Were you feeling neglected?" She thrust her hands into his fur and he practically knocked her over when he put his weight into pushing further into her hand. "Whoa, easy. What should I call you? I know Mitchell is still in there, but you aren't him. I've deemed Ren's alter ego 'Wolfie', but who are you?" He sat back straight as a board and held his chin high. Then Aggie knew who he was. "Alpha! That's what I'm going to call you." He let himself loosen just a little and licked her hand, seemingly giving his approval. "Well, now that we have that settled, do you boys want to do your thing and we'll just be over here discussing stuff?" Stretching down on his front legs, Alpha pounced on Wolfie's back, surprising him because Wolfie was distracted by Aggie's other hand. Quickly, the wolves were rolling around, playing with each other and wrestling. Aggie couldn't help but smile at their antics.

Turning back to see that Kyrel and Eldon still remained and were quietly waiting for her attention to return. "Well now, where were we?"

"We were busy in the hallway, and I think I should have whisked you away to my own room. Then we wouldn't have gotten so rudely interrupted." Eldon puffed out his chest and squared his shoulders. This wasn't the shy, quiet guy she had known before their encounter in the hall.

"I didn't want to interrupt. I was content just *listening* in on you from behind my door. You two were truly connected and it was magnificent." Kyrel licked his lips as though he had just eaten the best steak dinner money could buy. Aggie scrunched up her face at him. His behavior that night was out of sorts, as was everyone's.

"I think you had a great idea." She glanced toward Eldon. "I'm happy to go back to your room while these pups have their play time. I could always just come back and sleep later since this is where everyone has deemed me the safest for now."

"I agree, we should go back to Eldon's room." Kyrel interjected his plans and Aggie looked at him in disbelief.

"Uh, I don't know about you," hooking her thumb back at Eldon and absently considering how much she wished she had painted her nails before this excursion to faraway lands, "but I'm not sure I'm ready for two at a time." Eldon didn't say anything, but looked like he was considering his options.

"It's okay, I'm just planning on watching. Unless you decide to change your mind. I could use a release as well, but don't want to impose. I'll be there in spirit anyway, so to speak. His room is right next to mine. I don't have to see you but it would make things more enjoyable for me." Kyrel's grey eyes caught the light and they looked like they were sparkling from the excitement of what was to come.

"I'll leave that up to you, Eldon. At this point, I'm just ready to get back to what we started." Aggie sauntered over to him and placed a hand on his waist and leaned in towards him.

"As long as you behave yourself and don't increase anything with your propensity for leaking or helping, I don't see why you couldn't observe. If the mood changes, we will let you know. Does that seem reasonable?" Eldon wrapped both arms around Aggie and pulled her in close and kissed the top of her head.

"That seems fair enough. I promise to keep myself reined in and just absorb what you give off. I can't leave a perfectly good meal floating around for anyone else to absorb. I promise to keep my hands and my powers to myself." Eldon nodded, accepting Kyrel at his word. This situation was strange to Aggie, but if she ultimately would be with all of them, alone or not, she would have to get used to the idea of others being around. The lack of jealousy is what confused her the most. Without another word, Eldon led her from the room. The wolves snuffed their acknowledgment but didn't stop them from making their exit.

"I'll be back later; you two behave and don't destroy the room with your games." Aggie felt like she was reassuring a pet. That was strange, because she knew Mitchell and Ren were in there. She made a mental note to ask how aware they were in that state as to what was going on around them.

Eldon guided them to his room. Aggie was still intrigued by the door and how it shimmered almost as though it moved. The iridescent color was almost ethereal. Placing his hand firmly on the knob, it clicked and released immediately. It was like the door knew how badly they all wanted to enter. His room wasn't ornate or overly cluttered. He kept everything very clean; Aggie didn't see any scattering of clothes on the floor or any items out of place. He had a reading nook in the window, sandwiched by a bookshelf on either side. The books were filling every inch and Aggie was envious of his collection.

"It seems you are quite the reader." She motioned towards the shelves and the window seat.

"I love to read, but most of those books are historical accounts of the different races or realms. I like to keep up-to-date on whatever we might encounter." Eldon's answer was precise and very much his personality.

Kyrel came in and found a seat in the chair by the fireplace, which was mysteriously already lit. "Is that magic?"

"In a way; there is a central unit in the center of the castle. When it is lit, the connected fireplaces ignite automatically. It is something like your central heat in the human realm." Eldon loosened his shirt from his pants and unbuttoned it as he spoke.

Aggie became so distracted by the exposed skin that she nearly forgot what they were talking about.

"Oh, well, that's a perfect option then. I'm glad some of the technology isn't lost on the other realms. I'm also thankful you've figured out plumbing in some way, too." She kicked herself for bringing up bathroom maintenance at a time like this. Who talks about anything besides hot baths or sexy shower sessions when getting ready to have sex. Especially hot sex with a gorgeous Fae, and a dreamy Incubus watching. Aggie wondered if she had died and gone to her dream heaven. "Ouch!"

"Are you all right?" Eldon's instant concern made her feel stupid.

"No, I just pinched myself because all of this is so surreal. I thought I might not actually be here with you, both of you." Aggie felt her cheeks heat and quickly turned away to hide it. She didn't like feeling lesser or not enough. She was always in control of her situation or anything that might happen.

"Hey, don't turn away from me. I want to see you, all of you." Eldon approached her from behind but didn't turn her right away. His hand traveled from her shoulders down the sides of her top. When they found the bottom, his fingers trailed up, grazing every inch of skin and setting it aflame in their wake. Her nipples peaked again at his touch and her mouth opened slightly as she enjoyed the feeling. Her shirt pulled as he lifted his hands. Soon he pulled it over her head, leaving her open to him. Her modesty was only covered by a lacy black bra, leaving little to the imagination. Eldon leaned down and his teeth scraped over the side of her neck, eliciting a soft moan from her lips.

"You are the most beautiful creature I have ever seen." His words were felt by the breath sweeping lightly across her neck. His hands traveled to her breasts and he squeezed, softly kneading them with his fingers. He pulled the fabric of her bra down, letting their natural weight drop into his waiting hand, one at a time. Grazing each nipple with his trimmed nails, he pinched them between his thumb and forefinger. He held it just long enough to sting and then massaged the pain away. Still he didn't turn her around.

Unable to control herself she pressed her backside into his growing erection, causing him to move his hand further down. Hands flat against her skin, he traveled down her body. When he reached her pants he flipped the button with practiced skill. He didn't waste any time with her zipper and slipped under her panties, deftly finding her clit and applying the pressure she needed. She was already soaked and knew that little preparation would be required, but she still hadn't seen or felt his actual size. They were interrupted before she got that far before.

Reaching behind her and knowing that it lifted her breasts and perked them up for anyone watching to see better, she threaded her fingers through Eldon's hair. The fact that he hadn't removed her bra left them shelved and on display. Eldon brought his free hand up to tease her nipples to points and Aggie heard a moan from across the room. Sparing a glance, she saw Kyrel was unfastening his pants and drawing out his length. What she saw left her breathless and she forced her ass back into Eldon's length to cause some friction, resulting from what her eyes were taking in. He was engorged and the girth was beyond belief, even his own hand barely wrapped around it. The cliché, "Is that going to fit?" ran through her mind, causing fear and anticipation all at the same time.

Eldon suddenly shifted; while keeping his right hand firmly seated against her sensitive spot, he used his free hand to reach behind and slip her pants and panties off her in one clean sweep. Only then did she realize that he was still much too dressed for what was happening. Turning abruptly, she knocked his hand loose from where he was rubbing her and bringing her closer and closer to her own release, stopping all progress.

"I think you have some catching up to do." Dropping to her knees, Aggie was almost eye level with his crotch. Slipping her fingers into his waistband, Eldon's head fell back and he sighed with pleasure. He knew what she was planning and she wasn't going to disappoint him. Opening his button and undoing his fly, Aggie separated the fabric as far as she could in order to make this easier for her. He was pressed so tightly against his own pants that his cock had to be in pain yet again. She instantly felt bad for putting him through that all over again. Quickly, she gripped the top of his jeans and yanked hard. Pulling them halfway down, Eldon helped her out by stepping free of them to make the process easier. He wore boxer briefs and the idea made her smile. For some reason, being so connected to nature, she expected him to be going commando. Gripping his taut ass cheeks, she reveled in his tightening and releasing them to her grip. Her face mere inches from his cock still in his underwear, she could just lean forward slightly and touch it with her mouth. Not to waste any more time, Aggie slipped the band down and gently pulled until his cock sprang free, bobbing happily in front of her face. She had to lean back slightly to avoid it smacking her in the process.

Nothing was there to stop her so she leaned forward and pressed her tongue to the tip, tasting his salty drop waiting for her. His sigh turned into a deep moan at the contact. Without taking down his clothes any farther, Aggie gripped the base of his cock and squeezed tightly, not wanting him to get ahead of her. Flattening her tongue, she ran it from base to tip and sealed her lips over the bulbous head. He wasn't as thick as Kyrel, who was still sitting and stroking his own cock from the nearby vantage point. Aggie was starting to second-guess her plans to not involve him. Eldon's head was large enough that her mouth widened to go around it. She didn't let that stop her from bobbing a few times to satisfy herself. She needed him to know she appreciated all that he had done for her. On her last drop, she reached back with her free hand and lightly caressed his balls. The skin was soft and smooth, making her want them more. So, she released his head and sucked one into her mouth, moaning her enjoyment.

"You need to stop that now. I want to be inside you before you tease me into oblivion. I plan to make you enjoy every second with me and not be lacking in any way." He pulled her to her feet and his cock bounced along her stomach. She wanted to climb him and seat herself on it. He leaned down and sucked in one of her nipples and bit down just enough for her to cry out. Then he laved the area with his tongue to soothe the ache. "Go and lie down on the bed. I want to taste you before I ruin you forever."

While she was no virgin, Aggie went weak in the knees at his words. Hurrying to avoid falling, she made her way to the bed on wobbly legs and climbed on top. Both men crooned their appreciation for the view of her backside as she climbed atop the bed. That gave Aggie an idea, but she wasn't ready to voice it yet. She wanted to be sure Eldon was okay with it.

Eldon followed her up and soon she was flat on the bed, his face between her parted legs. Without preamble he licked up her wetness. "Mmhmm, you are delicious. I could live off your nectar." If he was any other guy from any other place Aggie would have chalked that up to another line to win her over, but not Eldon. He seemed genuine in everything he ever did. He didn't spend much time working her over, but slipped in two fingers to stretch her a little. She could only imagine the damage he or even Kyrel would do to her without a little preparation, now that she had seen them both. She knew wetness wouldn't be an issue, but she had never considered size being this big of a problem, no pun intended.

"Eldon, if you don't mind, I think Ky might like to at least come a little closer. It will be harder for him to see from over there." She didn't know Eldon's true viewpoint, so she wasn't going to push her luck.

Eldon turned to Ky. "Is that right?"

"I'll stay where you want me, but I would love to watch her face as you enter her." Kyrel wasn't shy, but he was respectful.

"Why don't you climb up here on the bed. There is plenty of room and you will have a better view." Eldon was more gracious than Aggie expected. Perhaps he had a similar idea. Kyrel didn't waste a minute. He shucked his pants and made his way over.

"I hope you don't mind but seeing as how I wasn't going to be putting this away, those pants were just going to make the climb more difficult."

"I don't mind, but only if you don't mind if in the heat of the moment I reach out and touch it myself." Aggie was feeling brave, and freer than she ever had before. She'd never experienced a high like this, to have someone watch while she got sexual with another man. It was stimulating and her hormones were working overtime.

"You are welcome to touch any part of me you wish." Kyrel's smile spoke volumes and Aggie returned it.

"Will that bother you, Eldon? I'd hate to do anything to ruin what we already have going." Aggie wanted his okay to include Kyrel in their escapades, but she wasn't asking for permission to have fun with Kyrel. That was her decision and hers alone.

"I'm happy if you're happy. I only want to please you. Kyrel is no threat to me and I know we will have fun either way." Aggie breathed a sigh of relief. It amazed her how well Eldon was handling another man in his bed.

"Now, if you don't mind, could we get on with this? I'm worried someone is going to come in and stop us again and you'll end up with blue balls as bad as whatever it is women get, and I've had enough of it." They all laughed with her and Eldon dropped his head back between her legs. His eyes never left hers and she glanced over at Kyrel, who continued working himself again with slow even strokes, his eyes firmly on where Eldon's face was lapping and fingers pumping and stretching. Aggie moaned and pumped her hips. It was hard not to rub her clit and press it into his face. She didn't want to take the control away from him.

She let her eyes travel over to Ky again. "Ky, will you take off your shirt? I'd like you to feel more included." A grin broke out on his face and he did as she asked without complaint. It seemed all the men she'd seen or felt were just as built, and all she wanted to do was feel his muscles that were flexing underneath his tanned skin. Reaching for him, he leaned toward her. Running her fingers over his chest she dragged her nails down the exposed skin, squeezing him, and Eldon added a third finger and pumped them in deeper. She cried out and arched forward. Pulling out his fingers Eldon quickly lined himself up with her entrance, easing himself in, but Aggie felt no pain. He pressed in further and soon was seated fully. Frozen in time, Aggie enjoyed the full sensation of Eldon's cock pressed deeply into her and tightly against her inner walls.

"If you don't move soon, I'm going to have to do it for you." Aggie cried out as the pressure was building inside of her. She wanted to feel his cock pumping in and out more than anything. Eldon chuckled deeply, the sound vibrating through her, but quickly complied with her request. As Eldon picked up speed, Aggie felt herself climbing toward her own release. Turning to look at Kyrel, she saw he was pumping his own dick faster than ever. "You need to bring that over here and I'll handle it for you." Kyrel froze, but that award-winning smile broke the tension as he got up on his knees and crawled to her.

Seated on his heels, his cock stood proudly between his legs and the tip glistened with early release, begging to be tasted. Propped up on her elbows, she gripped him as best she could from the base, gently pulled him closer, and brought the tip to her lips. Her other hand openly stroked his sac. Ky's eyes never left her face, watching her every move. She glanced back and saw Eldon, who was also watching her holding Ky's cock. Eyes wide with interest he watched her lick the tip slowly, drawing out the pleasure for them all. The sight made Eldon move faster inside her. She felt his dick flex with the approval of her ministrations and Ky relaxed toward her, allowing her to do anything she wanted.

Pressing the overly thick cock back to her lips, she opened around them. While she wasn't going to get very far, she would do her best. Aggie moaned around the massive erection in her mouth and twisted her hand up and down tightly, enjoying the sensation of both men. Then, while her eyes were closed, a hand wrapped around one breast and a set of lips sucked the other nipple into its mouth. Opening her eyes, she saw both men captivated by her nipples fully erect, waiting to be played with and teased. When Ky squeezed her available nipple closest to him, she screamed and found her release instantly. It had always been a hair trigger for her; he must have sensed that. Eldon followed her quickly, and after one more long suck from Aggie's plump lips Ky was hot on their heels, exploding his load into her waiting mouth.

She swallowed every drop and wiped anything that escaped before she leaned forward to kiss Ky on the mouth. She realized then that she had openly sucked his cock before actually kissing him to invite him into their inner circle created by her and Eldon. Eldon kissed her neck, making room and somehow not making her feel cramped at all. They stayed wrapped up, kissing for a few more minutes before Aggie fell back with a flop of exhaustion.

"Oh, my God, that was amazing! Is sex with all of you always going to be like that, or was that just because it was my first time with two men at the same time? Do you realize how big of a turn-on it was to have you silently watching from a distance, Ky?"

Aggie was out of breath and completely sated from their bedroom escapades.

"I know, watching the two of you was truly the best thing I've seen in ages." Aggie assumed that meant a lot, because Kyrel had likely seen a lot in his day. "I also love that you have chosen to shorten my name. The sound of it from your lips is the greatest gift you could ever give me."

"Also, I should probably say that you felt like that because of the transfer of power. Since you and I are now mated, your body took on more than the average human. I will say you were worth it. I can't say I've ever felt that wonderful with any woman. I'm blessed that you chose me to be your first." Eldon's words were spoken softly, and Aggie tried not to let it grate on her that he was mentioning his other conquests mere moments after being inside her. The rest of what he was saying made her feel special. She hadn't thought about it being him first or another waiting, she just had a connection with him throughout the day. Everything just clicked with him. If she was going to have sex with all of them to complete her role as the ninth, then she wanted it to happen organically and not be forced. Sort of like adding Kyrel to the mix. That wasn't the original plan, but at the moment it felt right.

"Does that mean that we are also mated because we also had..." Aggie didn't finish her thought because he knew what they had done, and to say it out loud felt stupid. She wasn't ashamed of what she had done, but sometimes the words don't matter as much as the feeling.

"No, that isn't how it works. Each time you have natural sexual intercourse with one of us, we are able to break the spell by spilling inside of you. While you won't be able to get pregnant the first time with us, it is required to break the magic placed upon us by our oath." Kyrel sounded a bit disappointed by the thought of not being mated to her.

"Wait, I don't want to get pregnant. That isn't in my game plan right now." Aggie's voice rose as she panicked a little.

"Not to worry; Gryson can create an individual spell for each of us. That way we aren't at risk, and we aren't inhibited either." Eldon didn't sound concerned in the least, so Aggie calmed down. The men lay down on either side of her.

"Given that information, if I take any of you in my mouth or in my…" Aggie hesitated because she had never considered any of the alternatives before, and now the idea of multiple partners gave her pause. "If I take anyone in my ass, does that mean I'm not mated with them and therefore won't take on any new magic?" She was never one who openly talked about sex or sexually-related things, but this seemed different somehow. Like she wasn't talking about sex, but what would happen to her afterward. With her muscles still languid she didn't feel the need to move or turn her head to look at either. Whoever decided to answer was up to them.

"You can have as many or few partners as you want, whenever you choose. If you don't want to mate anyone else for a time, you can just provide them an alternative position." Eldon seemed cautious, "Are you upset that we are now mated and I didn't clarify this before we proceeded this evening?"

"No, not at all; I'm just trying to make sense of it all." She reached for Eldon with heavy arms and wondered why he felt different, and why it was so hard to reach for him. She understood post-sex bliss, but this was ridiculous. Instead of the sharp sense of butterflies across her skin it was more like they were a part of her now, not simply trying to gain access. They were inside and all around her like a warm blanket, covering and protecting her. "Oddly enough, I just feel extra tired."

"That is not just your average exhaustion. Likely, your body is trying to reallocate where to put your magic. It should manifest itself soon, and we will know what you need to learn in order to control it. That can be added to your training schedule when you begin your defense training tomorrow." Eldon caressed her head and she closed her eyes, still fighting not to let the sleep overtake her. "I should carry you back over to the other room, so you can get settled. I'll let the guys know what is happening and they will keep an extra close eye on you."

# Chapter 14

When Aggie woke up, she was wrapped in the warmest blanket she had ever felt. Snuggling deeper, she realized that she bumped into what felt like something furry resting against her shoulder. Opening her eyes just a slit, she saw a black-as-night snout sitting there. She tried not to move so she wouldn't disturb Alpha, but she smiled that he was wrapped around her like a fur blanket. The only way he could have gotten any closer would have been to sleep completely on top of her.

"He hasn't moved from that spot all night. When Eldon carried you in, his wolf went crazy. Mitchell couldn't contain him and had to shift. That says a lot because the Alpha has the most control. My wolf didn't go as crazy once he knew Mitchell had you under control." Ren was sitting across the room, in a high-backed, dark red chair and his feet propped on a stool. He ran his hand through his sandy hair and stretched his back out.

"Did you sleep in the chair all night?" Aggie scooted out from under Alpha's head, causing him to growl lightly. She placed her hand on his neck and he calmed immediately. Sitting up on her elbows, she got a better look at Ren across the room.

"Someone had to keep an eye on you two." He shot her a lopsided smile and scooted forward so he could rest his arms on his legs.

"That couldn't have been comfortable at all. Why didn't you just crawl into bed with us?" Aggie pressed her hand into her hair and brushed her hair back. "God, my hair feels like Medusa's snakes."

"I think it looks hot, and I didn't want to disturb you two; you looked so cozy. Not to mention, I didn't want to make you feel uncomfortable if you woke up sandwiched between us." Ren's words were spoken on a whisper, as he was trying to not wake his sleeping brother.

"Get over here, you look like death on a stick." Aggie lay back down and pulled the blanket down behind her. Snuggling into Alpha's thick, soft fur, the bed dipped as she felt Ren press up against her back. She rolled over slowly, meeting Ren's piercing gaze. "See? Was that so hard?"

"No, but it will be." Ren wrapped his arms around her and kissed her right on the nose. Aggie giggled until she felt a similar body pressed up against her back. Turning to look over her shoulder, she was surprised to see Mitchell had taken control again and shifted back while her back was turned. She noticed something rather quickly: he was completely naked and his dick was pressed against her ass, hard as a rock.

"Now, this is an awkward position you have me in here, boys. Did you plan this?" Aggie shifted slightly so she could look at them both at once. Unfortunately, in doing so, she pressed a bit hard against Mitchell's nakedness under the blankets, causing him to groan, and his dick twitched in response. Eyes wide she said, "I'm so sorry. I didn't mean to do that."

"It's not your fault; you're in  bed with us and we are drawn to you like moths to a flame." Mitchell nuzzled his nose into her neck, just as Alpha had done.

"Are you awake when your wolf has control?" As usual, blurting was Aggie's go-to when a question was burning. Now that Mitchell could speak to her, it was the only thing she wanted to know.

A husky laugh and a rare smile was the answer she got, and his kisses trailed down her neck to her collarbone. She felt her nipples perk up and scrape across the fabric of the shirt she was wearing. Glancing down, Aggie realized it wasn't her shirt. Lifting the collar, she inhaled deeply and caught a whiff of earth and a light petal scent. Smiling, she knew it was Eldon's shirt. He always smelled like a walk through a garden. She couldn't help the giggle that bubbled out. He always swore he wasn't a fairy like Tinker Bell or other TV concoctions, but he smelled like she imagined one would.

"You didn't answer my question, pup." Aggie knew she was poking the bear, or wolf, but she didn't care. She wanted her answer

"Who are you calling a pup?" Though he was growly, Mitchell was smiling through gritted teeth. He pressed his very large cock into her ass for good measure. "I will show you how much of a pup I am if you keep pressing." He then proceeded to tickle her with a vengeance and she thrashed left and right to try and break free. Unable to speak through her laughter, except for broken words, she pleaded with her eyes to get Ren to help her.

"Help? You want me to help? You insulted my brother's manhood, my Alpha, and you expect me to help you? I don't think I can do that in good conscience." With that he held her down and started to tickle her feet while she was locked at the knees by his muscled arm. There was no way she would escape. The best she could do was thrust back and forth from her hips in hopes to throw them off. Sadly, that only resulted in her inching closer and closer to the edge of the bed. With Ren now at the foot of the bed, holding her down, that meant there was no one there to stop her from, *THUMP!* Without warning she fell to the floor. All horseplay stopped instantly.

"Are you all right?" The twins echoed each other, and for the first time actually sounded like what one would expect of a twin, Finishing each other's sentences and reading each other's minds.

To their surprise, Aggie just found herself laughing at the insanity of it all. "I'm fine, I'm just glad I fell before you two made me pee myself. I ask a simple question and you two gang up on me." She was laughing hysterically now and the guys joined her. It took a couple minutes for them to calm down. She crawled back into the bed between them.

"I pick up the stronger feelings. Mostly from my wolf, whom I believe you named, Alpha, am I correct?" Aggie felt a blush rise in her cheeks; these guys were good at getting her to do that. "No, he likes it. I do, too, mostly because you understand that we might be connected but our wolves are separate in their own right. It changes things when people understand that."

"I didn't want to keep calling him 'Mitchell's wolf' all the time. I thought that was worse than naming him." She turned to Ren. "You don't mind me calling your wolf 'Wolfie', do you?"

"If I recall correctly, you called me 'Wolfie' before you deemed it my wolf's name." Ren winked and his hand crept up her hip, under her shirt, and slid closer to her.

"Well, I think you might have been acting rather wolfish at the time." She smirked and poked him in the ribs.

"Don't start that again. You just fell off the bed a moment ago; I'd hate for you to repeat that." Ren rolled over and pushed her hand back. Leveraging himself, he leaned upon his forearm and kissed her passionately, but this didn't stop Mitchell from keeping his hands busy with her breasts beneath her shirt. Aggie decided she was enjoying their ministrations too much. Stopping them wasn't worth it. They obviously knew that she had been with Eldon the night before and that didn't bother them. Why should she let it bother her? Sharing wasn't an issue for them, so she was going to enjoy whatever attention they graced her with.

Just as Ren let his free hands wander to the top of her panties, Aggie knew this was going to be a fun way to wake up. Reaching up she laced her fingers in each of the brother's hair, running her nails across their scalps.

In the still slightly darkened room, not yet kissed by the morning sunrise, sparks skittered out from Aggie's hands right off the heads of both guys. Aggie screeched and held her hands aloft as they continued to glow. The twins leaped from the bed at speeds Aggie didn't know were possible and wondered if they were actually descendants of *The Flash*. Ren was frantically brushing his head and Aggie was worried she had hurt him. Mitchell, the ever stoic one, had his gaze firmly locked on Aggie and her suspended hands. She realized that it looked like she was a criminal standing off against the police.

"I don't know what's happening. Did I hurt you? I'm so sorry. I didn't mean to." Aggie's words were a jumble and she barely let a single breath in between them. Panic was painted on her face and she was afraid to lower her hands for fear of what would happen.

"Your hands…" Ren stated the obvious and Mitchell elbowed him for his insensitive remark.

"We're fine. Are you okay?" Mitchell's voice was gruff and to the point. She realized it wasn't for lack of caring but just trying to get down to business to sort it all out. Aggie looked at her hands and didn't know what to say. She just looked back at them in horror. Mitchell approached her cautiously. "This must be your power making itself known, and it must be connected to your emotions. You need to try to calm down."

"I don't want to hurt you." Her words were soft and trembling. It was obvious she was terrified. If they needed any other proof her hands were shaking as well, causing the sparks to shoot toward the ceiling every few seconds. Luckily, they dissipated before reaching an actual surface.

"You won't hurt us. Any feelings you have toward us should flow through your magic, the same way I knew my wolf wouldn't hurt you when we changed yesterday. He just needed to meet you. Your magic got a taste of us upon initial appearance, and now your fear is the only thing keeping it active right now. You need to relax as best you can. Don't fear it. Embrace it, let it meld with you. Ren, go get Eldon. He might be the only one who can talk her through this effectively. All I can do is try my best to calm her." Ren followed Mitchell's direction, and only hesitated once before walking through the door.

"Hang in there, I'll be right back with Eldon. It's going to be okay." Ren blasted through the door with the same speed she saw him and his brother use moments before. Mitchell gently lay his hand on her leg and smoothed it up and down. He didn't speak, so she closed her eyes and focused on the sensation of his hand on her body. Every nerve in her body felt like it was alive. She had a new awareness of her body from head to toe. This was all so overwhelming and scary.

"Will it ever go away and let me go back to normal? I don't know if I can handle this. I'm not built for this. I'm not the right person." Aggie threw out all of her insecurities because they all made more sense now. "What were you guys thinking? I'm not the one you need. I'm weak and can't take all these changes." Tears slipped from her closed eyes; she refused to open them, not wanting to see the disappointment sure to be painted across Mitchell's face. She wasn't strong enough for them and to take on the role of their Ninth. Her arms were growing tired but in order to not strike the men she was growing to care for very deeply, she forced herself to hold them up.

Without warning, she felt two hands encircle her arms just below her elbows. They didn't feel rough like Mitchell's, and her body was instantly filled with butterflies. Eldon. Parting her eyelids just slightly, her line of vision was filled with his face. She didn't see a look of disappointment or anger, but a compassionate expression. She allowed him to hold the weight of her arms and her shoulders relaxed. The relief was instant and Aggie sighed. "I think you can put these down now." Eldon's lyrical voice filled Aggie with relief. "You have been a warrior among women today. Not many would have thought as quickly as you."

"I don't want to hurt anyone." Sniffing her sobs back, Aggie's arms trembled for fear of him pulling them down without her consent.

"As you can see for yourself, you have nothing to be concerned with." Aggie looked up upon hearing Eldon's words, and to her surprise the magic was no longer visible. All that was left was her hands hanging in the air and her fingers curled slightly and protective. She must have been subconsciously trying to keep them from shooting out.

"How did you do that?" Aggie was sure Eldon had come in and waved his magic around the room. She pictured a flourish and a swoosh as though he'd had to clear the air.

"That was all you, my dear. You have been given a great gift and your magic will respond to your bidding. Even if that means you have to concentrate really hard on what you want it to do while you are still new to it. Soon it will become easier and then second-nature." Eldon pulled her to him and she slowly dropped her arms, letting the blood flow return to them. He embraced her tightly and she collapsed into him.

"Mitchell told me to relax; I thought it was impossible to do that and keep enough control and not throw whatever that was around the room." Aggie leaned back and rubbed her arms to help the blood flow, but Eldon quickly took over for her.

"He was absolutely right. No one could do that for you; it had to come from within. I'm not sure what you did exactly, but it worked and you handled it like someone who knew it was coming. I'm sorry I wasn't here for when they manifested. It seems you are connected deeply with the nature aspect of the Fae powers. I'm not going to try to guess what was going through your mind that jumpstarted them, but the glimpse I got when I arrived of the lightning crackling between your grasp was well controlled." Eldon's hands massaged her cramped muscles from overworking them while trying to retain control, it seemed, without actually to attaining it fully.

"That was controlled? Wow, I'm not sure I want to see what out of control looks like." Ren smirked at her and then winked, so she knew he was joking to lighten the mood of the room.

"Actually, she could have easily taken out the entire room and set fire to many of the items in here." The pride in Eldon's voice wasn't missed, and Aggie felt herself blush.

"Either we need to get my room fixed or get me assigned a new space of my own. I don't want to put any of you in this situation. While you say I wouldn't have hurt any of you, I'd hate to destroy your spaces because my magic is majorly wonky." Aggie felt tears slip from her eyes, but quickly wiped them away. She wasn't a crier at all, but when one's life had been flipped upside-down and sideways in just a few days it couldn't be faulted.

"You will stay with me until we can get this under control. If one of you wants to stay with us that is fine, but I won't let her out of my sight." He directed that at the twins, but his words were firm. With that he lifted Aggie from the bed and carried her back to his room.

"I'm more than capable of walking, unlike when you brought me in last night." Aggie flushed, thinking about the previous circumstances Eldon was forced to carry her across the hall.

Breathing deeply, she knew Eldon could likely smell her arousal. "I will carry you if I choose to and this has nothing to with how capable you are. If my guess is correct, though, you might want to try to control your desires or extracurricular thoughts for a bit, until we get your magic to a comfortable level." Groaning, Aggie redirected her thoughts the best she could.

"Are you saying I'll have to limit my sexual thoughts and interaction because I might react magically again?" She wiped her hand over her face in an attempt to clear the images of the previous night and that morning from her brain. "If that's the case, then I definitely need my own space. This isn't going to work."

"I will train you and we will start the moment I get you settled. I think a hot bath to relax you is necessary first." Eldon pressed his door open and placed her on his bed. "I'll go start your bath."

"I think a shower would be better." Aggie had another sexual memory from the tub and she didn't think water and electricity would mix well.

"As you wish, my little warrior." Eldon left the room and headed for the bathroom. Aggie forced herself off the bed because her most recent memories of it were likely going to make an appearance sooner than later, left to her own thoughts.

Eldon appeared moments later and gave her a quizzical look, his head leaning slightly to the right and his eyebrow raised. "I have the water started and laid a towel out for you."

"I suppose asking you to join me would be out of the question?" Smiling to show him she was joking, her heart didn't feel it. What had happened to her life? Everything was a mess of epic proportions. How was she supposed to help, now that she needed to be trained to control her emotions so she didn't set fire to anything or worse?

*****

Towel wrapped around her body Aggie appeared back in the bedroom, feeling loose from the shower beating out all her tense muscles. This still-short day had already been very trying. A movement caught her attention and she realized that both the twins were sitting at the table along with Eldon. They all turned their attention to her and the heated looks they all gave her weren't helping her. She immediately felt the hairs on her arms stand on end, and even her wet hair that was draped around her shoulders began to move. In a moment it was standing on end as well.

Eldon jumped from his seat and pulled her back into the bathroom. His hands on her bare shoulders sent the butterflies running through her and her nerves settled. Closing the door behind them, she felt like someone flipped a switch and her hair fell back to rest on her shoulders. "This isn't going to work. What am I supposed to do? Not to mention, that bitch destroyed my room and all my clothes. I have nothing to wear!" Eldon wrapped her up in his embrace, squeezing tightly. She felt a tingling sensation, and when he backed away the towel fell from her. It was so unexpected that when she reached for it, she missed and it fell to the floor. Only, the body she saw in the mirror wasn't naked. It was clothed in a beautiful moss-colored wrap dress. Upon closer examination she realized it was made out of actual moss. She touched it and was at a loss for words. The dress was stunning, but that wasn't what had her captivated. Eldon had created this with his bare hands and magic.

"I thought this might help you channel your magic. Also, I think it looks perfect and suits you." His eyes were hungry as they roved over her body. It didn't fire her magic, thankfully, but she wanted nothing more than to have him take her all over again.

Now that she was covered, they escaped the bathroom once again. The brothers were still seated at the table and the heated look they gave her didn't have the same effect on her body as before. For that she was grateful. It seemed this scrap of fabric—no, nature—was acting as some sort of shield. Aggie wrapped her arms around herself and hugged the dress, and it hummed in answer.

"Did you add something to this dress?" She didn't know how to describe it but it felt different.

"No, aside from something to raise your breasts to eye level for my pleasure. I do love to see them whenever possible." The brothers grunted in appreciation and Aggie looked down, noticing for the first time that this strapless *dress* was indeed accentuating her rack, which was always very full. So, she spilled over the top with perfect round mounds. It even made them look balanced, which she had never been able to achieve before in any of her earthly clothes. Not in the least bit embarrassed by the display, she was thankful they were taking in the view. She appreciated that her body didn't react with crazy powers or anything new.

"Well, whatever you did, thank you. I already feel more under control." Aggie smoothed her hands over the moss, intrigued by the hum it radiated back at her.

"It is the connection as I suspected. You are using the dress as a grounding point for your natural instincts. Instead of needing to release it, the moss is absorbing it. When you need to use your magic it will be there, but it will be more like you are one with it. It should never feel like something separate." Eldon sounded matter-of-fact but not clinical, and that helped Aggie relate to him better.

"I see, so what sort of training are we going to do?" She wasn't so sure about using her powers, but she also didn't want to set fires or make anything worse than it already was.

"I've been chatting with Ren and Mitchell about that. While this will be new to all of us, they will have a better idea of how to help you with the fact that I'm sure it feels like something has invaded your body." Aggie nodded enthusiastically, because that is exactly what it felt like; something running over her skin, looking for a place to burrow. "Yes, that is what I thought. I will help you find a place where you can communicate with your new gift. Once you find a place where you are equals, it will be easier to channel it."

"What does that mean, exactly?" Aggie sat down beside them all at the table, still slightly hugging her new dress as it calmed her nerves.

"Meditation." Eldon's words were direct and to the point. No mincing words adding to any confusion.

Aggie couldn't help the laugh that broke free from her lips. "Seriously? I've never meditated a day in my life. I can barely sit still to ride in a car, let alone if you want me to concentrate while doing it. This is going to be a disaster."

"We will all be here, helping you along. It will be easier than you think." Eldon was the only one speaking, but the twins were agreeing with his every word. Ren was leaning back, relaxed in his chair, nodding enthusiastically. Mitchell was leaned forward with his elbows resting on the table, arms crossed. His agreement was a bit subtler and more in his wheelhouse. A stern, barely noticeable, head shake and focused eyes that never left Aggie's face.

"Okay, I'm willing to do anything to get a handle on this because, as much as I love this dress, and it is more than comfortable, I don't think it's really appropriate for mixed company." Smoothing her hands absentmindedly down the dress, Aggie glanced at each of the men individually.

"Let's all sit on the floor; it would be better if we could be outside but, given the weather, I think this will have to do. The castle's stone will have some residual energy." They all followed Eldon's request and quickly arranged themselves on the floor in a small circle. With their legs crossed, it wasn't difficult to stay connected with each of them because their knees all touched around the circle.

"Everyone, close your eyes and think of something relaxing. The goal is to clear your head so that nothing can get in the way of your magic's essence." Eldon's words seemed easily done, but the more Aggie tried the more difficult it became.

After what felt like an eternity, Aggie cried out in frustration, "Argh! This is pointless. Why can't I do this?" Finally, she resolved she'd never get it. "It just isn't worth it; it would be easier to just wing it and hope for the best. Surely the magic in me can't be that strong. I'm just a human." There was nothing else she could think of to try, but through her entire rant not once did Aggie open her eyes nor did the guys say anything. When she was finished she was about to get up from the circle, but a finger reached across and touched the bare skin of her wrist. Only one finger, not an entire hand, and since it was on her right Aggie knew it was Ren. Then, as if sensing his twin, Mitchell repeated the exact same action on her left.

For whatever reason, Aggie felt her mind start to drift. Slowly, like she was being pulled from her body and flying through the sky. It was a strange sensation, but she no longer had any trouble focusing on the task at hand. Her mind no longer wandered, taking in the sounds around her. Now the only thing she heard was the sound of the breeze and rushing water. The trees blew in that wind lightly and she heard the leaves rustle.

Taking a deep breath, she actually smelled flowers. It took her a moment to realize she wasn't in Eldon's room anymore and he hadn't procured or created another bouquet for her. This all felt real, like she was walking through a meadow. Then, off in the distance, Aggie saw a person walking towards her. She hesitated because none of the guys were with her, and she didn't know who it was coming at her. As the person got closer, Aggie realized it was a woman with dark hair about the same height as herself.

The woman looked up from her steps and met Aggie's eyes, and Aggie gasped when she saw the face was her own. "Is this some sort of trick?" Aggie questioned the woman, now standing right in front of her, unmoving.

"This is no trick." The lookalike's voice was Aggie's voice, but with a lyrical note to it similar to Eldon's own voice. Aggie stared at her in disbelief.

Reaching up, Aggie tucked her own hair behind her ear but stopped mid-motion because her lookalike did the same with her hand. Aggie slowly proceeded and watched it play out in front of her. Only, when the other Aggie reached the top of her ear it was slightly pointed, though still a bit rounded as though she were Fae. Aggie gasped and squeaked her surprise. "What are you?" Her words were but a whisper and what she was seeing was hard to believe.

"I'm you, well, your magic I suppose is the best way to phrase it. This is my home. Don't you just love it?" Aggie looked around and took in her surroundings. The trees above her head were tall. They created a full canopy of the forest they were standing in. Animals ran on the branches but didn't scurry out of sight upon seeing them. They just looked on curiously, more like they wanted to come down for a visit but didn't think it was the right time or their turn. The flowers lined the path she walked on in every variety. Some she knew and some she didn't. They were pristine as though they had just bloomed that day. No decay or fallen petals could be seen on any of them. Aggie's mind was put at ease just by taking in the scene around her.

"Yes, this place is breathtaking." Realizing she was here for a purpose, and now that Aggie knew her doppelganger wasn't a threat, the next step meant getting down to business. "Well, I suppose I'm here to talk to you but I'm not sure what about. Do you have anything you need me to do or tell me perhaps?" Aggie's magic chose then to sit down gracefully on the bed of grass below her feet. That was something Aggie didn't know was possible for her own body. So, in an effort to prove herself wrong, she tried to mimic her, only she failed miserably and ended up collapsing in a heap. Luck was on her side and she didn't land on her head.

Once Aggie had righted herself, her mirror image leaned in as though to tell Aggie a secret only meant for their ears. "You have done all you need to do. We are now acquainted, and with that we will be able to work as one. You will be able to call on me in times of need, and I will no longer worry when your emotions are out of control. I can feel as you do now and will be able to tell the difference."

"That's all? No need to do any special training or merging our minds? I won't potentially be killing anyone with a thought anymore?" Aggie was relieved to hear this, but she wanted to clarify just in case there was some catch.

"Not unless you want to kill someone I suppose. Then we will do it together." The Fae version of Aggie was very straightforward and to the point, and for that Aggie was thankful.

Considering her words very carefully, Aggie found accepting them was easier somehow. "What if I want to talk to you or just check in on you? Is that possible?"

"While you can always come here to my home the same way you did just now, that isn't the only way to commune with me. As you have noticed, since you are wearing something from the earth it helped make the connection."

"Actually," Aggie interrupted her Fae self, "I think the twins might have had a hand—or at least a couple fingers—in doing that."

"No, they merely helped clear your mind. You brought yourself here on your own with a grounding connection of your choice of dress. It is lovely, by the way." With that, her Fae self swirled her hands above her head and adopted a similar style dress of her own design and draped it over her body. Aggie looked down and saw she was no longer wearing her own dress, but a cotton dress and a wristlet of ivy entwined with tiny white daisy like flowers entwined. "As long as you wear something connected to nature, you will always feel our connection. No matter how big or how small the item is, you will feel me all the same."

With that Aggie was whisked back the way she came, almost feeling ripped back to Eldon's room. She was just thankful she was already sitting on the floor because the impact would have been dreadful.

"What are you wearing?" Eldon's words were the first she heard.

Glancing down, Aggie saw the cotton dress in place of the moss one created by Eldon. Lifting her wrist, she noticed the bracelet created by her magical self was still sitting there undisturbed. "I found her."

"Her? Did you connect with your magic?" Ren twisted so he could sit up on his knees, in a more comfortable position.

"Yes and she looked just like me, but a little different." Aggie's gaze fell to Eldon and her eyes shifted to take in his ears. The corners of her mouth tilted up. "She was Fae."

Never looking away from Eldon, the twins' reaction was somehow less important. She needed to know how Eldon felt about all of this. At first, he was frozen as though in time or ice. She worried he was in shock and wasn't going to respond, until a grin broke out on his face and morphed into the biggest smile she had ever seen him wear. "You are now a part of me, my one true mate. Your power has emerged and you have accepted her, therefore accepting me. That is the greatest gift you could ever give me." With that, he rose from his spot on the floor and scooped her into his arms. Twirling her around, Aggie laughed at his antics. He joined her laughing and they were lost in the moment.

"Now that you have them contained, you should begin to train." Mitchell was back to business, and Aggie wondered where the happier version of him had gone to.

"Actually, that's the best part. She told me I don't need anything special. It's an innate power and all I have to do is call on it." Aggie loved that she knew something he didn't, and she was going to relish it.

"That can't be; prove it." Mitchell was going to hold her to her word. Aggie didn't know what she was doing but she was going to trust her alter-ego at her word.

"I'm not sure what I should do." Then she had an idea. Closing her hands around each other, she thought about what she wanted. Just as the idea came to fruition, she opened her eyes and the guys all looked at her like someone had taken over her body. As she finished her design, she opened her hands slowly and there lay a perfect, long-stemmed red rose.

Eldon reached out and took it from her gently. He twisted it back and forth in his fingers, holding it up to the light. "This is magnificent. It took me six years to make one this flawless."

"Your eyes." Mitchell's voice was awed.

Aggie reached for her face and touched her eyes. "What? Is everything okay?" Her hands flew over her face, frantically looking for any sign of what Mitchell might have been referring to.

"They glowed," Ren replied, with just a few words as Mitchell.

Aggie's mouth dropped open and she couldn't make words form. Instead she scrambled to the bathroom. Standing in front of the mirror, she repeated the process. Placing her hands together, this time she didn't close her eyes. She stared at her reflection in the mirror. Staring back at her she saw the second-most beautiful pair of iridescent eyes she had ever seen.

# Chapter 15

"What do you mean, Aggie is part Fae? We know her lineage, and her family has always been one hundred percent human, unless…" Mathius' eyebrows rose in understanding. "Did you guys…" The question was left unsaid, but everyone knew what he was talking about.

Aggie just smiled and produced a black rose, just for Mathius, the way she had before. "Does this answer your question?" Then she turned her attention back to Eldon. "I really need to learn other things than this party trick. Perhaps something more useful." The group laughed at her light-hearted sarcasm and Eldon smiled reassuringly.

"I think we can add that to your fight training. Who is taking first shift on that?" Looking around the room, Eldon's eyes fell on the twins with assumption in his eyes.

"Yes, we will have her in fighting shape before you know it." Mitchell's confidence was both endearing and terrifying. The idea that she would go from zero to hero in such a short period of time was outside of her comfort zone.

"I'll come in for the last part of each session and run magic drills. Before too long, you will be able to incorporate those into her fighting lessons and make everything a practical use of her time." Eldon turned back to Aggie. "In the meantime, why don't you consider what natural things feel the strongest to you—if it is your connection to the earth, the trees, or the sky. There might be a stronger aspect to your magic that you will want to focus on in the early stages. Then your practical fighting will go easier in the beginning. When we have more time, we can focus on your weaker elements and see what we can do with them." This made sense to Aggie and she hoped her connection to the bracelet would help her figure out the answer.

"Where are you guys at on figuring out where the Wanderer is located? Is she really just called 'the Wanderer'? Doesn't she have another name we can use? I feel silly calling her that." Aggie might have addressed her question to Mathius but it was a general question, as everyone had a role to play in all of this.

"I believe we are making a little progress on the location, but it's still slow going. I have narrowed it down to the east side of the town due to the terrain. Unfortunately, that is also the side with more land owners and therefore more properties to search." Liel wasn't as rigid as usual, and Aggie wondered if he was just tired.

"Did you guys work through the night?" Aggie's stomach clenched, waiting for their answer.

"We were still a bit worked up from the evening's events, and with Walpurgisnacht Roodmas now less than five days away I'm not sure how much time these kids have left." Mathius' words hit home and tears welled in her eyes. If crying was a new side effect of the acceptance of her new power, perhaps taking on any more wasn't a good idea. At least, not until she got a handle on these hormonal changes or whatever they were.

"I get it, and now I feel bad for letting you guys stay up all night alone. Why don't you two get some rest. Gryson and Kyrel, do you think you could pick up where they left off?" Aggie tried to stealthily wipe the water from her eyes as she addressed them all.

"I need to see if I can scry for her using that fabric you found anyway. It might take a few tries, as it is badly damaged. I'm afraid whatever substance that she soaked it in will dampen the results, as it won't have the same elemental compound of her own chemical makeup." Gryson was already consulting Liel to get the rundown on what to expect.

"Are you telling me that magic and science are friends?" Aggie was dumbfounded. School subjects she hated were never supposed to become practical in her everyday life. She placed her hand over her eyes and groaned, which earned her a chuckle from Gryson but he chose not to respond to her question.

"Let's go down to the gym, Aggie girl. I'd love to show you around. Then we can get started on your training." Ren reached for her hand, but before he could clasp it Mathius redirected her.

"I might be tired, but I think that dress might not be the best gym-appropriate attire. Don't get me wrong, that dress is perfect on you, but I have something else in mind."  He placed his hands around her body but didn't touch her. She felt a warm current run through her body, yet no pain. When she looked down again, she was clothed in black leathers with a gorgeous silver belt and collar. Ironically, or not, it was the same shade as Mathius' eyes as he created the design.

Smoothing her hands over the material, Aggie was surprised to find it soft to the touch. Bending her knees a few times, she realized while they weren't yoga pants they had enough give that she could easily work out in them, even if they were formed right along her skin. If he hadn't magically created them Aggie wasn't sure how she would have pulled them on. Visions of butter ran through her head, and she quickly shook them loose.

"Is this how I'm to get my clothes from now on? Not that I'm complaining; so far, the options have been beyond belief, but I'm not going to run around naked until one of you magic-wielders comes along to clothe me." Aggie was still feeling the rich leather and in awe of how perfect it was on her. Only thing she was missing was a mirror so she could strut her stuff and see how it really looked from all angles.

"I think it will have to do until you figure it out on your own, but don't take it away completely. At least until I get my turn." Gryson winked at her from across the room.

"Well, now that she is dressed more appropriately for the gym, are we allowed to get to work now?" Ren rolled his eyes at everyone's antics, but Aggie wasn't fooled. He was just as caught up in it as everyone else.

*****

Ren opened the door to the gym and Aggie burst out laughing, "Really? This looks like every gym in the history of gyms. Here I was, thinking being in a demon realm I would be seeing something new and spectacular. Nope! All I see are weights and machines. The epitome of a gym rat's wet dream."

"It isn't quite that bad; look there is a fighting pit over here. Not many Earth places have these." Mitchell was getting defensive, but Aggie didn't care. She wasn't going to lose this one.

"Nope, only every one that trains fighters or boxers. They're common enough they made an entire movie series about it. You have spent time on Earth you said, so maybe you've heard of them? Rocky?" Snapping her hand on her hip and shifting her weight off that leg, Aggie stood there waiting for his rebuttal.

Sighing, Mitchell walked further into the room. Aggie was disappointed he gave up the fight so easily. While it wasn't life or death, she loved that he was the one who always challenged her. Out of frustration, she imagined a strong gust of wind and blew lightly from her mouth. With little effort, she had pushed enough air from her lips toward him that Mitchell was forced to stumble slightly forward. The moment was short-lived however.

"I wouldn't have done that if I were you." Ren was half laughing at her and half warning her. Aggie turned her attention back to Ren, just starting to roll her eyes, when out of nowhere she was knocked to the ground by an unseen force that knocked the wind out of her. It took a moment to regain her breath, but when she looked up at the weight that was on top of her it was Mitchell. His nostrils were flaring and his breath was ragged. He was practically panting.

"You want to pick a fight, I suggest you pick one you can win." Mitchell's words were stunted because of his labored breathing. Aggie assumed that was likely not caused by him being out of shape.

"Get off her, you overgrown hound; she has to learn before we can attack her like that." Ren pulled back on Mitchell's shoulders. When Mitchell didn't move fast enough, Ren put a little more muscle in it. The result was Mitchell flipped over on his back and about six feet away.

"How do you do that? Not only have I witnessed superhuman speed, but now strength." Aggie's eyes were widened and her mouth slack. She just stopped speaking and froze.

"What, that?" Ren chuckled low and slowly before continuing. "That is all part of the shifter gig. If you think we are fast, then you should see Xavier when he lets loose."

"Now, that I can't believe; he moves practically like a floating statue. How am I supposed to imagine that moving faster than what I just witnessed with you two more than once?" Aggie slowly pushed off the floor to stand. Ren reached down and she took his hand gratefully.

"That is just a ruse and more of his way of staying closer to human speeds. If he walked normal for him, it would be supersonic to the rest of us. Now, let's get on track; how much training do you personally have?" Ren got down to business, and had she not already figured out how to tell them apart this would have made it difficult. It was like he was channeling Mitchell.

"Did you two ever try and fool people into thinking you were each other as kids?" As usual, blurting just happened, but she never regretted it. This was how she got to the bottom of her burning questions and it had always worked.

"Yes, but it never worked, so we gave it up. The wolves always scented us before we made it very far. By the time we left for Earth, we had outgrown that kind of childish behavior." Mitchell had calmed down but he still wasn't snapping like normal. It was strange, and actually made Aggie feel more uncomfortable around him.

"I have to admit it still would have been fun to try; a little hair dye or temporary color and you could have anyone fooled." She smiled at the thought. "Now, about my training or previous experience, let's just say it's basically nonexistent. I'm not a fan of working out and it isn't my idea of fun. I can think of plenty of other things to do that are actual fun activities."

"I guess that means we are starting at the basics. I need to see what you are capable of now. Do you think you can do some basic moves with me? You had high school PE, right?" Ren was in his element, and the fun-loving guy she had grown accustomed to was nowhere to be found.

"Yes, but PE was evil, right up there with that stupid rope. I never was able to climb that rope." She kicked the floor in frustration. Aggie was sure that small statement was going to dig her grave. They were going to write her off and send her packing. She wasn't cut out to be their Ninth. She would just slow them down. Even now when they all could be doing something else to help these poor kids who were missing, they were standing in a gym full of equipment Aggie didn't even begin to know anything about.

To her surprise, Ren didn't seem surprised or put off by her statement. "Okay, then I will have the opportunity to mold you into who we want and you will fight in a way we expect. Not to mention the more powers you take on, it will make your instincts stronger and more attuned." Aggie groaned at the idea; she had already decided she needed to wait on that and not speed up the process. She wasn't going to tolerate them pressing the issue for very long.

For the next two hours Aggie, Ren, and Mitchell went through squats, lunges, chest presses, minor weight training, and an entire gamut of things Aggie couldn't remember the name of for long enough to perform it. The machines were easier than the free weights, but overall none of it was outside of her ability to control. While she struggled on a few things, it seemed the bracelet she wore infused her with a little more energy to push through them in the long run.

Dripping with sweat and a little dehydrated Aggie sagged to the floor quickly, falling to her back and wheezing. "Okay, enough. I think I'm dying." She guzzled water like it was somehow magically going to fix all her aches and pains. Ren and Mitchell just looked on with pleased smiles plastered on their faces. "Was that your plan? Did you want to exhaust me beyond the capability of moving?"

"While that wasn't the plan, I'm more pleased that you were able to keep up. The level of competition you have coursing in you was admirable. It makes me want to push you that much harder tomorrow." Mitchell was back. No more overly nice, super sweet, annoyingly accommodating Mitchell. Nope, he was back to his frustrating self, even if just a little bit.

"I don't know, I kinda felt bad for her towards the end. I would have rather left her with enough energy to move on her own. Then perhaps we could have persuaded her to test that magical control in our bed tonight. I'm curious if what she says is true, and she won't lose control even under the most emotionally heated circumstances."

Swinging her leg toward Ren, Aggie attempted to kick him. Unfortunately, given her current state and position on the floor, that only resulted in her hurting herself further. Then movement out the corner of her eye caught her attention. "Thank God! Eldon, why didn't you come sooner? They were trying to kill me here." Aggie might have been exaggerating, but she didn't care; right now, he was her white knight and she was gonna take it.

Calling for the power within her bracelet, Aggie built enough strength to move herself to a seated position. "You definitely look worse for wear. Is there something I can do for you before we get started? Perhaps a snack?" With that, he procured something Aggie didn't expect and, had she been able to move it, might have been the only thing to get her on her feet. There in Eldon's hand was a package of Nutty Buddy's and they were both there.  It was like a mirage in the desert, and it crossed her mind that she was imagining it. So, with every bit of willpower she could muster Aggie pulled herself to her own feet and trudged as quickly as her sore muscles would allow and snatched the bar from his hand.

"You are my hero. These two, I'm starting to wonder if they're related to Satan himself. Do you think maybe they've just been in the demon realm too long? Does Satan actually live here somewhere or is he on an entirely different plane all together?" Exhaustion led to rambling and Aggie had it bad. Instead of waiting for answers to her random questions, she tore into her first chocolatey goodness and savored the peanut butter as she chewed slowly. Going any faster would result in her missing out on much needed rest time. The last thing she wanted was to finish and be dragged off and on to a new daunting task.

"Let's take your treat over to the mats. It will be a more comfortable place to sit and we can talk. Then I will give you a few things to try. My goal is to give you practical skills you can use in combat. Then when those two goons start to teach you any fighting skills, you can fend them off." Eldon took her hand and walked her over to the mat. Not once did she relinquish her food or offer to share. This was hers and, given the guys' ability to get almost anything, she didn't even bother to ask where he acquired it. For all she knew, a Brownie could have sent it over.

Legs crisscrossed on the mat Aggie faced Eldon head on, but this time they didn't touch. Between mouthfuls and a couple times without bothering to empty her mouth she said, "They put me through the ringer, but it was all strength training. They said from here on out they'll do the first session like today and the second with fighting skills training. Total of two hours a day until I don't tire as easily."

"That will come easier as you get used to the magic inside you. The magic will reset your system as you go." Eldon leaned back on his hands as they spoke, making Aggie feel more relaxed as well. That was something Eldon was always good at; he could calm her down in an instant.

"I noticed that this," Aggie held her bracelet up to show him, "my Fae self told me would help me channel my magic and control it. If not this," she shook her bracelet again as she referenced it, "specifically, then anything connected to nature directly contacting my skin. I realized whenever I needed a boost or felt like I would drop, I could draw a little from the bracelet and I was able to keep going. I didn't do it much but I realized it when I almost keeled over a couple times. The energy was just there and I was back moving again."

"That sounds about right; you are channeling your magic and you don't even know it. The bracelet, while it helps you connect, is really just a symbol for you to focus on in times of need. Your Fae is quite wise to have given you that focal point. Now, if you could, would you try something for me? I would like you to visualize wind in your head and focus on creating a tiny tornado in the palm of your hand." Eldon really had big plans for her; it seemed he was starting out with the big guns.

"Wow, nothing like taking it slow. Oh, I should tell you I breathed a wind today and knocked Mitchell over. So, this shouldn't be too hard, but I did that with my mouth before." Aggie got so excited over the food he brought her that she had almost forgotten to tell him about her manifestation of her powers.

"This shouldn't be too difficult then, but just picture capturing that tornado under a glass, similar to a snow globe. Only this one will be called a tornado globe, purely for observation not destruction." Aggie giggled at his description even though it was a tad odd; it did make it easier to paint the idea in her mind. Without saying anything she held up her palm face up and stared at it. She was making an extra effort to not close her eyes. She wanted to see it form, and she knew how pretty her eyes would become as they transformed into the Fae version of her own.

Seconds later, she started to feel the air move across her hand. A smile broke out on her face because it felt just like before, except this time it came from everywhere and not from her lips. Quickly that wind took shape, swirling like a tumbleweed around her hand. She had the concept, but it was still a bit rough and not anywhere like a globe covering it. Aggie focused a bit harder and she pictured a glass floating above her hand and easing it over the billowing bundle. Once she had it trapped from above, she sealed the invisible glass over her palm and closed the escape for good. Now the tornado began to spin and twirl, but never got any bigger than a garden gnome. The thought made her giggle, because the tornado looked very similar to that gnome's upturned hat.

"I did it! Look at it El, it's magnificent." Aggie wanted to jump up and down for joy but she was afraid the imaginary glass would fall from her hand, letting the tornado escape and wreak havoc on the space.

"Once again, like an age-old Fae you have now mastered the power of the wind, just as you took to creation. I'm so proud of you." Slowly she let the wind recede, and as it calmed she mentally raised the invisible glass. With that, all the wind dispersed into the room naturally and Aggie let her eyes lift and meet Eldon's. She could see the pride shining in his eyes and it warmed her from the inside out. Not that she never had that as a child, but she had never done something like this that would warrant such a reaction. She wasn't very much of a go-getter in high school academically. She opted for the 'just get by' approach. This, on the other hand, was the perfect reaction and just what she needed.

"Teach me something else; I want to knock Mitchell on his ass tomorrow. I'd really love it if it packed enough of a punch to keep him down for a minute, as I might need time to make a fast getaway." Aggie winked at Eldon so he'd know she was kidding, at least about the running away part. "No, if I knock him down, no matter how hard it will be enough. I'll stand and fight whatever he throws back at me."

"Good; there would be no point in training you magically or otherwise if you are planning to just run away when the first threat appeared." Eldon wasn't upset, more like stating the obvious. "I think the best thing you could do that would be both surprising and still big enough to make a statement would be a vine."

"You mean I'm going to conjure a vine from thin air?" Aggie was impressed, but a little skeptical seeing as she wouldn't be outside and the bracelet might not be a big enough connection for this plan.

"Yes, but not technically from thin air. This castle, as I said, is made of natural stone, but because it is stone there are gaps in between that are made from a dirt paste, or mortar. You can use that to your advantage here. It will just take a bit more concentration to control it, but thankfully it isn't as dangerous as the tornado you just contained." Eldon stood from the mat they were on and Aggie followed suit.

"Should I take off my shoes? I feel like connection will be key here and I'm not sure my bracelet will be enough." Aggie hesitated, but decided telling him about her insecurities was better than hiding them at this point.

"Let's leave them on; I'd hate for Mitchell to get a clue before you nail him." Eldon's wide grin was contagious, and Aggie found herself enjoying this moment right along with him.

# Chapter 16

The next morning Aggie was sore, but it was a good sore. The kind of pain that let you know you had muscles, but not enough to be immobile. Breakfast was the usual spread and, after their workout the day before as well as the plan to repeat it that day, Aggie planned to load up on calories so she wouldn't crap out too soon. Piling her plate high with eggs and bacon, she threw on a couple pancakes and slathered everything with syrup. As she sat down, a cup appeared in front of her. Glancing around she saw that no one was anywhere near her. "Who did that?"

No one said a word, but Gryson's smile slipped on his face. Aggie nodded her head as she took that first sip. It ran through her body like liquid energy. Then it hit her, "Eldon, is it possible that foods and anything that comes right from the ground will affect me differently now?" She didn't know how to describe it but coffee had always felt like a life-giving brew, and that morning it was literal. She felt renewed.

"I can't say exactly how it would work on you. What I can say is, I feel a bit more spry after my meals. Since I've always been that way it isn't something I really notice all that often as something of significance. We can watch it and see how you react before and after eating." Eldon scooped up another bite of his breakfast.

Deciding to test this theory, Aggie jumped from her chair and grabbed a second plate of food; this time she chose only from the fruit table. Selecting a piece of cantaloupe, Aggie took a bite. The juices ran down her arm and she slurped up what she could to not let it escape. The flavor burst in her mouth as though it were the first time she had ever tasted it. Sweet and light in flavor and perfect in every way. With eyes wide like a child Aggie looked around the table, but to her disappointment none of the guys was paying any attention to her. So she chose to enjoy the rest of her meal in peace.

Aggie quickly realized that only the grown food reacted in the magically new way as the cantaloupe. The pancakes, eggs and bacon, while good, weren't explosive on her tongue the same as the fruit. To Aggie's surprise, she finished everything and wasn't overly stuffed. If she didn't want to make headway and get to the gym, she would have gone back for seconds. She was dressed in another set of leathers, this time created by Liel. He met her at the twins' door before breakfast and Aggie was grateful. While Eldon had walked her back to the twins' room, he was kind enough to transform her previous leathers into a beautiful silk nightgown trimmed in lace.  Liel's version of the leathers from the previous day were practical, and the same buttery soft and pliable. She never would have realized how functional this material was until she worked out the previous day, vigorously with no complications. Liel's accent color was beautiful sweeping greens of different shades waving across her right torso. They ran diagonally, twirling at the ends and twining the individual strands and colors together into one on both ends. Her boots were the perfect size and all black. Aggie felt like she could go on a super-secret mission after dark and fit in perfectly.

Scraping her chair back from the table ready to start the day, she asked, "So, what's on the agenda today?" While she was leading the conversation, she didn't want to dictate today.

"I made some headway with my scrying yesterday, but I'm having trouble narrowing it down. I'm hoping with Mathius' help I can narrow down what I'm seeing. I don't know the terrain and can't figure out what the interference might be at this time." Gryson looked exhausted, but more disappointed than anything. His hair was out of place for the first time since she had met him, as though he had been constantly running his hands through it.

"I think that's a good plan. Mathius, do you have any plans today?" Aggie wanted them to cheer up and know they were on track.

"Nothing that can't be held off for a while. I was just going to do rounds and see if anything had changed." Mathius moved over beside Gryson and the other two men. Liel decided to pick up his original role in the search, and they made their way to what Aggie assumed was the Security room.

"Anyone else have any wonderful plans today?" Aggie scanned the room, but the remaining men just shrugged noncommittally. Raising one eyebrow, Aggie silently questioned their response.

"Well, Ren and I are going to be picking up your training from where we left off yesterday. I'm planning to incorporate some actual fighting today, but you aren't going to like it. Chances are you will be on your ass so much today, it's going to be sore." Mitchell snickered at his own words, and Aggie scowled at him.

"Well, since that's our plan and no one has anything else they want to share, let's get this ass beating under way." Aggie didn't want them to know she had an ace up her sleeve, so she played along and ho-hummed her way through, following the twins out and to the training gym.

*****

"I said keep your hands up; you are going to ruin that pretty face if you don't protect it. The entire point is to block yourself from attack. That means any attack. Try it again." Mitchell's gruff words made Aggie mad. They had been working for over an hour and she was exhausted. Her arms felt like they weighed a hundred pounds each. "You also need to keep moving; an opponent could get the jump on you at any time and you need to be on guard at all times, even if that is just staying in motion. Becoming stagnant for even just a moment could cost you your life. You also have to remember there will be magic in play, as well. Let me show you what I mean. Ren, care to help in this demonstration? We're going to show you how much quicker the reflexes can be from still and from already in motion. Even though he has no magic, with or without, just consider the consequences of one or the other if someone threw magic at you." Mitchell took up the stance he had taught her, legs spread shoulder width apart and knees slightly bent for mobility. Bouncing on the balls of his feet, shifting his weight back and forth, he brought his hands up in a light fist, right hand slightly in front of the left. Aggie understood the purpose of this motion, but her will to keep going was wavering. She wished she possessed the stamina to keep this up as long as Mitchell and Ren.

Then, without warning, Ren barreled down and attacked his brother, yelling and raising his leg in a side kick to try and take him down. Mitchell was ready for him and quickly dodged, able to step out of the way, and never had to raise a fist or arm to block him.

"Reset!" Mitchell yelled out. He didn't address Aggie between sets, but just spoke to his brother, who rounded back across the room to begin again. Mitchell reset his stance. Only, this time she noticed he didn't bounce on the balls of his feet. For a moment, he swayed back and forth just shifting his weight from hip to hip. This time he looked more like an impatient husband waiting for his wife to finish shopping. His hands were on his hips and not in a protective stance.

Ren's smile looked more like a malicious leer as he prepared to attack. This time, instead of a loud war cry, he approached more stealthily, and without warning. When he got to Mitchell, he was scanning the room with his back to him and Ren didn't hold back this time. With a quick jab, Ren punched Mitchell directly in his right kidney. While Aggie probably would have dropped to the floor, writhing in pain, Mitchell's face gave the slightest tensing. If Aggie didn't know better she would have thought he was wincing. Though Aggie knew that Ren hadn't pulled his punch, Mitchell was too much of an Alpha to show how much it actually hurt. He instead dropped to one knee to carry on with Aggie for the next few minutes. Not fooled one bit, Aggie knew he was regrouping because the punch wasn't a tame one.

"As you can see, I was better prepared and had a better reaction time when I was in proper form. When I was relaxed and just waiting for the next shoe to drop, that was when he got the better of me. Even though I knew he was coming, I couldn't react as quickly when I would have had to turn completely around and then still put my hands up to react. This is why always being ready in most situations, but especially the ones you expect a fight to break out, is best. Are you ready to go again?" While she completely understood the reasoning behind the mechanics, what she couldn't change was the sheer exhaustion that she felt in every inch of her body. If it weren't for those poor kids and the need to rush in there and save them, just as soon as they knew where they were, she would much rather go and take a nap.

"Actually, can I please take a break? I'd be happy with a fifteen-minute water and sit break. Nothing crazy, I promise. I just need to rest. We've been at this for over an hour now." Aggie saw Ren glance up at the clock and cringe.

"I'm sorry, Aggie. Yes, by all means, go take a rest. That will give Mitchell and me time to talk through your next set. Just think about the punches and kicks we have taught you. This will be a review session when you get back from your break." It was a wonder to Aggie how the twins worked seamlessly together, sharing the responsibilities while magically not stepping on each other's toes.

Sitting on the mat, she silently observed the guys as they discussed in the distance. While she couldn't hear their words, it was fun to watch them in silence. In her mind, she ad-libbed an entire conversation they were having about china dolls becoming a trend in Madagascar.

"No, seriously, they are having them imported via drones because they don't want the pilots to feel ultimately responsible for the dolls in the event of a crash," Aggie imagined Ren telling Mitchell.

As the conversation continued, Aggie fought a snicker at her own antics. "What do mean? Couldn't the drones crash just as easily?" Mitchell, ever the realist, countered his brother with a furrowed brow and a confused look on his face.

"No, with the drones they can fly lower and drop faster in the event of an emergency and not worry about any loss of pressure or risk to human lives. That allows them to set the drone and the load down faster, and there is less possibility of damages." Aggie lost it and couldn't hold back her mirth any longer, falling back on the mat, rolling with a huge burst of laughter. She had forgotten about doing that when she was younger with her Gran. They used to mute the TV and make up their own dialogue that they deemed more suited to the images on the screen.

She was still laughing when the guys approached her. "What are you laughing at?" Mitchell's scowl stopped her dead, but she still had to catch her breath so she wasn't as somber as his face said she should be. Taking two large breaths, she attempted to rein it in and settle herself.

"I don't know that I've ever seen you in that good of a mood. Whatever caused that, we are so going to repeat it later. Care to share whatever it was?" Ren always in good humor, but Mitchell didn't seem amused.

"I think if she is feeling that good we should be getting back to work. We still have a long way to go." Aggie knew he was right, but that didn't sit well with her. As they walked back to the training area, Aggie formulated her plan.

"Okay, Princess, let's go over what we have learned. I want to see what you have retained. Ren and I will alternate attacking you from different directions to help keep you moving. You either block us or dodge us. We won't throw a punch. This is just for you to practice staying on your guard, but if you have to hit or kick to get around us do so. I don't expect you to do anything that will cause lasting damage at this point." Mitchell's confidence in his words only revved Aggie up, and had her more determined that she would be carrying out her plan.

Getting into her starting position, Aggie motioned with the first two fingers on her right hand. "Bring it, boys. I think I'm in the mood for a challenge."

"That's what I like to hear. You are in it to win it; let's do this." Ren and Mitchell moved to their starting point, giving no inclination as to which one would move first and when. Aggie got up on the balls of her feet and started bouncing around back and forth every second. This gave her a prime view of both men with only a second or two delay. While they were fast, she should at least see them move.

Ren came at her first from the right. She dodged him easily, rolling to the left and out of his reach. Mitchell came next and very quickly, but she rolled back through her right shoulder, the entire time never losing her bounce in her step. Mitchell doubled back but she didn't have enough time to spin away; instead she connected with his jaw, using a right uppercut. She didn't do too much damage, as he shook it off and glared at her. Staying in motion, Ren sped up and ran straight forward, but with Mitchell still to her left she locked in and nailed Ren in the abdomen with a double jab, right then left.

Ren doubled over at the impact, making Aggie feel justified for the force she was packing. The only let-down was Ren's beaming grin shining back at her instead of a pain-laced grimace. Shrugging it off, she was thankful that she at least got part of a reaction.

"Is that all you've got?" Now Ren was taunting her and she wasn't going to let that slide. Deciding to take the game to them Aggie kept her bounce in her step, but flexed her fingers and arms loosely by her side. It looked a bit silly, she knew, but it was more of a distraction. Her shoulders twisted slightly, adding to the rubbery look of her arms.

The distraction was just what she needed as she reached for her powers, quickly hoping to achieve the final goal before they realized her eyes were glowing. Looking up slightly and closing her eyes, she looked like she was just shaking out her muscles.

Without warning Ren yelled and Mitchell bellowed as only he could, the sound carrying across the room. Not releasing the magic, Aggie opened her eyes as she placed her hands on her hips, smiling confidently. What she saw was just what she had designed. Both men were suspended in the air by a thick vine that twisted and turned through the space. It almost resembled a briar, but without thorns. She didn't have any plans to hurt them, but just remind them she wasn't relying solely on her ability to fight with her physical strength.

"Now boys, I think you should have a bit more awareness of what I'm capable of. I can do this anywhere. I just created this inside and not just outside. There's a limited list of places where my powers would be completely useless." Choosing to hold them both there a bit longer, Aggie just waited them out. When they were able to acknowledge her as more than just a simple girl, then she would let them down.

Just then a movement caught her eye. It was Eldon. She turned with a smile on her face, but quickly realized he wasn't there on a social call. He was moving a rapid speed, and with the concentrated look it was obvious he was attacking. Her hackles rose instantly, and she nearly missed the chance to get her hands up. She rolled to the left but not before he clipped her with his elbow, propelling her a bit farther than she had intended.

"What was that?" Aggie screeched at him, but she realized that in the loss of concentration she had lost her hold on the vines. They weren't gone, but the twins were working their way loose. So she quickly twisted them a few more times for good measure to limit their process. It was a good thought, too, because just then Kyrel dusted in front of her face and shoved her back.

While they weren't using full force, she was getting pissed because this was four to one and those odds weren't right. Letting out a frustrated yell, Aggie got herself into position. If they were going to gang up on her, she was going to put up a good fight. Her timing couldn't have been better because a swirl of wind was coming her way, and while she couldn't identify the source she assumed it was Eldon using his magic to create some sort of cover. Throwing her hand out, she imagined a rock-hard shield and braced herself against it. If nothing else, she hoped it would end up splitting the air and causing it to go around her.

Since the shield was invisible, the force didn't know what she had done. To Aggie's surprise, it impacted her with the force of a man made of stone himself. Xavier slammed into her, knocking her flat on her ass, hard. For her lack of awareness and preparation, she paid for it with the loss of all air she had in her lungs. Gasping for air, she fought to regain control. When the twins mentioned Xavier was fast, this wasn't anything like what she had imagined. She literally couldn't see him at the speed he was moving. It was as though he traveled through time. Had she not noticed the wind, it would have been worse without her shield in place.

Getting to her feet, Aggie knew they weren't going easy on her. While they weren't throwing punches and all out hitting her, this was a fight, and if she couldn't win she was damn well going to try. Putting her fists back up to protect herself, she bounced back on her feet, spinning around quickly so as not to miss her next attack. Kyrel dusted in again and she felt the air shift around her just before he reappeared. Hoping she wasn't wrong, she recalled his approximate height and reached where his head should be appearing. Using his own momentum, gripping the back of his scalp and latching onto his hair, she pulled him down quickly and brought her right knee up and slammed it into his nose. While she didn't cause any bloodshed, it was enough to slow him down.

Without missing a beat Eldon was back in the game, coming at her from the left. She met him with a right cross, twice to the face. She was finished dodging and was ready to bring the fight to them. They wanted to now gang up on her five to one, they would feel the pain of it all. She wasn't going to back down and let them win. This was her fight and she was planning to own it.

Xavier, who was the one she had to watch, was missing. She didn't know yet how to combat his speed, but she was still working it out. Then, from above, the first twin fell to the floor and landed in a roll. Aggie was a bit disoriented because she had been twisted and dropped and twirled around. She didn't realize which one it was until he popped up, and the furious grey eyes of Mitchell were piercing and he was barreling towards her. She raised her hands to the ready and still bouncing on the balls of her feet, for fear one of the other guys would attack at the same time. Mitchell got close and Aggie feigned to the right. He went with her but she recoiled quickly, twirling back around and got him with a left hook to the jaw. It all happened so fast, Aggie impressed herself with her fast planning.

"HA! Take that, you overgrown dog!" Aggie was so excited her skin was practically vibrating. The ideas were flowing through her head, and then from behind she felt a set of arms encircle her. Not knowing what else to do she didn't fight, but used her magic, turning the floor beneath her attacker to ice. The unexpected change of texture caused him to waver, giving Aggie enough room to break free and spin around. Her attacker was none other than her favorite twin, Ren. His eyes were huge, but more in awe of her process.

Xavier was still unaccounted, for but she didn't underestimate his plan. He was likely lurking in the shadows in wait. She was ready for him; nothing was going to stop her from dropping them all properly. Bouncing back into her ready stance, Aggie twirled for what felt like forever. None of the others attacked and she didn't know why, other than they were also waiting to see what the elusive vampire was waiting to do. Instead of waiting for him, she decided to reach out with her other senses. She closed her eyes and called on her magic. It was a dangerous move, to give up her primary defense and cut off her line of vision, but Aggie assumed he was going to sneak up on her with his speed anyway, so what the hell.

The air moved around her, and as she bounced around she noticed the slight differences. After a moment, she felt it shift and she followed it. It changed and grew and the pressure was full. Aggie knew this had to be Xavier. She followed with her eyes still closed, allowing her magic to lead her. Aggie only took three steps before she smelled the metallic tang, similar to what was in the goblet that fateful morning when she was introduced to his nature. Turning slightly, the air shifted and Aggie just knew. Opening her eyes, she saw him directly in front of her.

"Do you want to try this magically or on the level?" Aggie proposed since they both knew she could attack him with her magic with relative ease. That and he could run on her and disappear. They each had their own advantage.

"I'd be happy to go toe-to-toe with you, wee one. I'll even let you use whatever you need to and I'll stick to basic hand-to-hand combat, but I won't hurt you." He motioned for her to approach him, which was smart, given that if he took one step toward her she was going to unleash a tornado and swoop him up to the clouds.

"On the count of three, you're welcome to attack me." Aggie figured it was the best approach.

Sounding off her count, Xavier reached for her with both hands. That was an interesting plan given Aggie's propensity for dodging, but this wasn't her plan. As soon as Xavier moved, Aggie summoned energy from her magic into her right leg. With every bit of force she could manage, Aggie kicked straight out and forced Xavier from her. Only, what she didn't expect was for him to fly back at least eight feet from her, landing on his ass.

# Chapter 17

Walking back to the common room, Ren exclaimed, "That was epic!" He was practically bouncing down the hallway, unable to contain his excitement. Aggie was still a bit shocked by what had transpired. "Can you believe what she did? Xavier, I've never seen anyone take you down like that. Can you imagine what she will do when she takes on more of our powers?"

"That wasn't her powers." Eldon was deep in thought and nowhere near as excited as Ren. Aggie snuck a glance at him and was worried he was upset by what she just did. "I think this is a development of her true nature. As the Gatekeeper, she is stronger than the average human. She is embracing who she is now. That is something that her ancestors haven't done for many years."

"I'm not sure what it was." Aggie finally decided she wasn't going to let them make her feel bad for her actions. "I know I felt my magic under my skin, waiting to be needed. While I did use it on some things," she gave a pointed look at Mitchell and Ren, "I didn't call on it to take on Xavier, per se. I used my senses and what I assume was my magic or instinct to find you in the dark, but then I just replenished my energy before I kicked. It was no different than when I used it to top off my resources when *Thing One* and *Thing Two*," Aggie pointed with her thumb at the twins, "overworked me on the mats. Not to mention you were all ganging up on me. If it had been an actual fight you would be patting me on the back, not trying to sort it all out."

"Well, I'm going to guess something else was at play there." Xavier's words were spoken softly, as though he didn't want anyone to hear. Aggie also noticed he was walking behind them all. As she glanced back quickly, it looked like he was rubbing his ass.

"You aren't still hurt, are you?" Aggie was worried she had harmed him beyond repair, and for that she felt a bit guilty. It wasn't her intention to hurt any of them, ever.

"No, more confusion and memory of the pain. I'm not one who retains injuries for long. Usually, I don't even feel the pain, but for some reason this time I felt it, even if it was only briefly." Xavier, the man of few words, had just given her a glimpse into his world. While it wasn't much, it was something she could stew over for a bit. Just as quickly as she had noticed his slip, he was back to stone wall as though nothing was bothering him.

"I think with a bit more training, she will be ready to take on anything." Mitchell's words rang home to Aggie, and for once they didn't make her want to lash out at him. "She performed well today." The words of affirmation filled her soul with hope. Maybe things would work out after all.

Before they could reach the common room, a crash and a commotion caught their attention. Sparing a glance between them, it was decided they needed to go check this out. Xavier, who was still behind them, became the leader and they were off; some a bit faster than others, but overall they all stayed together. Twisting around hallways and through corridors, Aggie wondered where they were headed. It couldn't have been that far away since they heard the scuttle so clearly. To Aggie's surprise, when they stopped it was at the front gates. "How did we hear anything this far away so clearly?"

"It's the hallways; they make sound travel differently," Eldon answered, but she wasn't satisfied.

"Then how did you know where to go?" Aggie insisted before they were able to proceed.

"Xavier." The words took a moment to register to Aggie. Then it dawned on her. He was in the lead and she hadn't been watching him the entire time. He must have run ahead and returned before anyone even noticed him missing. *That speed is a real asset, all things considered.* Her thoughts were cut short as they approached the now-open front gates. A horde of people had stormed the gate. Torches that were once hanging from the wall were lying on the floor. The commotion must have knocked them from their resting place.

The people were all gathered around, forcing them to push their way through. Guards parted for them, but it was the other side of the gate that held the most people. What Aggie saw took her breath away. Mathius had mentioned at one point the vast number of demon species was more than she could fathom.

Most looked human like Mathius, but many carried different features that would never pass as normal on Earth. Well, unless you went to the 'special' parts of town. Aggie recalled seeing a few strange piercings and implants a time or two. That and, given the number of tattoos on some bodies, it was a wonder they weren't deemed alien or something.

This was different, though. She saw men who stood eight or nine feet tall with blood-red faces, as though they had stood in lava or boiling water for too long, permanently scarring their faces with the color of the heat that must radiate through them. She saw what she thought was a woman with horns coming out the side of her head like a bull, with broader shoulders than the man standing next to her. He was shorter, but looked more like he belonged in the water. Even from a distance, she saw the slime that was covering him. Another person she saw looked like they glowed, but she couldn't tell if they were male or female. Their skin was bioluminescent in a way, and Aggie was definitely intrigued. This was just a fraction of the faces she saw in this sea bombarding the castle gates.

"What's going on?" Aggie asked and was thankful that, even though her men didn't seem to know, a guard heard her and answered.

"A child has made its way from the outer lands. No one knows from where exactly, but he came home this morning. After a little food and some rest, the parents have brought him here to speak to the king." She nodded her understanding to the guard, but her brain was overworking. *A child? Home? Could this be one of the missing children?* Aggie was so caught up in her train of thought, she didn't realize the rest of her men had gathered around her.

"Bring the child to us." Mathius' voice rang through the space and was more of a bellow that bounced from wall to wall, carrying as far as they could see. Turning to look at him, she saw him there in all his glory. One wouldn't doubt he was the head of the guard. He wore full leathers and a scowl that matched the fiercest warrior's. Aggie was proud of him but, given the fact they were meeting a child, she was instantly on guard.

"Mathius, dear?" She used a sing-songy voice to show she meant no offense. This was his territory and all, but she needed to offer some guidance.  He looked at her with a puzzled expression and she took that as a green light. Shuffling a tad closer to him, she said on a hushed breath, "You might want to lose the scowl. I suggest something softer. You're dealing with a child of unknown age. The last thing you want him to do is clam up, because you're a bit scary right now." Aggie shrugged unapologetically. He needed to consider what he was going into and it wasn't a battle, at least not yet.

It took him a moment, but Aggie knew the instant it sank in, as his eyebrows softened and the fierce crease in his forehead smoothed. He once again became the gentler version of himself.

While they waited, Aggie decided now would be a good time to get some answers. "Since we have a moment, care to enlighten me as to what I'm seeing here?" She indicated the sea of demons standing in front of her.

"What would you like to know?" Mathius waited for her to answer, as opposed to carrying on about histories and lifestyles like Liel likely would have.

"Just tell me a little about what kind of demons I'm seeing. I've met Delia, but I don't see any one like her that I can tell." Aggie scanned the crowd and, while Delia was a more visually tame demon unless you looked very closely, it didn't seem there were any of her kin lurking at the castle gates that day.

"Well, Tiran there," Mathius indicated the smaller man who looked to have come from the sea, "is a Kappa. His kind is aquatic, but can live on land for a time. He just has to get a daily dose of water to survive." Mathius didn't go into length about powers or anything. He just covered the basics and gave Aggie a better understanding of the different races of demons.

"Arina," he nodded his head in the direction of the woman who wore horns the size of a grown bull, "is a Shedu. They have the horns of a bull and the wings of an eagle." Aggie hadn't noticed her wings, but that could have been due to the trench coat she was wearing over her Hulk-like shoulders.

"Now Ragror," Mitchell's gaze was in the direction of a man Aggie hadn't noticed before. He looked more human than demon and so Aggie's gaze didn't settle on him in her previous sweep of the crowd. "His kind is a bit rare, Rokurokubi. They have the ability to stretch their necks farther than one could imagine." Aggie was enthralled by his every word. The thought that these people could possess such powers that on Earth would be unfathomable.

"What about that man?" Aggie indicated the man whose face looked to have been left out in the sun much too long.

"That is Belthazar." He left it at that, as though Aggie should know who he was.

"Unless, he is *the* Belthazar, and Phoebe has been reunited with him, you're going to have to give me a little bit more to go on for now." Mathius looked at her like she had grown horns herself.

"Belthazar is considered Satan's right-hand man. His family lives here and he spends most of his time here these days. That is unless the big man needs him for an important task." It was Aggie's turn to look dumbfounded.

She didn't have time to linger on it, because right then the guards brought up a small blond-haired boy who couldn't have been over the age of eleven even by a day. He was shaking and looked to be bone-thin. He was accompanied by a stout woman wrapped in a quaint shawl that was draped over her head. Aggie looked closer and she was very human in her appearance. In the back of her mind, she wondered what this demon woman was. His father was on the tall side, but more average tall in Earth terms. He had sandy blond hair like his son and didn't have any outstanding demonic traits. Aggie assumed one of them likely had nature-driven powers if this is one of the boys who was taken. Chances were in her favor that magic was like character traits for humans.

"Hello, young one. What is your name?" Aggie was proud of Mathius for holding his softer side in light of the child's possible trauma.

"Navian, sir." The boy's voice was small and still very shaky. Aggie thought they said he had gotten some rest, but perhaps he needed more like one or two weeks of bed rest to build his strength back up. She could only imagine the nightmare the past few days had been for him.

"Well, Navian, I'm Mathius, head of the guard. This is my team." Mathius indicated the rest of the guardians and they each nodded stoically, except Aggie who beamed at the sweet boy. She felt sorry for him and wanted to wrap him up and hug his fears away. "Would you and your family follow us? We can discuss what brings you here today." All his questions were directed at Navian. Mathius was making him the only focus, and his parents were just standing there as props to complete a set.

"Yes, sir." Navian was completely respectful and Aggie thought the world of his parents for instilling that sort of behavior in him. The boy and his family followed Mathius, while the rest of the team fell in step behind them. Mathius led them to the common room and everyone filed inside.

"Please, take a seat anywhere and we can get started." Aggie watched the boy's eyes travel to the buffet that was set up for lunch. His wide eyes took in every inch, and Aggie thought she heard his stomach growl.

"First, why don't we all grab a plate of food. I'm don't know about everyone else, but I worked up quite an appetite today during training." Aggie gestured toward the food, encouraging the boy to get his first. Mathius gave her a look of indignation, but it was quickly wiped away when she motioned towards the boy. He was ravenously grabbing piles of food, as though he hadn't been fed in months. Nodding, his anger subsided quickly.

After everyone had their plates and found seats, Mathius began again. "Young man, what has brought you here today?" Even though they all had their assumptions, it made sense to Aggie that Navian should say it and confirm their suspicions.

"I just got home." He paused, but Aggie could tell he was just getting started. "I never thought I'd ever see my parents again. She was a monster and I thought she was going to kill me." Aggie thought it was ironic that he called her a monster, given the people he was surrounded by every day. That must mean she was A game monster and not B movie grade.

"Who are you talking about, Navian?" Mathius was asking questions to draw out his story and not feeding him anything. The rest of the room remained silent and merely observed what the two were doing.  His parents even stayed quiet, like they knew this wasn't the time for them to offer their opinions or help Navian through. Aggie couldn't think of a single parent on Earth who would sit silently and watch their kids going through any of this alone. She was definitely seeing some cultural differences between them.

"I don't know her name; she never let us address her or even speak. It took days before another showed up, but that didn't ease the burden on me. I think she pushed me harder and, oh, the pain. It hurt so bad." Navian shuddered at the memory and Aggie's heart broke for him.

"What did they do that hurt so badly?" Mathius calmly pressed him for more answers. These weren't even the hard ones yet and Aggie was becoming protective of this little boy. It took all she had to stay in her chair and not jump between him and Mathius. The last thing Aggie wanted was to make this boy relive the pain of his ordeal.

"It began with a disgusting drink she made. I was forced to drink it all and she said some words I didn't understand. I thought they sounded funny, like a made-up language. Soon I fell asleep, and when I woke up I couldn't move my arms. They were tied to the wall, but not with rope. I couldn't see what held them there, so it must have been magic." Navian absently rubbed his wrists, presumably where the restraints had been.

"Did you see anything around that might have told you where you were?" Mathius pressed again for more details, and Aggie was so enthralled by the story that she didn't need to take notes.

It was as though it were being etched on her mind as Navian spoke.

"It was dark, and the floor was cold and damp. I never left the room I was chained in the entire time I was there. After they finished with me I fell asleep, and one day just woke up in the grass. I didn't know where I was then, either. Nothing was around. I followed the river back to the city. It was so cold and all I wore was my night clothes." Then his mother decided to chime in for the first time, and her voice was rough as though she had overused it recently or had a cold.

"He appeared by our bed, blue from the cold and bare from the waist down. His night shirt barely covered to his knees, but he was taken in the night, so no shoes or pants were there to protect him from the elements. It was dark and icy, as these storms have increased. It took me hours to warm him back up by the fire and with blankets. I feared bathing him for fear of doing irreversible damage to his limbs. I was terrified I'd never see my baby again. He is our only child and I was only blessed to have one. No matter our trying, it was not in our cards." Navian's mother began to sob softly. Aggie understood it wasn't grief, but just an overwhelming sense of emotion. Her child was home. A child she didn't know if she would ever see again. By some unknown power, he had been returned to her like a ghost on the wind.

"Do you remember anything else, or do you think you could tell us where it was you woke up? That could help us narrow down our search for the remaining children. Did you see the other children?" Mathius was throwing questions at him now in a sense of urgency. They only had a little over a day left to find the children before they potentially met their untimely demise. Aggie rested her hand on Mathius' shoulder to settle him. She didn't think scaring Navian or his parents was the solution to any of this.

Taking a steadying breath, Mathius paused his questions and waited. Navian considered all that he was asked. "I do remember the other children. I don't know who they were, as it was very dark, but I remember we used to talk. I don't know all the children, but I do recall one of them far away from the rest. His name sounded a lot like the prince's name. I don't recall what it was exactly, as it was hard to hear from that distance." That perked everyone up and gave them hope that at least Prince Rikan was still alive. "I also don't know if I can tell you exactly how to get back to where I woke up, because I was so tired and hungry that it took all my strength to keep moving. Also, the elements usually don't bother me, as I just use my magic to heat me, but it wasn't working and hasn't worked since I was released. I don't know what's wrong with it, but perhaps it's just that my body is too run- down to keep up with it." A grave look passed over everyone faces, including Navian's parents. Aggie didn't know what that meant, but a subtle head shake from Kyrel told her not to ask any questions. "It was all I could do to stay awake, walking through the cold."

"Gryson." Mathius only said that one thing and Gryson nodded. No other words were had between the two.

"If it is all right with you both, "Mathius directed the question to Navian's parents, "I'd like to check his memory for the information we need. Chances are he has that information there, but it is locked up in a way he can't retrieve it himself." Mathius didn't go into any more detail and the parents didn't seem concerned. This must be something that was common for the guardians. Aggie just hoped it wasn't invasive and poor little Navian didn't have to go through much more heartache.

Not waiting for any more permission, Gryson rose from his seat and knelt beside Navian. "My name is Gryson. I'm going to look inside your mind for just a moment and see if anything you saw in the past few days matches anything I've been researching. Don't worry, it won't hurt a bit; if anything you might feel a little tickle, right here." He pressed his finger to the back of Navian's neck just below his hairline and next to his spine. Navian nodded and Gryson closed his eyes, pressing his left hand to Navian's neck and the other to Navian's temple. The room fell silent, a natural response to the need for concentration. A serene look passed over Navian's face. It was the most relaxed Aggie had seen him yet. It was the look every kid got while they were sleeping. Gran used to say Aggie looked so peaceful while she slept, but Aggie always felt restless and thought she tossed and turned. Perhaps that was all inside her head after all.

"I have a location," Gryson simply stated as he lowered his hands from the boy who was left smiling. A look Aggie didn't expect from the traumatized boy. Raising an eyebrow at him, Gryson nodded. In a hushed tone, he said, "I also left him with some more pleasant memories of his time for the past few weeks. I hope you don't mind. Now his most recent events have faded into distant memories. While the trauma isn't gone, it seems like something that happened long ago and not so new and raw. I hope that was all right. I couldn't think to have him be unable to sleep or get on with his life."

"Thank you, that is wonderful. Please, let me give you something in return." Navian's mother was sobbing again, only this time in gratitude. "I know my son will never see his magic again, but you have given us a great gift that will help that transition. I would only like to give you the same courtesy."

"We didn't do this for a reward. Our only purpose is to help and do our best to rescue the remaining children if it is in our power," Gryson reassured Navian's mother. There was no need payment for helping their son through what was bound to be a rough period of his life.

"I'm a seer; please, I insist." Without warning, she gripped Gryson's hand and her eyes rolled back, only showing the whites. Had she not just mentioned she was a seer and they were already in a demonic realm, Aggie would have assumed that she was possessed. "Dragons. The prophecy is true." Her words made no sense to Aggie, but she waited patiently for her to come out of the trance. She looked around and the big eyes mixed with astonished faces had her worried.

"The Dragon Warrior, destined to take on the Great Darkness, will save us all." Her eyes quickly returned to normal and fell on Aggie. With a low bow she fell to her face, soon followed by her husband, and he pulled Navian down with him.

Aggie took three huge steps back. "What are you doing?" Her men all dropped to one knee, showing the same respect, but Aggie was still confused. "Get up, all of you, this instant. I don't know what's going on, but someone had better start explaining."

One by one they all got to their feet. The seer stepped toward Aggie and took her hand. "You are the Dragon Warrior, dear. You were prophesied hundreds of years ago, but it is more folklore now. If I had not just seen that with my own eyes, I wouldn't have believed. You have a long road ahead of you and many battles. But you will save us all from a great darkness that is coming. Without you, it will consume everything in every realm." Aggie was speechless. There was no way this was her destiny. The guys had just told her she was destined to be the Ninth Guardian, but now some foretold future was going to play out? She had no words; what could she say to that? 'Sorry, I'm not the one. I can't be a dragon, I'm human.' Something told her that wasn't the proper response to being told you're the savior of all the realms. Instead of waiting for clarification, she turned and left the room.

# Chapter 18

*I'm not a dragon. I'm not a dragon. I'm not a dragon.* Aggie sat on Mitchell's bed, repeating the words, trying to make herself believe them. Everything she had seen since entering the Gateway had proven to be true. This was the one thing she didn't think she could handle. Then she remembered the tapestry she saw on her way in that first day. Realization dawned on her; it was the prophecy. Just like the one marked 'The Wanderer' was an omen.

Aggie then began to hyperventilate, putting her head between her legs she tried to regain control. She was supposedly this foretold creature, person, magical dragon. Not only was she the Gatekeeper, the Ninth Guardian, the final link, but she was now Dragon.

A knock sounded at the door, but Aggie still hadn't regained control. She heard the door click open, followed by a trail of soft footsteps. Aggie looked up, still breathing rapidly, and her heart melted. Not one or even two of her guys stood there, but every single one of them.

"Are you okay?" Eldon was the first to speak and came over to her, placing his hand on the side of her head, cupping it and leaning in close.

Nodding, Aggie still wasn't ready to speak. Glancing around the room, she realized that each and every face that looked back at her spoke of concern for her. She could tell right then and there that every one of them was meant for her and she was made for them. No one cared this deeply over someone not meant for them.

"I suppose we should give you a little more of a history lesson about the Dragon Warrior." Mathius approached her and settled himself on the bed beside her.

"Is there more I should know, or did the seer cover the basics?" Her voice was small and weak, having only just caught her breath.

"She got the gist of it. There is a version of that story in each of the realms," Ren clarified for her, but only just.

"How am I supposed to be the final Guardian, the Gatekeeper, and now this Dragon Warrior?" Aggie was more than lost at this point and was grasping at straws to figure out any little bit of information.

"We had no idea you were meant to hold this burden, but the good news is you have a solid support system unlike anyone else would have. While it isn't unheard of for our women to hold a harem, you will have the strongest and one of the largest amongst the realms. You also have a link with every realm, where others wouldn't because it isn't common to breed between races." Xavier was feeling extra chatty; it seemed this was his preferred topic.

"I don't know if I'm cut out for all of this. When you all told me it was my choice to be the Ninth, I had no idea there was an *epic battle* in my future." Aggie knew she sounded like she was whining but this was important to her. If she was going to give up her life for all of this, all the cards should have been laid out before she jumped in head-first.

"All our battles are epic. What do you think we are preparing for to get these kids out?" Mitchell, the battle- hungry Alpha wolf, had a point. That didn't mean she was ready for any of it.

"Well, given the fact that I can seem to change my destiny, let's discuss where we are with Navian and the information you got from his mind meld." Aggie squared her shoulders and decided, since fate can't be changed, she would accept what she could change and that was getting these kids out alive rather than dead.

"It was dark when they dropped him outside, but I saw some landmarks and places that I've pinned while scrying. I'm still not one hundred percent sure where they are. It's like they just up and vanished into thin air." Gryson snarled out of frustration, which surprised Aggie enough that she actually jumped.

"Then maybe we just need to take a road trip." Aggie hesitated at her choice of words. "Perhaps that was wrong; it would be more of a hike in this case. Either way, we need to just head out there and figure out what we're missing. Take what we know from Navian and then what you've gathered from scrying and see what we find."

"I think a hunting party might be a wise choice, but I don't want all of us to go on this wild goose chase. What if that is what they are hoping for and then use that to attack in our absence?" Mathius pointed out

"Who do you want to leave? You won't be leaving me behind because, if you do, I'll just accuse you of trying to lock me in a tower for my own wellbeing. I'll tell you right now that isn't happening. You brought me along, changed my life for the crazier, trained me to fight, gave me magic, and I've been here every step of the way without argument. So, I think that's earned me a role in the rescue of these kids." Aggie wasn't going to back down even an inch on this. They wanted her? Well, now they had her.

"I agree, she has proven herself in training today. She can hold her own, and with us there I don't foresee any problems." Mitchell's words once again proved to be more shocking than expected. He had paid her a compliment. While not exactly a direct one, Aggie decided she would take it on principle.

"How did she go from basic training to fight-ready in one day?" Mathius was skeptical and rightly so, but this was a story Aggie wanted to sit back and listen to, if only to revel in the tale.

Listening to the guys carry on about how they felt when they saw her take one another down was captivating. Aggie giggled a bit and then found herself lying down on the bed, propped up by her elbow, taking in all the details.

"You missed it—she knocked him clean on his ass. It was epic!" Ren continued his way of thinking from earlier.

"It was definitely a surprising course of action." Xavier wasn't upset and sulking anymore, and Aggie got to hear his true thoughts given his time to think them over. "She was just there when she wasn't moments before. Then when I thought I had the upper hand, she proved me wrong rather quickly."

"I'm not sure any of us was expecting her to get the hang of it as quickly as she did. It was like second-nature to her." Kyrel had leaned against the wall, singing her praises.

"It was indeed a surprising turn of events. I expected the magic, just because we worked on control yesterday. What I didn't expect was everything else that came along with it. She acted like she had been fighting her entire life." Eldon sounded proud now that he'd had more time to consider the events at hand.

"Are you saying you had a hand in the dirty trick she played on us?" Mitchell wasn't upset, but he was surprised that Eldon played a part.

"In his defense, I asked him to help me sort it out. I wanted to knock you on your ass, but that was a thousand times better since it got you out of my hair. Which seemed to be the best course of action since you had plotted against me as well. What was the big idea, pitting all the guys against me at the same time? Were you hoping I would fail?" Aggie was a tad bothered again that they all had ganged up on her, even though it all came out okay in the end.

"I wanted you to see that you still had to stay active in the moment. You struggled with that and I needed you to know why. None of the guys was actually attacking you or hitting you. It was just a training exercise." Mitchell defended his actions to the letter, and Aggie couldn't fault him for that. She did learn some valuable lessons in all of it.

"It's a good thing she has taken to fighting so well, because this trip to find the children isn't going to be a walk in the park. There will likely be bloodshed." Liel sounded a bit forlorn and Aggie was a bit startled by his tone. She had never heard him sound even a bit emotional.

"I'm just glad we don't have to worry about her as much. This is a day of great news. I would like to leave as soon as possible." Mathius rose to his feet and started pacing the room, showing how anxious he really was after all the news they had received.

"I'm going to take a stab in the dark and say that Liel, Eldon, and Kyrel would be the best choices to leave here. Then, when we find the children, they can either be here to help in case of attack or help get the children where they need to be. Mathius could even sift back here and bring them back to us if we need the extra manpower." Aggie had watched them all interact, so she was getting a pretty good idea as to what their strengths were.

"In this case, Mitchell and Ren would likely be best in their wolf forms. That would help the group blend in with a smaller group. They can run ahead and, between their senses, be able to get a feel for where they need to go. Gryson has been scrying and that, mixed with the visions he saw in Navian's head, would help us know if we were going the right way. Xavier could blend into the darkness better than anyone and give them more of the element of surprise. Even if the captors saw them coming, they wouldn't necessarily see Xavier. Mathius knows the terrain better than any of them and would be needed to help guide them in the right direction for where this Wanderer should be."

"Let's gear up and then we can head out. I'll need you to set up a triage station somewhere here at the castle. While I hope it isn't necessary, I'd rather be prepared." Mathius directed this to Eldon, and that piqued Aggie's interest.

"Tell me why Eldon is the one you asked to do that. I'm sure you have a reason and it wasn't just a random choice."

"Eldon, would you like to share that with her while the rest of us go gear up? You can bring her down to get ready afterward or go ahead and prep her with what she needs. We'll meet in the common area." Mathius and the rest of the guys made their way out of the room. Eldon came up and took Aggie's hand and gently caressed it.

"Care to fill me in there, earth boy?" Aggie smiled at him to show she meant that in the nicest way possible. Then she turned and sat cross-legged, facing her Fae mate.

"As a child, I was something of a legend. While most children struggled to master this skill or that, I was proficient in all of them within weeks of developing each new facet of my powers. That garnered a lot of attention and my parents were the quiet sort. While they weren't ashamed of me, it was too much for them to handle. I was sent away to live with the priests of our clan. While I was with them, I saw things kids weren't usually subjected to. I saw sickness and death along with the shunned from one of our cities, sent to ask for pity from the priests." Aggie's heart was breaking for him though she didn't know what to say, but he continued with his story, giving her more time to digest everything.

"One day, the high priest noticed I didn't shy away from the most gruesome of men. He was probably in his middle years, full of disease and writhing in pain. I was drawn to him for some reason. I had an innate need to touch him. The priest tried to stop me, but before he could my fingers connected with the diseased man's skin. It was like a calm came over me and I pushed my energy into him. When I opened my eyes, the man looked different. Not just was he healed, but his aged skin was repaired and his features were youthful once again. It was as though I had taken him back to his teenage years. I was so surprised that I fell back onto my hands and scrambled to run away. I thought I would be in trouble."

"Why would you have been in trouble?" Aggie was confused because, first, he was just a child, and he had just saved a dying man. Who would punish a child for any of those things?

"No one had shown signs of this power for thousands of years. I was also the youngest. Most who develop it are later in life and not still in their growing years. I had at that point developed every known power and then some. My parents thought I was distraction before. With this power the priests had to create a schedule, and I wasn't permitted to freely walk the grounds anymore. I became more of a hermit because it was less stressful. They brought me the worst of the worst that the doctors couldn't heal organically. I spent my time indoors during the day and chose to go out at night to avoid human interaction." That was probably why Eldon was so quiet when they first met. One thing they had in common: she didn't handle people well either. If she didn't piss them off by opening her mouth, then she was just inadvertently rude because she didn't know what to say.

"Over time I learned to control it and not take years away from them. Those early ones, while they were happy with their youthful appearance, found integrating back into regular life with a younger look provoked jealousy and bickering amongst the townspeople. I was thankful when I was able to rein in that power."

"Do you think that's why I'm able to control my powers so well, since you're the one who gifted them to me?" Aggie hadn't considered this because she didn't have any reason to believe it was unheard of in his world. This sounded like it was more Eldon-related after all.

"It is possible, and I've considered this myself. I'm not ruling anything out at this point with you. I'm beyond impressed by your abilities so far and can't wait to see what else develops." The look Eldon shot her made Aggie's heart swoon. He didn't even say anything particularly affectionate, but he was proud of her and ready to see what else developed. Which could be something magical or their relationship developing; either would be just as perfect.

# Chapter 19

Eldon dressed Aggie in her leathers again, but this time with his signature mossy undertone. Her boots wrapped up her legs to her knees, with a slight fold over them. Eldon said that was necessary for added protection. When she bent down she saw his iridescent coloring gleaming on the inside of the fabric from the inner stitching, along with a ring of tiny red roses stitched into the inside edging. That small touch made her happy to have a piece of him with her while they left him behind. She understood the need, but it was still hard to leave him while they stormed off toward unknown danger.

The guys were waiting in the common room for them when they arrived. It took a lot for Aggie not to drool over them each individually in their armor. While it wasn't metal and rather leather like her own, with all the weapons strapped to them it made them look all the more manly and frightening all at once. The kind of guys you wouldn't want to meet in a dark alley.

Even Eldon, Liel, and Kyrel had donned their battle gear. Eldon carried what looked like a walking stick, but Aggie assumed it was more like something used in hand-to-hand combat fighting. Liel's long hair was tied back with a vine-like fastener. This gave his cheekbones a striking appearance, leaving his face in a fierce expression. He wore a bow across his chest and a quiver over his shoulder. She thought he must have a keen eyesight and he did say he was the strongest Elven warrior in thousands of years. This just proved he had other skills as well that Aggie hadn't figured out yet. Kyrel's blonde hair curled loosely over his ears. He looked relaxed as he leaned against the wall with two large metal circles hanging from his sides. They looked oddly familiar to Aggie and she had to wrack her brain to figure it out. Then she remembered in her history class in school, they had done a lesson on ancient weapons. Those looked a lot like the chakram in the textbook. Never having seen one in real life, she wasn't positive.

Mathius had two large broad swords strapped to his back, and Aggie only had to use a little imagination to envision him wielding them with precision. Gryson had a belt of daggers strapped on, and Aggie wondered if there wasn't a magical element to each of them given what looked like their specific placement around his waist. Xavier, to her surprise, wasn't in a three-piece suit, but leathers like the rest. Though he didn't seem to have any weapons on his person. Aggie was a little concerned for his safety, but tried to ignore it for a while.

The twins only wore their leather pants; Aggie assumed it was because they wouldn't be in their human form the entire time. In the back of her mind, she wondered if anyone carried backup pants for them or perhaps she should be the one to do that. They didn't have any additional weapons on them like the rest, given the fact that they were their own best weapon. That was when Aggie realized the weight of all of this.

There hadn't been a time yet that she had seen them all dressed in battle gear. The reality of it all was like getting smacked in the face. Even though she hoped they would come out of this unscathed, the opposite was also possible. The latter possibility made it difficult to just leave and not say or do anything. While she would be taking most of them with her some would remain, and there was always a chance she wouldn't see them again.

Seeing that she had more time with the ones going with her, she approached each of the men who were staying individually.

"Kyrel, this is stupid of me I know, but on the off chance we might not see each other again I needed to say goodbye a bit more than just a head nod and a wave. We don't know each other well, and after this I plan to spend more time with each of you if I'm given the chance. I know you each mean something different to me, I just haven't figured out what yet." With that she leaned up and kissed him softly, closing her eyes and enjoying the feel of him on her skin. Breaking the kiss after a moment, she turned to Liel.

She knew nearly nothing about him and hadn't spent nearly enough time trying to figure him out. There was surely someone deep down that she could relate to. Either way, she was still going to be forced to leave him behind and run the risk of never knowing. "Liel, I know you least of anyone and for that I'm sorry. You were the first to trust me and bring me into this beautifully chaotic world. What would I have done without you? If we make it out of this alive, promise me you and I will set aside some time to figure each other out?" Liel nodded but didn't say anything, though he wore a look of confusion. Aggie leaned up and kissed him on the cheek, feeling like anything else was too familiar with their undefined relationship.

She had saved Eldon for last, not because he was any lesser but because she had more to say to him. The words didn't come easily, but she would do her best not to become a sappy mess. The last thing she needed was to full-on ugly cry before she made her way off to battle. "El, I'm going to miss you most of all. I know you're needed here more in this case and I respect you for that, but leaving you is one of the hardest things I've ever had to do. Our connection is growing every day and I don't know what I would ever do if I lost you. So, do me a favor," she paused right there and waited, unsure if she wanted to finish her thought. "Don't die!" With that she stood up high on her tiptoes to reach his height, pulling with her hands on his shoulders and causing him to bend down to meet her. Their lips connected in a passionate kiss, hotter than any she had ever experienced in her life. What she would have done for this type of connection on Earth. She knew right then that she was the luckiest girl alive.

*****

"Don't you think you got a bit sappy back there?" Ren asked, still dying from laughter over her emotional overload at the castle. They had only been walking for a few minutes before Ren started in on her.

"No, not at all; this is my first mission with you guys. For all I know, I might be used as bait and this could go south very quickly." Not that Aggie believed a word of what she said, though it was always possible since that bitch destroyed Aggie's room and none of the guys' inner sanctums.

"I'd never use you as bait, Schnookums." Ren used an overly lovey voice that Aggie couldn't help but laugh at.

"Of course, you would say that. Why would you want me to know I'm about to walk into a situation that would likely end in my death?" Aggie realized what she was saying and reconsidered. "Heck, why should I care? The goal is to get the kids out, and if I'm the reason we get them out, then I'm not the bait. I'm still their savior. Unfortunately, you'll get all the credit for your plan to send me in first after all." Aggie winked at him, but her thoughts were only tamed slightly. While she didn't have a death wish, she would do anything it took to save those kids and bring them home alive.

They were just getting through town and Aggie realized she was so distracted she didn't really see any of it. Disappointment settled inside her, but she tried to shove it away. Gryson led the group, followed only closely by Mathius. They were having a conversation that Aggie couldn't hear at her distance.

"Can you hear what they're talking about?" Her question directed at Ren, who kept pace with her. She wasn't used to this much exercise, and on Earth this trip would have been made by at least a car and only rarely on foot. The terrain wasn't impossible, but Aggie was very aware of how out of shape she really was. Closing her eyes, she slowed her pace and reached out for the elements around her and fed her own energy to make up for her lack of muscles.

"They are deciding if the visions are better to follow now, or wait until they are out farther past the map Gryson made with his scry notes." Ren hadn't even broken a sweat and for that Aggie was jealous. She was thankful she thought to put her long hair up in a bun before meeting up with the guys in the common area.

"Do the map and the visions currently differ, I wonder?" Aggie didn't know why that would be. "If they're the same it shouldn't be an issue, but if they're different, I wonder why." Instead of waiting for Ren to answer she jogged ahead, though her body cried with each bounce of her step. There were bigger and better things she needed to do, and crying over pain in her body wasn't one of them. When she got to Gryson and Mathius, it seemed they were in a debate about what to do.

"I'm not sure how they could be different. Unless the boy was sent as a decoy and he didn't escape." Gryson seemed confident in his own magic and that made Aggie feel better. Everyone should know what they're capable of, and trust was all they could be offered in return.

"That child was malnourished and half dead when he arrived at his parents' door. It is possible his thoughts were askew and you didn't see past the error in his mind." Mathius' voice was grumbling, as usual, but Aggie could hear the frustration as well.

"Didn't we bring our team with the exact purpose that each had a specific role to carry out?" Aggie startled them both and for that she was secretly proud of herself. They were so caught up in their own conversation they didn't notice her approach.

"What are you trying to say?" Mathius barked at her, making her square her shoulders and stand up to him.

"I'm saying we have at least three members of our team who can scout ahead on both paths. If you believe the boy's mind to be inaccurate, then why don't you send Xavier on that path? He can keep himself hidden from anyone who might have set a trap for us. Then, when he reports back to us, we will know for sure." Aggie was frustrated that they were arguing about this when the solution seemed plain as day. Not to mention, she was still having trouble figuring out who made these decisions before she came along.

"I don't want them running around willy-nilly. I would rather us take a break, so they know where to find us upon their return. Also, then we aren't making any needless backtracking trips because we need to go the other direction." Mathius huffed, but didn't shoot down her idea.

"I would want the twins to scout ahead on Gryson's scry path. That way we have a better idea of what we should expect to see along the way. We wouldn't want any surprises in the other direction after all." Gryson nodded his agreement and Mathius called for the rest of the team who weren't far off.

"Gryson, care to show me your map before we shift?" Mitchell proved they were all listening from afar and Aggie felt like the low man on the totem pole because she had to ask for assistance in her eavesdropping attempt. The two men scooted off to the side of the path to review what Gryson had decided was the best course.

Xavier approached them as well. "If you could share your vision from Navian, I will make my way along that road. Then I can get back sooner with my findings." Noting once again that he wasn't armed, Aggie decided to question it.

"Will you be okay out there all by yourself?" Aggie didn't want to sound like he wasn't capable, but she needed to be reassured.

Xavier smiled wickedly, and for the first time Aggie saw them. Caught in the moonlight Aggie didn't know if it was the late hour or her imagination, but his fangs were practically illuminated in the natural light. "My dearest Aggie, you have nothing to worry about. The darkness is a second home to me; there is nothing to fear. If I get into a situation, I have more of a chance than anyone of surviving because that is what my kind does. Survive."

Aggie, on impulse, reached up and for the first-time initiated contact with him. She wrapped her arms around him tightly. He returned her embrace and she leaned up and whispered in his ear, "You'd better come back in one piece or I'll kill you myself." Her threat was meant to lighten the mood, but it didn't do anything for the burning concern radiating through her chest. As soon as she released him, he was gone into the darkness without a trace.

"Please tell me you aren't planning on giving us a tearful goodbye." Mitchell's words startled her out of watching where she assumed Xavier was off to.

"Well, not you now. I'll save all the blubbering tears for your brother. You can get eaten by a bear, for all I care." Aggie, of course, didn't wish that upon Mitchell, but he was hot or cold and mostly freezing towards her. While he had shown her some concern a time or two, she thought his wolf was the only one who really cared about her in the least. "Ren, I only want you to do one thing for me."

"You know I would do anything for you, Aggie girl. Just name it and it's yours." Ren picked her up and swung her around playfully. She loved his ability to lighten the mood no matter how grey it seemed.

"Don't get dead." Pressing her head against his forehead, she was grateful he had picked her up. While her words were intended to be funny, she still meant them deep down.

"So long as you do the same. I can't have my girl crapping out on me before I get a chance to show her exactly what I'm made of, now, can I?" Ren leaned the fraction of an inch closer and kissed her lips quickly. Nothing passionate or overstepping, but just to solidify their connection. Then he turned quickly and joined his already- shifted brother. Taking his time, he unfastened his pants and put on a little show of slipping them off his waist, until Alpha headbutted him and Ren shifted right there. With a soft growl, Wolfie showed his displeasure with being rushed. Aggie noticed his pants were slightly ripped from the transformation. The wolves scampered off to investigate their trail.

"How long do you think it will take them?" Aggie's gaze moved back and forth in the directions that the guys just left in. She sighed and sank to the ground. Just before she connected with the earth, a stone appeared below her and she landed on it instead. Glancing around, Aggie realized that no one was looking at her and the bracelet on her wrist warmed slightly. Her magic was talking to her. Fiddling with the band, she tried to thank it in her own way.

"There's no telling how long we will be waiting, but I'm sure they will go as quickly as they possibly can." Mathius sat down beside her and she willed her magic to create a larger stone for him to sit on. When he connected to the surface quicker than expected he startled slightly, but quickly recovered. He nodded his appreciation. "Your magic is quite strong. It will serve you well if it comes down to a fight, as I fear it will. She's not going to give up the children easily. Especially if they are supplying her with any form of magic. She has been without for years. I only hope she hasn't seen or gotten word of our arrival and Xavier doesn't run into any traps. He can hold his own, but I still don't like any of us to be fighting alone."

"We passed through town so quickly, I missed my opportunity to look around. Tell me about Ahael, please. It will take my mind off what we're waiting for." Aggie leaned over to lean on Mathius' arm. He didn't shove her off so she remained, quietly hoping he wouldn't deny her request.

"I'm not sure what to tell you. I grew up in the castle. My father was a guard, as I later became. I seldom went out to the city for fun and games." Then a smile crossed his face and Aggie's ears perked up. "I do recall one time when I ventured out into the city market. It was on a holiday and there were many varieties of demons in to celebrate. Demons don't travel much to different areas or take vacations, but some of our holidays are more important than others, like Walpurgisnacht Roodmas Day for example. This was the first time I had ventured out of the castle alone, and the different demons were fascinating to me. It isn't unheard of to never see some varieties of demon.

"Kyrel is from another city, where his kind prefer, and has his own gate to guard. Since they are only visible to those with magic it makes it a little easier, but they have to know where they want to go. Most of the demons don't even use the gateway to travel, because the locations are kept a secret to protect against anyone stumbling into a realm they don't belong or into your backyard.

"This time in particular there was a fair of sorts. They had native food booths set up with demon delicacies. Most don't get multicultural food very often in their own city. I saw a Nickar seated at the water's edge, sampling from a vendor. It was the wildest demon I had ever seen. He had scales over every inch of his skin, but he looked like a man. Where his ears should have been were gills, moving in and out with each breath he took. His nose was more of a snout than the cropped version we wear. Then, when he opened his mouth, he had teeth as sharp as razors and I knew then that I wanted to see every kind of creature that I could and learn about them. Walking through the bazar, I saw Gorgons, Levianthans, Aggadah, and even the tiny Jinn. I loved watching them walk through the entire city, and the games the children played weren't anything I'd ever seen before. All I wanted to do with my time was observe each and every little thing. It was the most exciting time I recall as a child."

"After all this is over, will you walk me through the city and show me around? I hope by then it will back to its proper glory and seasonally appropriate weather." Aggie was a bit nervous to be asking him because they still didn't know much about each other, but she was going to take life by the horns and go for it.

"It would be my honor to do just that." Smiling, she gazed upon this man with new eyes. He had shared with her a story from his childhood. Since they had time, this might be a good time to reciprocate and get to know each other a little better.

"I remember one time Gran took me to the county fair. On Earth, we have rides and games and more food than anyone could ever imagine. I begged and begged for weeks to have her take me, and finally the day arrived and she gave in to my pleading. She told me I could get whatever I wanted for dinner since it was a special treat. So, I walked up and down the boulevard to see what my options were. I decided I needed a special deep-fried corn dog. Then I stopped at the next vendor and I needed a funnel cake, but I was only able to finish half of it before I saw the Spin-A-Nator. All my friends had said it was an awesome ride. I dumped all my leftovers in Gran's hands and got in line. Bouncing up and down, I couldn't wait to get on and desperately wanted the front row. The adrenaline rush and the feel of the wind spinning past me was all I could think about. Before I knew it, the line opened up and it was my turn to ride. I shoved my way to the front of the group and made it to the front car. It was everything I ever dreamed it would be."

Aggie sighed at the memory, and she knew that was where the happiness ended. It took all of her nerve to continue the story. Mathius was captivated and listening to her every word. "As the ride started, my heart was racing and I wanted nothing more than to be a part of the hands-free group. So, as it picked up speed, I released my hands and raised them into the air. The ride twisted and turned in a figure eight as the ride went faster and faster. Just before the ride reached top speed, I realized I wasn't cut out for this ride. To this day, I don't know whether it was the food or just my stomach didn't agree with the ride, but instead of coming off the ride in the same condition I went on I was quite the worse for wear. Just before the final fast rotation, my stomach released everything I had eaten. I don't know if I felt sorrier for the people who had to clean up or the people on the ride behind me." She cringed at the memory and second-guessed even telling him. Though her story followed the same line of thought with his, even if hers was a bit more embarrassing, it seemed like the right thing to do at the time. Covering her face with her hands, Aggie was worried about his reaction. Then, out of no-where, she heard the sexiest, deepest rumbling laugh she had ever heard, coming from right beside her. Opening her hands one finger at a time she cautiously looked up at Mathius, to find him smiling wide and laughing at her story.

"I would have loved to have been there to see that, but I think we will keep the roller coaster rides to a minimum for you. Maybe I'll save that little bit for a fun surprise for one of the guys." Still chuckling as he thought about it, Aggie was glad they had found some common ground.

# Chapter 20

What felt like forever later, Mathius informing her it was only about twenty minutes, Xavier made his way back, quickly followed by the twins. Aggie had no idea how far they had traveled but, given their abilities to move rather quickly, she feared they were actually going to be walking the rest of the night before they arrived wherever they were going.

"What do we know?" Aggie wanted to get moving again and stop killing time.

"It seems the paths were connected, as we ran into each other on the opposite side. So, what we have concluded is that they sent Navian down the path least traveled so he would be less likely to draw anyone back to them." Xavier didn't look like he had encountered any attackers on his little excursion.

"The place where they come together, though, is odd. Like there was a house there at one point, but it is just gone now." Ren had changed back and was standing in the meadow just beyond the path, hanging out in all his glory.

"Okay, hold on, you're going to have to put on your pants or there will be a completely different train of thought here and we need to focus." Aggie only hoped they were still wearable with his speedy removal before.

As Ren complied, his brother filled in the missing details. "We couldn't get a read on when it was last there or how it was torn down. The foundation hasn't grown over with grass completely yet, but it was a rather large accommodation in its prime."

"I agree with their assumption. We didn't want to get too close to the area in case anyone was watching. Our task was to deduce which way led us to where we wanted to be, and it seems that either way is fine. I think the way along the water is actually a bit out of the way and the twins' route was a bit more direct." Xavier was very intense and Aggie had never seen him like this. She also had never seen him in utter darkness, as it was his perfect element. He had never given her cause for concern before, and she only hoped he wasn't feeling the need for a little snack.

"Do you all agree with his assessment?" Mathius posed the question to the twins. Gryson looked on intently.

"It really is the best. I didn't see anything to cause alarm, but we might want to stick to the shadows as we get closer. Xavier, I want you to stick to the darkness. Ren and I will go in wolf form. We will be a bit more inconspicuous than six full grown adults will be." Mitchell was in full Alpha mode and more than happy to dictate what they should and shouldn't do. If he didn't get on Aggie's nerves so much, she would have been turned on by his dominance.

On Mitchell's advice, they started toward this mysterious location to get a better look at this property and get to the bottom of where the house might have gone. In the back of Aggie's mind, questions rolled. *Where could an entire house go? What if the house isn't gone? Could someone actually just make a house invisible? How did they block the wolves from sensing anything?* The questions rolled on and on as they walked. Aggie was thankful that, given the amount of energy she was using, she wasn't feeling tired.

"It's time to take to the shadows." Mitchell's voice broke her thoughts. Aggie looked up and couldn't see anything different about this stretch of the road than the five miles previous. However, she trusted Mitchell's words, and slid to the side and followed the rest toward the tree line. Xavier disappeared completely from view, as he had on the training ground. Though Aggie could still sense him if she reached for him with her magic. The wolves were at her feet moments later and, reaching down, she scratched Alpha and Wolfie between the ears. It was her way of saying thank you and also letting them know she was all right.

"Lead the way, boys." Aggie nudged the wolves into the lead and everyone else fell into step behind them. Walking softly so as not to stir the leaves below their feet, Aggie was surprised they still crunched under foot with the crazy weather changes and ice-covered ground. Thankfully, given the colder temperatures, the thunderstorm had warmed things up a bit. She also was attributing her lack of shivering to her magic keeping her warm while walking all these miles to their unknown destination.

The closer they walked the slower their pace, the wolves guiding and setting the speed. No one walked around them, and everyone trusted they would keep everyone out of trouble. Suddenly, Alpha stopped dead in his tracks, and Wolfie split off to the side and flanked him, but stopped instantly as well. Everyone else froze a number of paces behind, leaving a large gap between them and the wolves. The reason for the sudden halt was unknown to everyone except the wolves.

Then Aggie saw Alpha raise his paw in the air and hold it out in front of him. She could have sworn she heard a low growl coming from him. It was a strange thing to see a wolf, or any animal who walked on all fours normally, do.

"What is he doing?" Aggie whispered to anyone close enough to hear.

"I'm not sure, but it looks like he's resting his paw on something." Gryson answered her in the same hushed tone. Aggie glanced around at everyone frozen and decided that none of them were going to get any answers this way. So, she tiptoed as silently as possible up to the area where the wolves had stopped. Taking a deep breath, she steeled herself and mirrored Alpha's action. When she connected with something solid she gasped.

"Get up here now!" Her tone still hushed but insistent Mathius and Gryson complied quickly. Mathius might have taken a slightly quicker approach, as he appeared right beside her in a breath of dust. His hand placed beside hers and she watched his face as the surface of something connected with his palm.

"What kind of magic is this?" Mathius' question was directed at Gryson, who was standing on his other side with a confused look on his face.

"I have never seen this kind of display in all my years. I don't know a single incantation or potion that will make anything this large invisible." Gryson started to walk along the wall to find the edge of it. He walked for at least seventy feet before he came to a corner. Luckily Wolfie had done the same on his end and only went about five feet before reaching an edge.

"If this structure is this long, how are we to know where the front is or how wide it sits on the property?" Aggie was cautious, and worried that they would be walking into danger without more information. "Does anyone have any ideas, besides blindly feeling our way around these walls?" Her voice was a bit louder as her frustration rose. She clasped her hand over her mouth in an effort to rein it in quickly. Taking a deep breath, she let it out slowly without saying another word. It wasn't helping her to freak out. They needed to put their heads together to figure things out.

"Why don't we leave the wolves here as a place marker and fall back to the tree line to discuss our options. Their hearing will allow them to not miss out on anything while they wait here." Mathius' suggestion was just what she needed. Anything to take a minute and regroup to get her head back on straight.

"I agree that's a good idea, but I don't like the thought of them being exposed like this. Can you boys lie down as close to the ground as possible to try and blend in a bit better?" Alpha and Wolfie complied immediately. Aggie patted them both in gratitude. At least she wouldn't have to worry about them being seen.

From the trees, Aggie noticed the wolves were barely seen. She hoped that she could only see them because she knew they were there. "Anyone have thoughts on this matter?" Xavier's voice startled her, as she'd missed his approaching footsteps. It was as though he was floating above the surface of the ground.

"That is what we're attempting to sort out. How do we get in without knowing which side is front-facing and where the possible dangers are?" Aggie was using everything in her to maintain a balance in her voice and not lose control.

"One of us could go in first, if we find a door and eliminate any possible threats." Mathius, ever the warrior and not one to back down from a fight, threw out the most preposterous idea.

"You mean, one of us could go in and get killed or taken captive. We don't want to create more work in the long run. Honestly, if we happen upon the children and avoid the mistress of the house, I'd be all for that course of action." Aggie was aware of how cowardly that sounded, but she was in a very honest mood. When she got worked up or nervous about anything it was like she had been doped with truth serum. She hated to be pulled over on Earth; the cops knew everything from what she ate for breakfast that day to when she last pooped or had her period. Those times weren't her proudest moments.

A movement caught Aggie's eye just as she finished her rant. Someone came over the hill from the main road and Aggie frantically got everyone's attention. Everyone fell instantly silent, as though she had cast a muting spell. As the person got closer

Aggie could tell it was female from the swish of her hips as she walked, even though the woman tried to hide her appearance under a cloak. They all watched, captivated, and wondered what this woman would do. Aggie just hoped Alpha and Wolfie were in a safe spot and wouldn't be discovered.

As she came within distance of touching the invisible structure, a hand appeared from inside the cloak. She waved it in front of the building and then froze. Eyes glowing red, she moved her hand back and forth until the walls began to appear. The house was large and bordering on mansion status, several stories tall and a square distance around. This house was almost half as wide as a football field. It was unbelievable. Why was a house this large sitting out there in the middle of nowhere?

Before stepping inside the front door, which opened with her magic, the woman lowered the cloak on her head to reveal a familiar silhouette. "Yavari." The name was said on a whisper, but Mathius' voice dripped with disdain. While Aggie didn't think it carried across the field, Yavari's head swiveled around to take in her surroundings before stepping inside. As her feet hit the floor inside, the image of the house faded with her and the door closed behind her.

"Well, now we know how to get in, and we know who is waiting inside to greet us. What would you like to do?" Gryson was no longer flustered by the magic and was ready to go, but he was letting someone else make the call.

"This is going to sound completely unlike me but, given the fact that she has such a sweet spot for you, Mathius, you're going in first." Aggie wasn't using him as bait, but more like getting even. She was mad that he let her use her royal status to play him for so long and get her way. Even if they weren't ever an actual thing, Aggie hated that he'd never actually told her no. This way he could show her what side of things he was actually on.

Xavier, who stood behind her, actually chuckled at her decision. Gryson just nodded, while Mathius growled his disapproval but didn't say a single word.

"Once you're inside, you can leave the door open just a hair. One of us will catch it and wait for you to distract Yavari. Try to get her into another room, the goal being to remove her from the direct line of sight of the door. If you can't do that then try to remove her from the room completely, no matter what you have to do. Getting five more of us into the room while you attempt this will be tricky enough. There's no room for error."

Approaching the house, Aggie flagged down the wolves and they fell in line behind the group. A surge of power made Aggie realize they had shifted back to human form.

"Is Mathius really going to play to her heartstrings to get us in?" Ren's words were unexpected, but not startling.

"You don't think I can handle this? If I can take on an opponent on the battlefield, what makes you think this would be any different?" Mathius grumbled, and Aggie felt a little remorse for making him do this, but she could think of no other way to get them in the door. Not much time had passed and there was a chance she was still close to the entrance.

Feeling the wall for a door, Mathius found the entrance quickly. He reached for the handle and they all held their breath. Given the fact that the house was hidden from view, the chances that it had a magical locking system were slim. Why else would they hide it from view? Seconds later the latch clicked and Mathius was on his way inside. Aggie reached up quickly and placed her hand in the crack of the door, preventing it from sealing. They all gathered close to hear for their cue to enter.

"Mathius, what a surprise to see you here." Yavari, always the politician, never faltered once.

"I saw you leave the castle this evening and, given the late hour, I was worried about you." If Aggie didn't know Mathius' true feelings for Yavari, she would have assumed he was actually worried.

"Oh, you needn't worry about me. I started taking late walks years ago, while still in my youth. I find they are calming to my nerves." She never gave anything away, causing Aggie to wonder what Mathius would try next.

"What is this place, Yavari? I haven't come across it before on scouting trips. I would think you would steer clear of strange places, given your status. Had I not seen it change upon you entering I never would have given it a second glance. How did you happen upon it?" Mathius was using her name more, and she preened under his watchful eye. She was lapping up the attention like a two-dollar whore. Aggie wanted to throw up or at least gag at the display if it wouldn't have drawn unwanted attention to them standing outside. Given the darkness, no one had noticed the door being left ajar.

"This is my thinking space. I found it abandoned years ago and claimed it for my own. I come here when life in the castle gets to be too much." Aggie couldn't believe how she didn't even flinch or quiver in the slightest. Then Mathius reached for her shoulder and guided her toward another room.

"Surely this is too much space for just yourself. Don't you get lonely here?" Yavari leaned into his touch and he gently pulled her from the room. That was their moment. Aggie pushed the door open and they all crept in and Xavier silently latched the door behind them. Aggie heard Mathius one room over. "I'd love for you to show me around since I'm here. I feel like we never get to speak alone anymore, with your guards always around and my team listening in no matter where we are." That was their clue to look around.

Aggie took in the house. It was once a polished regal space. Perhaps one of an upper-class citizen, if Ahael had such a thing. She still didn't have a good grasp on society. The furniture didn't scream poverty, but not quite the same as the rooms in the castle either. It seemed those who lived there weren't lacking for anything. All their needs were met.

Hearing the sound of Mathius' voice get a bit farther, she motioned for Xavier to stay close to him. While she couldn't speak to him to instruct him, Xavier nodded and headed off in the direction of Mathius' fading voice.

Feeling a bit more at ease knowing that her team was at least in groups, Aggie motioned for the remaining three to follow her. They roamed through the house and she tried to let herself think like an insane person. *Where would I hide a bunch of children? Didn't Navian say they were in utter darkness?*

They had traveled a distance from the front entrance when they came across what she thought at one time might have been the servants' quarters. While they were empty now, Aggie felt it would be a good place to investigate farther. If she was right, there would be a back entrance to some of the places the owner might not want just anyone to see upon walking around.

# Chapter 21

Just when Aggie was about to give up hope, she found a tiny door located behind the kitchen. At first she thought it was just a pantry, but she decided it was worth a look. Wrapping her hand around the knob, she jerked her hand back instantly as a scalding heat flooded through her body. Looking at her hand, she sighed in relief; it only appeared red and not blistered as she feared.

Gryson was right there to grab her hand and inspect it. "What was that?" He smoothed his hand over hers and whispered an incantation. Immediately, the burning ceased and her hand no longer was in pain.

"I'm not sure, it just burned me instantly. I don't think that is just a pantry like I originally thought. Anyone have any ideas?" Aggie looked at the three men and waited, but Mitchell had his own plan.

Walking around Aggie, he placed his hand around the knob and gritted his teeth through the pain. Twisting slowly, his face contorted as the burning worked its way through his palm. Finally, he made it full circle and the latch released. Never once did Mitchell make a sound, but Aggie knew from his facial expressions that it had hurt.

"What was that? Now we're down a man because you couldn't stop being macho for five seconds to let us come up with a plan." Aggie was fuming, and yet still trying to keep her voice low to remain hidden from any other dwellers.

Mitchell took a cleansing breath and then flipped his hand over to show Aggie the damage. To Aggie's surprise, what should have been first-degree burns for as long as he held on to that knob was barely red. As she watched, the redness quickly faded to his normal white coloring. Shocked and a little sheepish over her previous reaction, Aggie just stood there gaping at him.

"I was the best choice. Ren would have been the second choice, but as Alpha I heal a touch faster than he does. This way the door is open and no one is damaged for the long haul." Proud of himself and as cocky as ever, he motioned for Ren and they both walked through the doorway first. It led to a narrow staircase that they had to travel single-file. The wolves could see in the dark, so it was their best option to let them go first, but Ren held back and brought up the rear.

It was a short set of stairs, as they reached the bottom rather quickly. Gryson whispered softly and a glow built in his hand much like that of a dim flashlight. Aggie was thankful not to have to rely on following Mitchell and the walls to keep from falling down.

Walking a few feet, Aggie nearly shouted with joy. There, strapped to the wall, was a tiny little boy. He looked sickly and barely conscious, but he was still breathing and that made Aggie happier than words could express. He was leaning against the wall and his body sagged with the strain of holding his arm aloft. Some invisible power was holding it up in the air and his hand was slightly discolored, as though the blood hadn't been in it for a long while.

Unable to control herself, and knowing that the guys were there and not distracted, Aggie ran to the little boy. As she got closer she realized he was only about five years old, and her heart broke. No one should have to go through any trauma like this, much less a child. The guys circled around her, facing out to watch for any unknown threats while she tried to figure out how to break this child free.

As she reached for his arm, the boy startled and started to breathe heavily. "*Shhh*, little one. I'm here to help. I want to take you home to your mama. Let me just get you loose." She felt up his wrist and realized there was a shackle attached to a chain holding him to the wall. None of this could she see with her own two eyes; she could only feel it with her hands.

"What do you think you are doing?" The voice of an unknown woman sounded like it came from everywhere. Everyone froze and instantly went on guard. "That is one of my pets and you won't take him without my permission. That is something you will never get from me." Her words scraped across Aggie's senses. She sounded more like Cruella de Vil and the epitome of villains than just some crazy cat lady. Just then she appeared from the stairwell, startling them because no one heard exactly where she was approaching from. She could have been appearing like the Cheshire Cat for all they knew.

"Who are you and why are you holding these children hostage?" Aggie's words were a bit shaky but she was trying her best to portray bravery and stand up to this bitch.

"I'm Alentra, and you are inside my family home. It was removed from my view, so I couldn't return here many years ago. When I found it I decided to keep it hidden and stay here comfortably. Soon I discovered a child that had wandered a little too close to my property, and trespassing is a sin I take very seriously. So, they were taken captive and I am using them for my various purposes." While she wasn't clear on her purpose for keeping the children she did give them more than Aggie asked for, and that gave her something to go on.

"You're The Wanderer, aren't you?" Matter of fact was usually the best approach when you're grasping at straws. Own your answer, and if you're wrong at least you gave it all you had.

Alentra screamed so loudly Aggie had to cover her ears. She noticed the guys wincing in pain but they held their ground between Aggie and this woman. "I hate that name and I refuse to answer to it. You will refer to me by my given name or I will end you now." With that a ball of lightning filled Alentra's hand, and it crackled and bounced in a tiny ball. Contained for the moment. What she didn't know was Aggie was prepared and two could play at that game.

"Oh, really? Did you want to play catch? I brought my own ball." Aggie's fingers quickly caught in her own ball of lightning with only the thought. She imagined that same glass she trapped the tornado inside to contain the storm building.

"I know who you are, and you don't have a clue what you are doing. I know you only just came to Ahael days ago. I have been wielding this power my entire life, while you are a baby compared to my skills." Alentra threw the ball, showing off. Aggie got tired of the game and threw her feelers out to figure out what this room was made of, and she was in luck. The edges of the floor had a wood base, which meant Aggie could reach for her powers. The stones had cracks in them just like the castle, and Aggie had done this before and successfully held back two strong-ass shifters. Still keeping the ball dancing under her invisible glass, Aggie summoned the vines again and added a level of thickness just for good measure. Never once giving a clue that she was adding to her ploy, Aggie faced off with Alentra as the guys stood vigilant.

Without warning the vines struck out, and wrapped and grew and knotted until Alentra was successfully entangled amongst the briars. Aggie did in this case add the thorns. She was unconcerned with how much damage was done. She wasn't protecting this source of evil who kidnapped kids and tortured them. Thrashing and throwing a fit, Alentra screamed at the top of her lungs to be released. Aggie only hoped she hadn't come into her full powers with the help of these children, or she might be able to sift right through the vines and into their space to attack unbeknownst to anyone.

Not letting a second lapse, she shouted, "Quick, Gry, we need to figure out how to get these kids free!" Gryson shown his light at a higher lumen and they counted the remaining four children as expected. She said a silent thank you that there weren't any extra kids unaccounted for without parents to claim them.

"I don't know this spell; I'm not sure how to decipher it if I can't see it. Whoever put the invisibility on these things has hidden the secondary power. It might even be what she is using to syphon the powers from these kids." Aggie's heart sank immediately.

"Tell us how to free these kids and we'll spare your life." Aggie pleaded with Alentra, knowing that it would take a miracle to bring her back from this evil.

"I'll never help you. The Master promised me powers beyond compare if I could succeed in my plan. I won't let him down." Alentra sounded like a crazy cult follower. Aggie had no clue what she was talking about.

"Master? Who's the Master?" Aggie was lost, but at least if she kept this nut talking it might result in her giving something away that was useful.

"He came to find me when I was lost. He wanted me to be whole again and told me how to find my power. I am almost there; I can feel the power inside me. It completes me and I need to finish the transfer. You won't take them from me. They are mine. I have taken them fair and square. If their parents even loved them a little they would have protected them better. It was so easy to get to them. My favorite is the little prince. He was just sleeping, and his wonderful aunt simply picked him up and cradled him until he was safe in my custody." Well ,that at least gave them reason to believe Yavari's hand in all of this, but there had to be more.

At that moment Alentra began to scream again, piercing to the ears and louder than before. Aggie closed her eyes and covered her ears. When the screaming stopped Aggie opened her eyes, and was startled to find Yavari standing there with Mathius in her grasp, a knife to his neck. Aggie was in denial; there was no way Mathius was overtaken by this bumbling idiot. Then, had she not been looking right at him with confusion, she would have missed his subtle wink. Aggie then knew he'd meant to be taken.

"Let her go or I'll take care of this one myself. I'd hate for you to lose one of your sacred harem, human." The last word was spoken with such disdain Aggie realized something. It hit her like a ton of bricks.

"It was you! You destroyed my room. Why would you frame The Wanderer if you did it all along? You would have been better off not leaving a clue for us to find." Aggie lifted her hand and another bolt of lightning just hovered there, no need for a glass because she intended to throw this one.

"Don't call me that! I said I hate that name!" Alentra screeched.

"I framed her because I don't want my nephew to die, but I am willing to let you two battle it out and see who wins. I won't, however, let you kill *my* Mathius in the process." Yavari gently scraped the blade across Mathius' jaw, in almost a loving way that was on edge of sick.

"Your Mathius? I think you have some wires crossed there." With that she let the bolt fly and envisioned it flying faster than the speed of light. Yavari, unable to react fast enough, took the blow to the shoulder, knocking the blade from her hand. Mathius kicked it out of the way and moved to stand between Yavari and Alentra.

"Do you think that will stop us? Those children are still spelled under my magic. Even killing me won't free them." Yavari was so proud of herself. "The Master will be pleased with me." There it was again, that name of some unknown person. Aggie assumed it was a man the way the two of them went doe-eyed on mentioning it.

Without warning, a bolt of lightning grazed Aggie's head, and she shrieked and ducked away. Feeling her face, it felt wet and she realized she was bleeding. Not wanting the kids to get caught in the crossfire, Aggie imagined a shield of wind surrounding them all. It was all she could think of and hoped it would be enough. Though it took a lot of concentration to hold, Aggie wasn't going to give up the fight. She looked back to Alentra and realized she had gotten one hand free. It was slow for her and Aggie assumed it was because she hadn't regained all of her magic. Just then a child cried out in pain. "I'll take what I need and I will win this." Alentra was reaching toward the child who was screaming, and Aggie could feel the power transfer as though it was palpable.

A growl echoed through the room and Aggie saw both shifters change form. Gryson was glowing with balls of magic in his hands and Mathius' eyes were full-on red as he channeled his demonic energy. Aggie realized his power was stronger than the other two demons in the room, but Alentra was still pulling from the children.

"Guards!" Yavari yelled toward the top of the stairs. They must have been waiting for things to get out of control, because they hadn't come down sooner. If Yavari thought she could persuade Aggie with the blade to Mathius' throat, she'd underestimated them.

Unfortunately, the number of guards who flooded inside was more than what anyone bargained for and filled the space. It was now hard to see the women; the men took to battling the guards. Mathius drew his blades and his magic traveled through them. Upon contact, it was as though they had been lit with Hell's fire. Instantly, they were set ablaze in a fire black as night and hotter than anyone could imagine.

Gryson fired balls of magic toward oncoming attackers, keeping them from Aggie who still stood behind him. She was focusing all her energy on protecting the children from the fight. The wolves grabbed any guard within reach in their jaws, ripping them to shreds in an instant. Then, as though he heard Aggie's worry, Xavier appeared amongst them, sinking his teeth into an unsuspecting guard approaching Aggie from the side. It was as though they were all told to attack her, as she was the weak target.

Thankfully her men stayed close, but somehow the guards were multiplying; for every one they took out another three appeared. They needed to end this and do anything it took to save these kids. Aggie only hoped that Yavari was bluffing about breaking the restraints, or she would take pity, not wanting her nephew to die as she said before.

Every once in a while, one of the guards got a little too close for Aggie's comfort and she would throw out a kick to the head or a right-cross to the jaw. She channeled as much energy into those as she could spare in order to do the most damage. None of them was as strong as Xavier, so they went down fairly easily.

Another child, a little girl near where Aggie stood, let out a bloodcurdling scream in one long breath, then suddenly stopped. Aggie glanced quickly to put eyes on this tormented creature and noted that she was now unconscious.

"What did you do?" Aggie growled at Alentra in an accusatory tone.

Alentra laughed haughtily. "Nothing, I just took what was waiting for me. It will be more than enough to finish this and get on with my plans." With that she let loose a storm inside that rivaled a tropical storm one would see in the coastal regions on Earth. Aggie fought against her impulse to cower. There were kids to protect at all costs.

Yavari cackled at the turn of events. "You can't win this. She has an endless supply of power, and at midnight it will be permanent." Aggie had no idea what time it was, but she knew it had been a few hours since it went fully dark. So, time was approaching quickly and they didn't have much left. The men were beginning to sweat with the energy expelled trying to keep the guards at bay. Aggie still didn't understand where they were all coming from.

"Enough!" Aggie was fed up with the antics of these two, and was willing to risk the power by attempting to break the chains herself in an attempt to save the lives of the children. She was finished waiting on Yavari. She conjured a tornado in her mind and sent it quickly. Navigating around her own men, the concentration was excruciating. She felt something drip from her face and chalked it up to sweat, like she saw on the guys fighting alongside her. She pushed through the pain and exhaustion. Dancing through the room, Aggie grabbed each guard and worked her way to the front by the stairs, where Yavari and Alentra never moved. Without another word, she scooped them up and entangled them both inside this twisting wind.

She felt Alentra's magic pressing against her own, but she just pushed herself a little more. Another drip fell from her face but there was too much at stake, so she brushed it on her arm and pushed harder. Fighting against the similar magic countering her from inside, Aggie fell to her knees to avoid losing control. Then she felt hands fold over each shoulder, one at her hip and one on the other side mirroring that, then an entire strong body pressed to her back.

Aggie knew it was her men, and their strength gave her strength. She pushed back to her feet and fought through, until she felt the magic lessen to a manageable level as it evened out throughout her body.

Aggie wasn't sure what to do; she needed to get the kids free. So, she dropped the wind shield from around the kids and that gave her a boost in power to keep her enemies contained. Then she threw her mind into the tornado to seek out Yavari. In one last burst of power, she separated Yavari from the twisting windy mess and wrapped her in a muddy, lightning-infused mold so only her head was still out.

"This is your last chance to save your nephew. You said you led us here because you wanted to save him. This doesn't look like saving him. How do we release their bonds?" Aggie's voice sounded different, but she didn't care. Anything to get her point across. It was more demanding and more powerful than her usual voice.

"Please, please don't let me die." Yavari's pleading was a given for anyone in her position. Aggie didn't want to hear her pleas, but rather a solution to the problem at hand.

"No! You *will* die if you don't free these children from whatever you have them trapped with." Her voice grew in intensity and power. It wasn't very human anymore.

"I'll release them, but it will kill Alentra. I can't keep them all alive." Yavari was stammering and stuttering, like a child learning to speak. She was scared, and she should be. Aggie wasn't playing and she was tired of people attacking them. Another drop dripped from her face, but a hand caught it this time. The same hand that was resting on her right shoulder, wiping it from her face without a word.

"All I care about are the children; she made her bed and she will lie in it no matter the consequences. These kids shouldn't have ever been put through this. No matter what you were told by this *Master* of yours." Aggie released one of Yavari's arms. "Know that if you try anything funny, I will kill you without a word."

Closing her eyes, Yavari's hands glowed slightly, and one by one the children's hands fell to the ground. Some that were awake grabbed their wrists to rub the blood back into them. Mathius approached the young girl who was still out from the power absorption moments before. He picked her up from the floor and was gone in an instant. Aggie didn't need to ask where he had gone. Eldon would be waiting for them and Aggie knew she would be fine.

"What kind of demon are you?" Aggie asked the now physically defeated Yavari.

"My mother was Gardarene, but my father was part Pockla. It seems my brother and I don't share the same father, and I was blessed with the power to make things and people invisible. It came in handy when I wanted to leave the castle as a child. Then I discovered I could hide other things with it as well. It allowed me to block my magic under a cloak, never to be noticed by anyone."

Mathius came back, with Kyrel hot on his heels. They scooped up two more children and were gone in the blink of an eye. Then and only then did Aggie relax, because they had most of them out and the odds were in their favor.

Xavier stepped between Aggie and her line of sight to Yavari. "Wee one, I fear you pushed yourself too far."

"Why would you say that? We won, didn't we?" Aggie was baffled by his approach. She looked around and saw Alentra unconscious under the pile of all the guards, who were slowly disintegrating into a pile of stone. Yavari seemed to have been creating guards from the bricks of the house itself. That was why they were coming and seemed to be never-ending.

Xavier reached up and wiped the space between her mouth and nose, only to come back red with blood. He slipped his finger into his mouth and closed his eyes in satisfaction. "Like a rare wine, only to be had on special occasions." His voice crooned his delight at the flavors dancing on his tongue. Aggie's eyes were wide with disbelief. Perhaps he was right; she had pushed herself too far. She felt her body draining as she pushed harder and harder to get the information she needed to save the children. She didn't care about herself in that moment—it was all about the children.

Then it hit her, she had been preaching to the guys to let everyone own their strengths. If they said they had something under control, then trust them to handle it. That's just what they did for her in that moment. While they saw her fading, they never stopped her. They only gave her what they could, and that was to know they were there for her no matter what.

# Chapter 22

Eldon had the kids well in hand by the time Mathius sifted everyone back to the castle. They did a final sweep of the invisible house and found no trace, other than sleeping quarters and the room the kids were held in. The thought made Aggie shiver even after it was all over.

"How are they?" Aggie wanted to get a handle on the situation before anyone dispersed for the night.

"Three of them are fine, as is the prince; just a little groggy and malnourished. Gryson had to put a dampener on their powers. He said it would wear off over time, as they aged and came into their powers naturally. They are just too young to have that much power all at once. It could actually kill them." Eldon was very serious, but still took his time and checked Aggie over for any residual pain. "How are you? Xavier said you took a beating out there, but you look perfectly fine."

"I'm fine, I just pushed myself too far when I took on Alentra and Yavari at the same time. I handled it, though; no loss of consciousness for me, but I can't say the same for them." Yavari and Alentra were taken to the depths of the castle, beyond the dungeon. Aggie didn't even know that was a thing, but she chose not to visit it and trusted that they guys had them secure. Had Alentra not died in releasing the children, she would have been sentenced to death for what she had done. Yavari, after finally came around, helped in the end to free the children, and would be given the chance to live but would be spending many more years locked away for her treachery. "Wait, did you say three of the children are fine? What about the fourth?" Aggie panicked and her heart started to race. The last things she wanted was for any of the children to have not survived.

"No, she is fine. Gryson said she was hit hard during the fight." Aggie thought back and realized he must have been talking about the little girl. "The problem is she exhausted her powers through the link. Without even a drop remaining, they can't regenerate on their own. She was essentially stripped of her powers, and I have no way of returning them to her without resulting in her death. You saw what the link did to her last time. With the strain on her body, there would be nothing to block her from the severity of the impact. She just can't support it anymore."

"Can't we wait until she's more recovered and then do it?" Aggie was grasping at straws, but she couldn't bear to see another kid so severely damaged and have to handle this for the rest of her life.

"I'm sorry, but the longer we wait to restore her powers the more her body becomes resistant to them. It would be like pushing something too large into a hole that is too small. You might get some of it in, but without the entire piece making it through it will just come right back out on its own." Eldon knew he was delivering bad news, but it was like a doctor telling you something bad. They have to do it no matter what, so it's better to just rip the band-aid off quickly.

"What can we do?" Aggie let out a long, low sigh as her shoulders slumped forward, her body drooping in defeat.

"Gryson is with her now. We decided it would be best to give her the same treatment he gave Navian. At least then she will have pleasant memories of what happened and that she lost her magic years ago and already have come to terms with it." Aggie wished she had a better way of showing her gratitude and pride in her men. Reaching up she threw her arms around Eldon, squeezing him tightly.

"Thank you for everything you've done here today. Without you this could have been far worse. Now, if I'm not needed any longer, I'd really love a hot shower to work out all this aggression that built up today."

"After that I'd love to take you out to be a part of the rest of the Walpurgisnacht Roodmas Day festivities." Mathius appeared out of nowhere, obviously catching the tail end of her conversation with Eldon. "The weather has already returned to normal. So please, wear something cool. I don't want you to overheat."

"That sounds absolutely wonderful." Mathius bowed a bit to Aggie and she nodded toward him. Making her way back to the twins' room, she was surprised to find her own door ajar. Deciding to peek inside, she saw Liel standing just over the threshold and out of the doorway. They shared a look but no words were said. Aggie glanced around the room and realized it was back to its previous glory. It was as though nothing had happened.

"What's going on?" Aggie couldn't hide the confusion in her voice as she turned to Liel for an explanation. They had been so busy preparing to rescue the children that she hadn't even though of her own room since the fire.

"The castle personnel have worked 'round the clock, trying to get this ready for you. I'm only sorry they didn't have it done sooner, or that any of this had ever happened to begin with." This was the first time Aggie and Liel had been able to have a private conversation. She noticed a change in him but she couldn't put her finger on it.

"It's beautiful; I wish I knew who to thank for orchestrating all of this." Aggie wanted to thank everyone personally but knew that was most likely an outrageous list.

"It was my honor to provide this for you. It was the least I could do for you since you are doing so much for us." Without a second thought she placed her hands on his chest, even though he was taller than her, and pressed up on her toes. She was thankful when he leaned down to meet her. Their lips pressed together innocently and Aggie knew right then that there was more to Liel, and she couldn't wait to discover what.

*****

After taking a very long, hot shower Aggie stood wrapped in a towel, trying to figure out what to do. She spent her entire shower thinking about how this outing with Mathius felt like a date. She thought, given what they have just been up to, that it was silly to think of something so trivial. Now she had to figure out what to wear. She was trying not to overthink it. Though, for some reason, she still wasn't able to conjure up clothes for herself. It made no sense that she could create a tornado from nothing but a thought, but something as simple as clothing was eluding her.

Holding on to her towel tightly Aggie walked around the room, trying to clear her head. She ran her hand along the table that looked exactly like the previous one and remembered her first day. It felt like so long ago and not just a handful of days that had passed. She approached the wardrobe and remembered all the beautiful dresses that were hanging in it, one in each of the guys' signature colors. She wished she had the chance to wear any of them before their tragic end.

Running her hands along the wood, it hummed underneath her fingertips. Like the nature and her magic were having a conversation. Then, on a whim, she gripped the handles and pulled open the doors. There in the vast space, where there was room for plenty of hangers to rest and hold countless outfits, was one lonely dress.

Nothing too fancy but, the color of the moonlight, it almost shimmered. The prettiest sundress she had ever seen. Quickly she shed her towel and slipped the light fabric over her skin. It hung perfectly, with an asymmetrical hem that fell from mid-thigh down to her knee. The neckline dipped low, revealing the line of her breasts, and it sat upon the thinnest straps that tied at the top.

Aggie twirled once just for good measure and giggled at the creation. She was worried she had zapped her magic in the fight and that it might be gone. *Was it just that I can't work this like the guys? Did I have to have a connection to my natural resource in order to make this?* Testing her theory, Aggie reached for the door of the wardrobe yet again. Feeling the hum again, she waited for the feeling to subside and then jerked the handles open. There on the floor was a pair of the daintiest sandals she'd ever seen, which matched the fabric of the dress perfectly. Slipping them on, the strap ran between her toes and buckled around the ankle. Nothing fancy, but they were the most comfortable shoes she'd ever worn.

Deciding that since she wasn't sure if this was a date, she would just let her hair dry naturally in some loose beachy waves. So as not to keep Mathius waiting, she made her way out of the room. Then she quickly remembered they hadn't discussed meeting anywhere and he wasn't in the hallway. So instead of standing there like a fool, she made her way to the triage area that Eldon had made up for the kids. Most of them were sleeping, but the girl whom she'd last seen passed out was wide awake, looking out the window.

"Hello, there. I'm Raleigha. Who are you?" The sweetest little voice called out to her as Aggie approached her bedside. She had bright turquoise eyes that reminded her of Kyrel's when his magic touched them.

"Hi, I'm Aggie. It's nice to meet you. How are you feeling?" Aggie kept her voice low, so she wouldn't wake the other children. They had all been through so much, rest was going to take precedence for a while as they recuperated.

"I'm okay. I just woke up and I feel much better." Aggie didn't ask her anything else, for fear of saying the wrong thing. "I wish the doctor would let me go, so I could go to the festival, but they want us to stay inside this year." The little girl looked so forlorn, but Aggie understood that they didn't need anything too overstimulating after what they had just come out of. Rest and relaxation was all they needed for a while.

"How about this—I've never been to the festival, so could you tell me your favorite thing that I just have to see? Also, if you could have one thing from the festival what would it be?" Aggie knew this girl had given up so much and, while all the kids had been to Hell and back, she had sacrificed more.

"I love the decorating egg run. It's my favorite and I can't play this year." Raleigha pouted silently and Aggie thought she looked adorable.

"I'll watch out for that, but what's the one thing you would want to have from the festival? I'll bring you back a present since I know missing out is hard." Aggie leaned forward and rested her elbows on Raleigha's bed.

"I want a timararoo." Licking her lips, Raleigha's eyes glazed over and she was lost in her thoughts.

"I don't know what that is, but I bet if you describe it to me I won't miss it." Aggie could tell by her reaction is was going to be a tasty treat.

"It's like a cake, but it's long and skinny. It's not completely sweet, but it melts on your tongue with each bite. I can't describe the flavor to you, as it's different for everyone. For me, it reminds me of a vacation I took with my parents years ago to visit my grandparents by the water's edge." Aggie didn't fully understand what that meant but it definitely caught her interest. It was the first time she would try their cultural food, as they'd always had Earthly food for her to eat in the common room, and for that she was grateful. It wasn't in her nature to branch out and try new things very often.

"Now, that sounds like something I want to try. I'll be sure you get one before the night is over." Aggie's promise was met with an instant hug, and she knew Raleigha was a new friend.

"Are you ready to head out?" Mathius' voice came from the doorway. He had let them have their privacy and waited until they were nearly finished before announcing himself.

Turning to Raleigha, Aggie checked in with her. "This is my festival escort. Do you think he's up for the job?"

Turning her head side to side she sized up Mathius, still standing in the doorway. "You're not just planning to take her to the feast, are you?" Mathius shook his head and she proceeded to interrogate him. "She needs to go to the shore line." Mathius smiled at the young girl and nodded again. "She needs to watch the decorating ceremony."

"Of course, I wouldn't let her miss that." Mathius didn't sound offended; it was a game at this point. Raleigha was very serious, though.

"She needs to try a timararoo for herself and other local food. You have made her miss out on so many things, as I bet you only allowed her to eat her own food while she has been here." Watching this little girl reprimand such a beast like Mathius, and with his position, was comical to Aggie. She did her best to refrain from laughing. Mathius was nothing but respectful, but she could see the mirth in his eyes.

"She needs one of those, too, by the way." Aggie interrupted their exchange, but it didn't stop Raleigha from staring down Mathius to make sure he knew she was serious.

"I think that is the least we can do for this little one." Mathius lifted his hand, but Aggie still didn't have Raleigha's approval, and even though she didn't need it this game was proving to be fun. Turning again, she deferred the decision to the girl.

Pursing her lips and putting her hand on her chin, Raleigha considered her decision. With a sigh, she said, "I suppose he will be a good enough guide. Don't make me regret that decision." Raleigha pointed her finger at Mathius to prove her point.

"I wouldn't dream of it." Mathius lifted his hand again and Aggie slipped hers inside.

Turning to leave, Aggie glanced back and saw Raleigha smiling in a way only a child who got their way could. She'd played Mathius, or so she thought.

"That little girl has taken a liking to you." Mathius transferred her hand to his elbow as he escorted her down the hallway to the gate of the castle. Aggie was excited to see the town in its element for the first time. Mathius was in the most casual clothes she had seen him in yet, but it wasn't something anyone on Earth would have worn. His leathers were modified into a sort of sleeveless vest. It reminded her of a guy who would wear his tuxedo vest without a shirt in a way. She loved the look of his muscles showing beneath the vest. She couldn't help but let her thoughts wander to running her hands over every exposed inch. His pants weren't full length but still looked like he could be armor-ready if the need arose. They were a tight, fitted leather, though cropped and stopping beneath his knees. She could only imagine how warm he would still be in that, given what she had heard about the weather shift.

"Raleigha is the sweetest thing. I'm thankful Gryson helped her with the memory of the events of late. I'd hate for her to be a lesser version of herself because of Alentra and Yavari." Aggie found herself caressing the exposed skin on his arm that she was wrapped around, but Mathius didn't complain, so she continued.

"He ended up doing something similar on varying levels for each of the kids. We were afraid the trauma would end up causing them lifelong grief. Instead, they now believe they have worked through it and can move on with their lives." Aggie squeezed his arm slightly. Knowing that they had done so much for these kids made her heart sing.

"That's the best news I've had all night. So, where are you taking me tonight?" A smile broke out on Mathius' face and Aggie was thrilled at the sight.

"I'm hoping to give you a dose of what it was like for me growing up in this world and make you love it as much as I do."

Aggie paused for a moment and just looked at him. "Wow, no pressure or anything. I hope this one night is enough for all of that."

"Well, then, it is a good thing for the holiday or it might have been more difficult." Grabbing her hand, he pulled her toward the door. The guard opened it upon seeing their approach. The light that shown through was blinding at first with the sudden transition. As her eyes adjusted Aggie saw what looked like giant birds flying through the sky, back and forth, gliding on the warm wind. The sky was more orange than blue, mirroring the heat she felt on the air. Hanging in the sky, adjacent to the sun that Aggie didn't dare gaze upon, was a moon that looked like it had rolling lava running across every visible surface. It wasn't hot, but more humid and muggy, like sitting inside a sauna all the time. Aggie was instantly thankful for the dress choice.

Flipping the hem of her dress to create a draft, Mathius took notice. "Who designed your dress? It's stunning." His eyes roved over her with a hungry flare of his nostrils.

"I did. It took me a bit but my magic sorted itself out. I just can't do it the same way as you guys. I have to use my wardrobe in some way. I'm not entirely sure how it worked, but I think it was the connection to the natural wood. Who knows how that will work when I get home. At least there I have a closet full of clothes. Although I was kind of enjoying the ability to think of something and it just appearing." Aggie walked absently as she described her design method, all while taking in her surroundings. When she came through before, she saw nothing but wintery mix scattered around. Now she could see the trees were like fire blazing amongst the leaves, with no real flames. The colors simulated it perfectly, and they emitted no heat. It was captivating and she found herself bouncing from tree to tree, taking in the elemental beauty.

"You will always have us to help you if the need arises. I quite enjoyed clothing you, but I'd love to reverse the process at some point as well." He wasn't shy about his intentions, and for that Aggie was thankful. Somehow that made this date seem less awkward. It wasn't like they were beating around the bush, worried to say this or that. She genuinely wanted to learn more about Mathius and his hot and cold personality. Unlike Mitchell, Mathius just seemed to not think and simply react. Sometimes that was heated and other times it was thoughtful; she just needed to learn not to let the gruffness be too off-putting. It would balance given time.

"Given this as your basis of inspiration," Aggie gestured to the natural surroundings that she never would have thought to consider beautiful days ago, but now she had a new basis of understanding, "I can imagine you are overflowing with ideas."

"You make the perfect inspiration."

Mathius turned her words on her and she preened at the compliment. She'd suffered so much grief recently it was nice to take a step back and just enjoy life.

"Where to first?" Sweeping her hand along the vast surroundings, Aggie didn't have a clue where they were headed.

"This way towards town; I want you to see the culture before I take you this evening to see the exceptional things that only happen once a year." Aggie let Mathius lead her along the path. Looking closer at the rocks underfoot, she realized they weren't just stone. It was more like a lava rock, a little bit dense, and as they rubbed together when compressed by their feet the soft grinding could be felt through her shoes. They didn't just roll away but worked between each other like sandpaper or a pumice stone. Black as night, they were stark against the contrast of the browning grass that Aggie realized wasn't dry, but just naturally colored that way.

It didn't take them long to enter the bustling city of Ahael. Aggie was so thrilled to be there she didn't know what to look at first. There were children running crazy through the dirt streets. They were carrying branches and vines like little ants in a path from the woods nearby. They traveled between the homes that Aggie marveled shared similar architecture to the castle. The glass walls weren't throughout, but there was at least one if not more on each home. The adults stood around near the homes as the children came and approached them. Each child would pass their load to an adult or a portion of a large load, split between two homes. They would promptly stick their hands out, looking for some sort of payment. What surprised Aggie was that they were given what looked to be an egg.

"What are they doing?" Aggie pointed, looking at Mathius for some sort of explanation.

"It is tradition to gather leaves, vines, and branches from the woods on Walpurgisnacht Roodmas to fashion around the exterior of the homes and some indoors." Mathius joined her in watching the action.

"What are they being paid with? I assume it's some sort of payment." Aggie couldn't take her eyes off the busy little kids and admired them for their drive.

"Eggs; they can take them to the vendors and get a prize. There is no limit to how many they can get and there is an unlimited supply of eggs for the adults to pass around, as they are magically supplied. So, no child is left out." Aggie was captivated watching this interaction, but she soon realized Mathius was watching her instead of the children.

"What?" Aggie wasn't embarrassed at all to find him staring at her, but he was obviously distracted.

"I like experiencing this with you. It makes me feel like I'm seeing it all with fresh eyes. While I knew showing you would be an experience, this is beyond what I expected. You see things that I think are old hat and make them new again."

"Then by all means show me more. I still have to try something called a timararoo, whatever that is; I'm not sure I fully understand." Aggie let Mathius lead her further into town. She was still captivated by everything she saw. The vendors were set up around what she assumed was the center of town. Little stations, with what looked like animal skins as the table coverings. Aggie was captivated by the fashion varying from simple cotton-like fabric to ornate leather pieces that Aggie would see as BDSM-wear on Earth. "Are those regular, everyday clothes?" Aggie didn't know a better way to ask that question without sounding rude.

"It's more like fighting attire. They keep it on hand because the guards are known to stay stocked up on fresh options since they wear them all the time." Mathius acted like this was everyday conversation.

"Wow, on Earth that would be considered bedroom attire to some people." Mathius gave her a look and she realized there was still a culture breakdown. While this wasn't slang or basic human language, this was a closed-door activity that he may not be aware of. "Are you familiar with BDSM?" She was praying that she wouldn't have to explain it to him.

Understanding lit his face and Aggie was instantly grateful. "I know what you mean but we don't call that anything special here, as most of us share those proclivities. A raised eyebrow was the only other thing he did, as if questioning her reaction to this.

"Oh, really? You said *us*, so I assume you are one of those?" Aggie had never participated in a relationship of this nature, but wasn't opposed to trying anything at least once. What was the worst that could happen?

"I like to have control in the bedroom, no matter what the other party has to give up in order to achieve it." A predatory smirk came across his face and Aggie felt a chill of anticipation run through her. She had no clue what the idea of the unknown would do to her. "Now, let's not discuss this now, as I have much to show you and I believe we have a treat to be delivered. I imagine there are a few children who need some more eggs, who would be happy to deliver this for us. That will give us more time to take in the scenery." Mathius took her hand and pulled her toward a vendor located in the corner of the lot. It had a short line and Aggie could only imagine how popular they were throughout the day, given Raleigha's description.

"Do we pay in eggs as well?" Aggie was mostly joking, but secretly she wondered what their currency was here.

"No, the children only use the eggs to redeem special prizes from each vendor. They have different treats and gifts for them. It's a reward for helping. The more they help, the more things they can collect. If one gets something from a table that another wants, they just turn in one of their eggs there or go get more to turn in." Aggie looked around and realized there had to be at least forty vendors, possibly more.

"They would need a wagon to haul all their goodies by the end of the day." She chuckled at her own thought as Mathius made it to the counter.

"I need two, please." Mathius handed him two silver coins that Aggie didn't get a good look at, but felt confident that it proved they had a standard form of currency. The vendor handed him two wrapped timararoos. Mathius immediately flagged down two young boys about the same age as Raleigha. "I'll pay you each three eggs if this makes it to the castle infirmary and to the girl they call Raleigha in once piece. You come back with a note from her and I'll pay you." The boys' eyes grew to the size of saucers. The job obviously didn't need two in order to complete it, but Mathius was being generous.

"Right away, sir." Mathius handed them the treat and they took off running.

"That was considerate of you." Aggie stretched up on her toes and kissed him on the cheek to show her gratitude. "I would have been happy to return it to her when we were finished."

"I have other plans for you, if I can persuade you with the remainder of your tour. I'm hoping it is very late or quite early before you are available again." Mathius' forward nature was very alluring to Aggie. While she may be with them to even out their internal battles and make decisions, it would be nice to let him take charge in the bedroom. It would be the one place she wouldn't have to make decisions. "Now it is time for you to taste this. As it is different for everyone, I can't tell you what to expect." That entire concept was amazing to Aggie.

"Is it laced with magic?" She hesitantly took the doughy creation from Mathius. It was shaped more like a churro, long and cylindrical.

"Not really, but the demonkind that make them have a way with the ingredients that I believe their magic hangs on during the process. They are Baku demons; they eat the dreams and nightmares of others." That thought scared Aggie a little.

"Should I be concerned about eating this? Is there going to be a demon in my head now?" She made to hand the timararoo back to Mathius. There was enough going on with her and she didn't need to add anything on top of any of that.

"Not at all, but really, don't you already have at least one demon in your head?" His voice dropped to a seductive tone on the last part. He leaned in and pressed a kiss to the back of her ear. Leaning into the sensation, Aggie couldn't respond right away. Instead, she gathered her nerves and took a bite of the cake-like confection.

Instantly she felt like she was flying, and in the back of her mind she hoped she wasn't wobbling on her feet. Even though she knew if she were to fall for any reason, Mathius was there for her. When she stilled, she immediately saw her mother. It had been so long since she had seen her, that Aggie's breath caught in her throat. Aggie was about three years old and they were at the park. The sun was shining and Aggie's younger self toddled between the swings and the slide. Her little self was laughing loudly as she slid down the slide and her mother was there to catch her. They both smiled and talked softly. Aggie couldn't hear the conversation and didn't remember this day before taking that bite.

Then her mother glanced up quickly, off in the distance, and a look crossed her face. Immediately she scooped up little Aggie and made to leave. This confused Aggie now that she was an adult. It seemed little Aggie had no idea what was happening. So now that she was able to see this as an onlooker, she looked off in the distance and saw a shadow of what looked like a man on the horizon. As soon as she saw it, the figure walked away.

When her mother and younger self were out of sight, Aggie started floating again. Before she knew it, she was back with Mathius.

"What did you see?" Mathius supported her back gently as she regained her bearings. When she knew she could stand on her own, she took a step away.

"I saw my mother and I think it was one of the last times I saw her. I was maybe three years old." She hesitated but then finished, "It was strange because it was as though I was just observing, and so I saw everything. Including a strange shadow of a man that seemed to run my mother off. She quickly scooped me up and we left." She didn't know what else to say. Not knowing what to make of the entire scene, she realized that the snack was gone from her hands. "Where did it go?" Looking on the ground, she couldn't imagine that it fell.

"You ate it. That is what prolongs the dream. Otherwise you wouldn't ever arrive at the final dream. You would stay floating. The eating of the timararoo becomes a mechanical action once it has induced the dream sequence." Aggie touched her mouth in amazement. It really didn't have a flavor, and there was no trace of it on her tongue.

"That's amazing; it's like a drug almost, because what happened on this side of the trance. I have no recollection of it and it's probably best you were with me when I did it. Who knows what would have happened if I were alone." Mathius rubbed her back reassuringly, and she leaned into his touch yet again.

"Who do you think the man was?" Now that she was calm, he seemed to be sticking on the one thing that had her unsettled.

"I'm not sure, but he definitely spooked my mom. She snatched me up faster than any other time I remember. She usually just bribed me to leave happy. That time, she didn't care if I wanted to leave or not. Then the man disappeared just as quickly." Rubbing her arms, she felt a ghostly chill run through her.

"Let's get you something to drink. Another festival must-have is our famous mead. We spend all year preparing it just for this holiday alone. The only time anyone is allowed to drink it is this time every year." He stopped at the next vendor with no line. "I need two glasses, please." Turning back to Aggie, he explained, "Each vendor has this, that is how popular it is." He paid the vendor and handed Aggie her mug.

Taking her first sip, Aggie sighed. "This is perfect." It was sweet and light and Mathius was right. Just what she needed. "Okay, let's keep going; I'm sure we still have lots to see."

They walked what felt like miles, but Aggie didn't complain once. It was the last thing she could think of when there was so much to see. They ate at the outdoor feast and Aggie tried many more things she wouldn't have normally. Most she didn't even remember the name of, but it didn't matter. As night approached, fires were lit around the town. Not small torches but complete bonfires, blazing high and lighting everything without any effort. They had their mugs filled every time they were emptied. Walking along Aggie felt a bit tipsy, but she burned it off quickly with their walking and had plenty of food as they went along.

"This is my favorite part." Mathius cryptically pointed toward the shoreline. The mountains off in the distance reflected the firelight onto the water. "You have to come down by the water. You won't regret this, I promise." There were many already standing between them and the water, but they parted when they saw Mathius. He was a bit of a household name, it seemed.

He took her right to the edge of the lapping water and wrapped his arms around her waist from behind her.

The view was breathtaking and Aggie knew she wouldn't soon forget this night. Then, just as the bell chimed in town, signifying midnight, something leapt from the water. Aggie flinched but Mathius held her tightly. She looked closer and realized there were some sort of demons in the water. They were throwing something from the water toward the shore. Then she saw the first ones break the shoreline and a rainbow band of sorts started spinning quickly around one bystanders. Soon there were lights flying from every direction, and more and more rainbows were spinning around. Then one came out and wrapped up Mathius and Aggie. She got lost in the colors that spun around them. Dizzy, she fell backwards and was thankful for Mathius' embrace.

*****

"Did I tell you the other most common thing during the festival?" Mathius and Aggie were walking back to the castle after taking in everything and then some of the town. Aggie glanced up at him; she clung to his arm as the roads were more difficult to travel at night. "Celebrations of fertility." He dropped the words like a bomb and left them to sizzle.

"Now that sounds intriguing, considering I'm only just coming into my fertile years as I've been told. Why shouldn't I celebrate them?" Aggie felt a sense of freedom with Mathius. She knew he would be the person who would give it to her straight and be a friend and lover. They might butt heads, but that would likely end in a vigorous session of make-up sex. Not to mention, she had so much food and wine to work off it was surprising he wasn't having to roll her back to the castle. "Yes, I think we should look further into the celebration." Aggie chose to sound very scientific and matter-of-fact. As though she were performing research for an upcoming project. Perhaps she was.

Walking down the hallway, they got to Aggie's room. "Did you know Liel had my room fixed up to its original state? I was so surprised. It was a thoughtful thing to do. I'm so happy to have my own space." She wrapped her hand around the handle and they walked inside. She was still enthralled by the beauty that was her room, she was surprised when Mathius came up behind her and pressed his lips to her neck. Leaning her neck away, she gave him more access. It was the prefect pressure and made her skin tingle at the contact. A moan escaped and her breathing increased.

"I'll have you doing more than moaning before we are finished." Mathius' promise had Aggie hanging on his every word. After the day they'd had, it was the perfect ending to a long day. Their date was more than she could have asked for.

"I want anything and everything you want to give me." Turning in his arms she sealed her lips over his, but he immediately gripped her arms and pulled her from him. Her eyes widened and she didn't understand what was happening. "What's wrong?"

"I told you earlier, this is my domain. No matter where it takes place, I'm in charge. You will follow my lead. If you can't listen, I will restrain you. I will never go farther than you are willing, and you can always stop me with a single word. You have to pick it, though." Mathius stroked her hair, never breaking contact with her.

"A word." Aggie couldn't think straight. She knew it had to be a word that wouldn't come up during the course of their interactions. "Porcupine." The word was blurted out without much thought. Then she covered her mouth in shock. "I don't know where that came from."

"I think it is perfect. It is the word that came up in your head, in the moment. You shouldn't accidently say it when you don't mean it, but you won't forget it either." Mathius gripped her shoulders and backed her to the edge of the bed. Slipping her right strap down, he kissed his way down her collarbone. The strap trapped her range of motion, but he didn't lower it any further. Matching the motion on the other side, she was successfully confined. One tiny push and she fell back onto the bed with a little bounce.

Mathius ran his hands slowly up both of her bare legs until he reached her core. He dipped his fingers under the seam and gently pulled the fabric down over her legs. Again he stopped short, at her knees, effectively trapping her again.

"Now you are going to be at my mercy. Do you have anything to say before I proceed to bring your evening to a perfect ending?" Mathius was very sure of himself and she only hoped he could live up to his own praise.

"I suppose you'd better get busy or you might not have enough time at this rate." Winking at him, she simply raised her dress a bit higher, exposing her intimate center.

With a roguish smile, Mathius knelt down and kissed her inner thigh on each side, effectively avoiding where she wanted him. When she lifted her hips to encourage him, he pressed her back down. "Now, now, if I have to get a stronger restraint I am more than willing." When she said nothing, he proceeded to trail his fingers over her hips lightly and ran one finger down her seam, separating the lips there slightly. "That is a beautiful pussy and I can't wait any longer to taste it." Mathius licked the length of it and crooned his approval at the taste of her. His slight scruff was just the right amount of pressure mixed with the vibration of his voice for her to want to press further into him for the full effect. She fought the urge and attempted to do as she was told and stay still.

"I will also request that you refrain from climaxing until I give you permission." Aggie moved to speak but he held her in place and placed a finger of his free hand over her lips to silence her. "Don't worry, it will be better for it and I won't put you through anything I don't know you can handle." He then sucked her pulsing bud into his mouth and alternated with his tongue inside her. She was practically writhing on the bed and it took all she could not to move. He gave her a little movement, and for that she was grateful. He must have realized how much effort she was putting into following instructions, and gave her some much-needed grace. When she thought she couldn't take anymore she started to speak, but he sensed her impending reaction.

"Just a moment longer." He pumped a second finger in and curled them forward, hitting the sensitive spot deep inside. "Now!" Aggie needed no further instruction, and she exploded as soon as the word left his lips. The orgasm took a few minutes to come down off of, as her body still twitched and spasmed its reward.

"See? I told you that you would be fine." Mathius' words came from a distance as she came back to her body. Her mind and body became one again from the fierce reaction.

"Wow, that was amazing. I have never done that before and I didn't think I would make it." Her words came out breathy, as she felt like she had held her breath forever as she came.

"That is just the beginning." Aggie had yet to catch a glimpse of his cock, and he hadn't pressed it against her when their escapades began. Staying far from her while he prepared her body, she had no idea what she was in for but, given the size of the bulge she could see as he stood up, she was in for a treat. Unfastening his pants, she itched to help him along. She was still mostly clothed. Having not put on a bra, she only wore the light fabric of the dress she designed. He was still removing his own clothes but left hers alone. Just before he removed his underwear, he leaned forward onto the bed and sealed his mouth over one of her covered breasts, soaking the fabric beneath. Her pert nipple stood at attention through the now-sheer fabric of her dress. He repeated the process on the other side, but bit down slightly before releasing. Aggie squeaked at the shock, but he silenced her with a deep, passionate kiss. She knew he was a man of layers and this only proved it.

Their tongues wrestled, but she didn't try to take over the kiss. Instead, Aggie submitted and left that for Mathius to control and direct. It was his plan and his time to unfold them as he saw fit. When he broke the kiss, Aggie was panting. The bulge in his underwear was straining. As he removed them, Aggie's breath caught. He was bigger than Eldon, but she didn't care. It wasn't about comparison and all about how the man wielded his sword.

Fingers itching to grip his cock and feel it in her hands, she wished she wasn't trapped. Also, she didn't want him to be upset with her, so she stayed as still as she could. Though she felt her body shaking with anticipation. Lining himself up with her, he leaned forward and toyed with her nipples under the wet fabric.

"I think I like this dress even more on you. It was the perfect choice for the evening." He gripped her breasts one last time before sinking deeply inside her. All coherent thoughts were gone at that point. All Aggie could think about was how deep and full she felt. He didn't stay still for long and for that she was grateful. She needed him to move as she adjusted to him. The feel of his cock pressed against her walls and she moaned loudly. Her second climax would come quickly at this rate.

"Remember, not until I say." His words were enunciated after each with a plunge of his dick. She screamed the punctuation for him. The way he worked inside her was perfect and just what she needed. With each pump of his cock she felt all of her tension leave, and any stresses of the day were drifting away. He knew just what she needed and how to bring out of her what he needed. "You are going to feel every inch of me, and one day I will open you up to things you've never dreamed of in your life."

Aggie stiffened at his words and bit her lip, all in an effort to control herself. He knew every string to pluck and could play her like an instrument. "You think you can't take it?"

She shook her head because she didn't trust her words. With that he reached between her and pressed down on her clit. "Come now!" The tenor of his voice dropped low and demanding and she cried out her pleasure. If it weren't for the soundproofing she knew was in the walls it would have been likely the entire town of Ahael heard her. Unfortunately, she was sure that the guys were well aware of her activities. Sadly, she was in such a state she didn't even care. They would handle themselves in one way or another. Mathius groaned and spilled his release into her a moment later, and she was completely sated.

"That was just what I needed," Aggie said, barely above a whisper and still very winded. Mathius pulled out after a moment and helped her to the head of the bed. Wrapping his arms around her, they promptly fell asleep. Their lovemaking on top of their already busy day had worn them out.

*****

The daylight poured through the window the following morning and Aggie stretched slowly in bed. Her bedroom playtime the previous night ran on a loop in her mind, and the soreness of her body was a pleasant reminder. Aggie rolled over and bumped into something solid. When her eyes made it to the top of the bed, she quickly realized Mathius had stayed the night.

Perfectly ready to get her fill of him and take over her side of things that she missed out on the night before, Aggie made her way under the covers to find a still very naked man lying there. She gripped him under the sheets and she felt him grow in her hand. He moaned his approval and flexed his hips. Just as Aggie was about to seal her mouth over his erect cock, her hands disappeared and she felt her entire body go limp. A moment later, she was standing alone in the hallway.

"What the hell just happened?"

# THANK YOU FOR READING!!!

**Curious about what happens next?**

Find out soon in the next installment of *The Gateway Saga*!

# Author's Note

Thank you so much for taking the time to read this book. It means so much to me. If you want to stay up-to-date on upcoming releases, follow me on Facebook at "Erin Thornton -Author". There is also a special reader group on Facebook just for the Gateway fans. You can chat about the books and which guys are your favorites or which ones you just haven't quite latched on to yet.

You need to follow me on Amazon if you want them to alert you to any new releases I might put out or to see the other books in my catalog. While this is my first Reverse Harem, I have three other books available right now.

So if you want to read more about Aggie, the guys, and their next adventure, you will need to follow me on social media. While I don't have a set release date, new installments will likely come sooner than you expect.

Last but not least, I have one more request. If you enjoyed this book, please leave me a review. If you are reading on a Kindle device, it should prompt you right after this page. It doesn't have to be anything fancy or of epic proportions. I just would like to know how much you loved Aggie and her guys. I also rely on those reviews for others who don't know me to decide to check out my writing.

www.ingramcontent.com/pod-product-compliance
Lightning Source LLC
Chambersburg PA
CBHW050603190726
48283CB00007B/2263